SPIRIT OF THE CENTURY™
PRESENTS

BEYOND DINOCALYPSE

BY
CHUCK
WENDIG

EVIL HAT
PRODUCTIONS

An Evil Hat Productions Publication
www.evilhat.com • feedback@evilhat.com
@EvilHatOfficial on Twitter
facebook.com/EvilHatProductions

First published in 2013 by Evil Hat Productions

Editor: Amanda Valentine
Proofreading: Karen Twelves
Art: Christian N. St. Pierre • Design: Fred Hicks
Branding: Chris Hanrahan

Hardcover ISBN: 978-1-61317-051-9
Softcover ISBN: 978-1-61317-016-8
Kindle ISBN: 978-1-61317-052-6
ePub ISBN: 978-1-61317-053-3

Printed in the USA

OTHER TITLES AVAILABLE OR COMING SOON FROM SPIRIT OF THE CENTURY™ PRESENTS:

THIS BOOK WAS MADE POSSIBLE WITH THE SUPPORT OF...

Michael Bowman *and a cast of hundreds, including*
"The Cap'n" Wayne Coburn, "The Professor" Eric Smailys, @aroberts72, @syntheticbrain, A. David Pinilla, Aaron Jones, Aaron Jurkis, Adam & Jayce Roberts, Adam B. Ross, Adam Rajski, Adan Tejada, AJ Medder, AJT, Alan Bellingham, Alan Hyde, Alan Winterrowd, Alex, Alien Zookeeper, Alisha "hostilecrayon" Miller, Alosia Sellers, Amy Collins, Amy Lambzilla Hamilton, Andrew Beirne, Andrew Byers, Andrew Guerr, Andrew Jensen, Andrew M. Kelly, Andrew Nicolle, Andrew Watson, Andy Blanchard, Andy Eaton, Angela Korra'ti, Anonymous Fan, Anthony Laffan, Anthony R. Cardno, April Fowler, Arck Perra, Ariel Pereira, Arnaud Walraevens, Arthur Santos Jr, Ashkai Sinclair, Autumn and Sean Stickney, Axisor, Bailey Shoemaker Richards, Barac Wiley, Barbara Hasebe, Barrett Bishop, Bartimeus, Beena Gohil, Ben Ames, Ben Barnett, Ben Bement, Ben Bryan, Bill Dodds, Bill Harting, Bill Segulin, Blackcoat, Bo Saxon, Bo Williams, Bob Bretz, Brandon H. Mila, Bret S. Moore, Esq., Brian Allred, Brian E. Williams, Brian Engard, Brian Isikoff, Brian Kelsay @ripcrd, Brian Nisbet, Brian Scott Walker, Brian Waite, Brian White, Bryan Sims, Bryce Perry, C.K. "Velocitycurve" Lee, Calum Watterson, Cameron Harris, Candlemark & Gleam, Carl Rigney, Carol Darnell, Carolyn Butler, Carolyn White, Casey & Adam Moeller, Catherine Mooney, CE Murphy, Centurion Eric Brenders, Charles Paradis, Chase Bolen, Cheers, Chip & Katie, Chris Bekofske, Chris Callahan, Chris Ellison, Chris Hatty, Chris Heilman, Chris Matosky, Chris Newton, Chris Norwood, Chris Perrin, Christian Lindke, Christina Lee, Christine Lorang, Christine Swendseid, Christopher Gronlund, Chrystin, Clark & Amanda Valentine, Clay Robeson, Corey Davidson, Corinne Erwin, Craig Maloney, Crazy J, Cyrano Jones, Dan Conley, Dan N, Dan Yarrington, Daniel C. Hutchison, Daniel Laloggia, Danielle Ingber, Darcy Casselman, Darren Davis, Darrin Shimer, Daryl Weir, Dave BW, Dave Steiger, David & Nyk, David Hines, David M., David Patri, Declan Feeney, Deepone, Demelza Beckly, Derrick Eaves, Dimitrios Lakoumentas, DJ Williams, DL Thurston, Doug Cornelius, Dover Whitecliff, Drew, drgnldy71, DU8, Dusty Swede, Dylan McIntosh, Ed Kowalczewski, edchuk, Edouard "Francesco", Edward J Smola III, Eleanor-Rose Begg, Eli "Ace" Katz, Ellie Reese, Elly & Andres, Emily Poole, Eric Asher, Eric Duncan, Eric Henson, Eric Lytle, Eric Paquette, Eric Smith, Eric Tilton, Eric B Vogel, Ernie Sawyer, Eva, Evan Denbaum, Evan Grummell, Ewen Albright, Explody, Eyal Teler, Fabrice Breau, Fade Manley, Fidel Jiron Jr., Frank "Grayhawk" Huminski, Frank Jarome, Frank Wuerbach, Frazer Porritt, Galen, Gareth-Michael Skarka, Garry Jenkins, Gary Hoggatt, Gary McBride, Gavran, Gemma Tapscott, Glenn, Greg Matyola, Greg Roy, Gregory Frank, Gregory G. Gieger, Gus Golden, Herefox, HPLustcraft, Hugh J. O'Donnell, Ian Llywelyn Brown, Ian Loo, Inder Rottger, Itamar Friedman, J. Layne Nelson, J.B. Mannon, J.C. Hutchins, Jack Gulick, Jake Reid, James "discord_inc" Fletcher, James Alley, James Ballard, James Champlin, James Husum, James Melzer, Jami Nord, Jared Leisner, Jarrod Coad, Jason Brezinski, Jason Kirk Butkans, Jason Kramer, Jason Leinbach, Jason Maltzen, Jayna Pavlin, Jayson VanBeusichem, Jean Acheson, Jeff Eaton, Jeff Macfee, Jeff Xilon, Jeff Zahnen, Jeffrey Allen Arnett, Jen Watkins, Jenevieve DeFer, Jenica Rogers, jennielf, Jennifer Steen, Jeremiah Robert Craig Shepersky, Jeremy Kostiew, Jeremy Tidwell, Jesse Pudewell, Jessica and Andrew Qualls, JF Paradis, Jill Hughes, Jill Valuet, Jim "Citizen Simian" Henley, Jim & Paula Kirk, Jim Burke in VT, Jim Waters, JLR, Joanne B, Jody Kline, Joe "Gasoline" Czyz, Joe Kavanagh, John Beattie, John Bogart, John Cmar, John D. Burnham, John Geyer/Wulfenbahr Arts, John Idlor, John Lambert, John Rogers, John Sureck, John Tanzer, John-Paul Holubek, Jon Nadeau, Jon Rosebaugh, Jonathan Howard, Jonathan Perrine, Jonathan S. Chance, José Luis Nunes Porfirio, Jose Ramon Vidal,

Joseph Blomquist, Josh Nolan, Josh Thomson, Joshua K. Martin, Joshua Little, JouleLee Perl Ruby Jade, Joy Jakubaitis, JP Sugarbroad, Jukka Koivisto, Justin Yeo, K. Malycha, Kai Nikulainen, Kairam Ahmed Hamdan, Kal Powell, Karen J. Grant, Kat & Jason Romero, Kate Kirby, Kate Malloy, Kathy Rogers, Katrina Lehto, Kaz, Keaton Bauman, Keith West, Kelly (rissatoo) Barnes, Kelly E, Ken Finlayson, Ken Wallo, Keri Orstad, Kevin Chauncey, Kevin Mayz, Kierabot, Kris Deters, Kristin (My Bookish Ways Reviews), Kristina VanHeeswijk, Kurt Ellison, Lady Kayla, Larry Garetto, Laura Kramarsky, Lily Katherine Underwood, Lisa & M3 Sweatt, Lisa Padol, litabeetle, Lord Max Moraes, Lorri-Lynne Brown, Lucas MFZB White, Lutz Ohl, Lyndon Riggall, M. Sean Molley, Maggie G., Manda Collis & Nick Peterson, Marcia Dougherty, Marcus McBolton (Salsa), Marguerite Kenner and Alasdair Stuart, Mark "Buzz" Delsing, Mark Cook, Mark Dwerlkotte, Mark MedievaMonkey, Mark O'Shea, Mark Truman of Magpie Games, Mark Widner, Marshall Vaughan, Martin Joyce, Mary Spila, Matt Barker, Matt Troedson, Matt Zitron & Family, Matthew Scoppetta, Max Temkin, Maxwell A Giesecke, May Claxton, MCpl Doug Hall, Meri and Allan Samuelson, Michael Erb, Michael Godesky, Michael Hill, Michael M. Jones, Michael May, michael orr, Michael Richards, Michael Thompson, Michael Tousignant, Michael Wolfe, Miguel Reyes, Mike "Mortagole" Gorgone, Mike Grace (The Root Of All Evil), Mike Kowalski, Mike Sherwood, Mike 'txMaddog' Jacobs, Mike Wickliff, Mikhail McMahon, Miranda "Giggles" Horner, Mitch A. Williams, Mitchell Young, Morgan Ellis, Mur Lafferty, Nancy Feldman, Nathan Alexander, Nathan Blumenfeld, Nestor D. Rodriguez, Nick Bate, Odysseas "Arxonti" Votsis, Owen "Sanguinist" Thompson, Pam Blome, Pamela Shaw, Paolo Carnevali, Pat Knuth, Patricia Bullington-McGuire, Paul A. Tayloe, Paul MacAlpine, Paul Weimer, Peggy Carpenter, Pete Baginski, Pete Sellers, Peter Oberley, Peter Sturdee, Phil Adler, Philip Reed, Philippe "Sanctaphrax" Saner, Poppy Arakelian, Priscilla Spencer, ProducerPaul, Quentin "Q" Hudspeth, Quinn Murphy, Rachel Coleman Finch, Rachel Narow, Ranger Dave Ross, Raymond Terada, Rebecca Woolford, Rhel ná DecVandé, Rich "Safari Jack Tallon" Thomas, Rich Panek, Richard "Cap'n Redshanks" McLean, Richard Monson-Haefel, Rick Jones, Rick Neal, Rick Smith, Rob and Rachel, Robert "Gundato" Pavel, Robert M. Everson, Robert Towell (Ndreare), Ross C. Hardy!, Rowan Cota, Ryan & Beth Perrin, Ryan Del Savio Riley, Ryan E. Mitchell, Ryan Hyland, Ryan Jassil, Ryan Patrick Dull, Ryan Worrell, S. L. Gray, Sabrina Ogden, Sal Manzo, Sally Qwill Janin, Sam Heymans, Sandro Tomasetti, Sarah Brooks, Saxony, Scott Acker, Scott E., Scott Russell Griffith, Sean Fadden, Sean Nittner, Sean O'Brien, Sean R. Jensen, Sean T. DeLap, Sean W, Sean Zimmermann, Sebastian Grey, Seth Swanson, Shai Norton, Shaun D. Burton, Shaun Dignan, Shawna Hogan, Shel Kennon, Sherry Menton, Shervyn, Shoshana Kessock, Simon "Tech Support" Strauss, Simone G. Abigail C. GameRageLive, Stacey Chancellor, Stephen Cheney, Stephen Figgins, Sterling Brucks, Steve Holder, Steve Sturm, Steven K. Watkins, Steven McGowan, Steven Rattelsdorfer, Steven Vest, T I Hely, Tantris Hernandez, Taylor "The Snarky Avenger" Kent, Team Milian, Teesa, Temoore Baber, Tess Snider, Tevel Drinkwater, The Amazing Enigma, The Axelrods, The fastest man wearing a jetpack, thank you, The Gollub Family, The Hayworths, The NY Coopers, The Sotos, The Vockerys, Theron "Tyrone" Teter, Tim "Buzz" Isakson, Tim Pettigrew, Tim Rodriguez of Dice + Food + Lodging, TimTheTree, TJ Robotham, TK Read, Toby Rodgers, Todd Furler, Tom Cadorette, Tom J Allen Jr, Tony Pierson, Tracy Hall, Travis Casey, Travis Lindquist, Vernatia, Victor V., Vidal Bairos, W. Adam Rinehart, W. Schaeffer Tolliver, Warren Nelson, Wil Jordan, Will Ashworth, Will H., William Clucus Woods...yes, "Clucus", William Hammock, William Huggins, William Pepper, Willow "Dinosaurs and apocalypse? How could I NOT back it?" Wood, wufl, wwwisata, Wythe Marschall, Yurath, Zakharov "Zaksquatch" Sawyer, Zalabar, Zalen Moore, and Zuki.

PART ONE:
THE RESISTANCE!

CHAPTER ONE

Jet Black fell.

He did not fall through open air. He did not plunge deep into water.

He tumbled through time and space. Everything was light and dark at the same time—bright flashes pulsing and long shadows stretching like cooling tar. It felt like he was falling through an endless tunnel, a pit-like perforation in the cosmic continuum.

All around him rose the voices and sounds of history: cannon-fire, erupting volcanoes, jackhammers breaking asphalt, the cheers and jeers of infinite crowds, the wailing of animals, the sobbing of children. All sounds warped, melting from one into another. A mad cacophony of noises kicking through his ear-drums and nesting deep in his mind.

It went on like this.

For a minute or a millennium, Jet could not say.

But for all the time, through all the space, one word formed crystalline in his mind, resonating like a fork tapping glass:

Sally.

When last he left her, Sally was crying his name. She reached out for him across the massive underground chamber, a sculpted space beneath Atlantis, as he hung frozen and limp in the invisible grasp of not one but *two* Doctor Methuselahs.

She had fired a sonic blast through the funnel-tube that wound around the chamber like a golden snake, and then everything *unstuck* as the platform dropped suddenly toward the whirling portal below, the two Doctors going with it. Jet suddenly flew forward, slamming hard into the side of the chamber—seeing stars, his head tolling like a bell—before dropping down toward the portal with all the others.

All the others except Sally.

Sally, left behind on the elevator platform.

Reaching. Yelling. Her body damaged by Methuselah's cruel mathemagic attack.

Jet plunged into the portal.

He didn't fall to the ground so much as the ground fell upward to meet him. There came the vacuum *pop* of Jet exiting the continuum of time and space and—

There he was. Standing on wobbly legs.

A wall of humid air, hot as a bull's breath, hit him in the face. Colors and light resolved into shape and object, and as Jet's internal compass spun slower and slower, he saw that he stood in the middle of a wild, verdant jungle. Vines thick as his thigh hung between twisted jungle trees, trees whose roots lay exposed, whose trunks were bulbous and bottle-shaped. The ground lay spongy beneath his feet. Everything felt wet. The air, heavy. Thick like in a cloud of steam.

A dragonfly flitted before him, herkily-jerkily darting left, then right, then up, then up again. Its eyes were like golden marbles. Its body, a knitting needle of sapphires.

And it was easily as big as Jet's hand. Hell, it was easily as big as Professor Khan's massive primate mitt.

Huge trees. Leaves so big you could use one as a parachute. Dragonflies large enough to carry away a newborn kitten.

Jet had no idea where he was.

But he damn sure knew when:

I've gone back in time.

Perhaps to the very beginning.

A moment of panic washed over him like a cold rush of water, turning his sweat icy. Again her name drifted across the surface of his mind: *Sally*. But no. This was not the time to dwell on the hopelessness of the situation. Hope was part of who they were, part of what they did. Without hope, any attempts at heroism would be dead in the water.

The dragonfly darted off to heights unseen.

The dragonfly, he decided, had the right idea.

Time to fly, he thought. Get a view of the forest—er, jungle—for the trees.

Jet kicked the air-booster on his jet-wing, launched himself straight up.

He flew ten feet. The jet-wing's air booster stuttered. The wing tilted. Jet's body corkscrewed suddenly, and before he knew it, he flew sideways into a tree whose trunk seemed a braid of several smaller trees.

Jet Black fell.

Only about twenty feet or so.

Just the same, it was enough to horse-kick the air out of his lungs.

Gaaaaasp.

Then, a roar came, echoing across the jungle.

An all-too-familiar roar. The roar of a gorilla.

In the canopy above, big colorful birds took flight.

"Professor," Jet gasped, wincing as he hurried to his feet. His jet-wing may have been broken, but he was who he was, and one of his fellow Centurions was in danger.

Professor Khan struck out with a fist, but his fist froze in mid-air. He grunted, snarled, tried to pull away—but it was held fast by an invisible hand.

Their powers are different here, he thought. *Stronger. Not just telepathic, but telekinetic.*

The psychosaurs—no longer sporting the illusion of human faces—came sweeping out of the jungle riding ostrich-sized dinosaurs (leading Khan to believe they were some manner of Ornithomimus). The psychic saurians hissed and gnashed their flat razor teeth. Three psychosaurs to the front of Khan, then three to the rear.

They held reins of golden fungus, strung up around the necks of their dinosaur mounts.

One of the mounts darted toward him with an open mouth—that's when Khan took a swing, but found his fist trapped suddenly. Khan reached for his one fist with his other, but found *that* hand pinned by invisible forces, too. Both arms wrenched suddenly backward, his arms burning at the shoulders with twin lightning bolts of pain.

The psychosaur ahead of him reached out a clawed hand, palm down.

As the psychosaur raised its hand, Khan also rose off the ground. Like a puppet.

Khan thrashed, and roared.

The second psychosaur to the right reached down to the side of its mount and uncoiled a long lash—this, too, made of the thumb-thick glowing fungus. The psychosaur whipped the lash forward, and Khan felt the fungus snake around his neck. It tightened there, as if pulled taut by psychic hands. He felt his head pounding. Darkness bled at the edges of his vision.

His body weakened.

At first, he thought he was hallucinating. To his right, the air rippled like pondwater hit by a thrown stone, and then a body appeared out of nowhere—

Another gorilla.

Father, the Professor thought, the word a betrayal of his own mind. *No! He is not your father, you daft ape!* The Conqueror lay still on the jungle floor, a shaft of sunlight illuminating his nose—the Professor saw the gorilla's prodigious nostrils flaring, revealing that he was not dead but unconscious.

Then—

The sound of swift footsteps.

A shape darted out of the jungle.

The monster tumbled off the Ornithomimus, and the Professor saw a familiar flying suit: Jet Black had come to save him.

Just because his jet-wing wouldn't take him high didn't mean it couldn't still offer some advantage. Jet burst through the jungle into the clearing and hit his air booster just as he took a running leap—the momentum carried him forward like a clumsy bullet tumbling end over end, and he crashed into the psychosaur holding the glowing whip.

The two of them thudded hard into the side of the next mount, causing that dinosaur to stagger suddenly, its rider tumbling over the side and on top of Jet.

Now Jet found himself beneath two hissing, writhing psychosaurs.

He brought a knee up, then lashed out with an elbow. Both found purchase and the two psychosaurs toppled off of him. "Offa me, you big palookas!"

Jet managed to stand. He hurried toward the Professor—

Then found his body jerked sharply backward. He was lifted into the air. Blood rushed to his temples, thrummed in his ears.

The invisible hands threw him.

Hard. And far.

He hurtled sideways high in the air, flung like a child's raggedy doll. Through the trees. Crashing through vines.

Jet landed hard against something that broke against his body.

Dizzy, he tried yet again to stand—planting a hand on a curved concrete shape to his right. A shape which had a match to his left. Between them (and beneath Jet): shattered planks of wood, once painted green, the paint mostly flaked away.

Jet pulled his palm away, found a small hunk of black asphalt beneath it.

A road.

A bench.

He pulled himself up, looked beyond it all—

Through the trees, he saw great canyons of stone pillars rising up. Pillars thick with moss. Choked by creeping green.

Except these were no stone pillars.

They were buildings.

A nearby street sign leaned crooked up against a tree, vines pulling it into a tangled embrace. The sign read: *6th Ave.*

"We're in New York," Jet said, breathless. *This isn't the past. This is the future.*

Behind him: a branch snap.

Jet wheeled. Two psychosaurs. Whether they were the ones he just knocked off their mounts or not, he couldn't know—they all looked the same. Suddenly, their faces flickered: human guises appeared and disappeared, and he felt their greasy unseen hands prying along the edges of his psyche. He felt at his temples, found the brass headband still in place—

But it no longer mattered.

Pressure closed around his throat. Invisible hands lifted him up. He felt the psychic barrier protecting his mind start to break apart like clods of desert-dry dirt between rubbing fingers. Fingers that then sunk deep into his consciousness—

The assault began anew.

You are weak.

YOU ARE WEAK.

YOU ARE WEAK!

Then, a sound—like something cutting air. A glinty flash caught a beam of sunlight and something whipped around in front of Jet, toward the psychosaurs. Both assailants shuddered.

Then the flashing shape was gone again.

Jet felt the psychic assault cease lickity-split. He fell to the ground on his tailbone.

The first psychosaur's head casually, as if pushed by the gentlest prod, fell off its shoulders and *fwudd*ed against the soft jungle earth below. Then the other's chin dipped forward, and the head left its mooring, too. The second decapitated head rolled into the first.

Both saurian stumps burbled black blood over the scaled necks and shoulders. Then the bodies fell in opposite directions.

Jet blinked.

And nearly wet himself when a hand grabbed his shoulder.

"Get up," came a voice. A familiar voice.

Sally.

He leapt to his feet, his heart leaping right along with him—

Another chill. Another bath of icy sweat.

This was... Sally?

She was older. Not *old*, but... time had changed her, worn her down, drawn a few lines around her eyes and her mouth, framing the scowl that sat plastered on her face. One eye lay hidden behind an octagonal black eyepatch. She wore a red jumpsuit whose material seemed as scaled and organic as the skin of the psychosaurs themselves.

In her hand, a bladed boomerang gleamed. She slid it into a holster hanging at her toolbelt, and there hung other implements of war: a cattle-prod, a hooked knife, an Atlantean sonic blaster.

But no wrench.

Jet said as much: "Sally. Your wrench."

She sniffed. A momentary sadness crossed the dark of her eye like a ship traversing a black ocean. "I lost it years ago."

"When are we?" he asked.

"No time to talk," she said. "We have psychosaurs to hunt and heroes to save. Stay behind me. Follow my lead. *Don't* get us killed."

And then she was off. Striding forward into the jungle without him.

Jet felt far more unsettled than he had when he was plummeting through the time-space tunnel—this was more than just his body going topsy-turvy. His heart and soul felt suddenly like they were spinning end over end, faster and faster, refusing to return to kilter.

"It's... good to see you," he said quietly, and hurried after this time-worn Sally Slick.

CHAPTER TWO

Saurian shrieks rose and echoed around them. Distant. But closing in.

Sally marched forth with grim determination, taking her razor-edged boomerang and using it to machete-hack her way through the jungle foliage of (and this is the part that still baked Jet's noodle) Central Park. Up ahead stood Professor Khan, the erudite ape picking leaves and dust from his fur, a concerned wrinkle crossing the dark dome of his massive head.

"Professor, we have to go," Sally said. Jet detected a flinty hardness in her voice he did not recall: this was new. At least, to him.

The Professor's head jerked up and he squinted at Sally.

"Sally Slick!" The ape chuffed a laugh and hurried over, arms wide. "As I live and breathe, it is most wonderful to see—"

Sally pushed past him. And stood over the still body of the Conqueror Ape. The *other* Khan. The progenitor of all talking apes and one of Doctor Methuselah's pet projects. She nudged the still body with a boot. The Conqueror moaned and shuddered but did not wake.

A look crossed her face. A flicker of question ended by the reaper's swipe of what must have been a very unpleasant answer. Next thing Jet knew, Sally had the boomerang high over her head, except this time she wasn't going to chop down an errant jungle vine—

She was going to bury it in the Conqueror's skull.

Both Jet and the Professor leapt forward—Khan the intellectual hunkered down over the body of his so-called "father" while Jet stayed the hand of Sally by grabbing her wrist.

The look she gave him burned like a cigar tip pressed against his cheek.

"Let me go," she growled through clenched teeth.

"We can't," Jet said. "That's not... this isn't how we do things."

"You have three seconds to let go."

"Wait!" the Professor barked. "*Wait*. I... have surmised, I believe correctly, that we are in some kind of *far-flung* future of New York City. Yes?"

"The year 2000."

"And the psychosaurs are dominant. Is that correct?"

"It is. And I'm growing impatient." As if on cue: more shrieks and screeches. Closer, this time. Accompanied by the sound of thrashing foliage. "Sounds like *they're* getting impatient, too."

"We can use him. The Conqueror Ape is the one who first shackled the psychosaurs in some prehistoric age. He can tell us things. He can help."

"He is a villain of the utmost order. I don't have time for villains."

Jet matched her stare. Tried to find something in the dark of her one good eye, some glimmer of the old Sally Slick. "Please. Sally. *Please*."

The unbroken gaze told him: *She's going to bury that thing in my head first.* But then, a moment when her eyelid flickered and she looked away.

The glinting boomerang lowered.

She sighed, began prodding the Conqueror in the head with the pointed tip of her boot. "Wake up, *Mighty Ape Lord*." That last, said with some sarcasm. "Wake up or you'll find my boot in a very uncomfortable place."

The Conqueror snuffled, sniffed, jerked awake.

His eyes first fell to the Professor. "Son."

Khan, *their* Khan, said: "Do not call me that."

"What's happening?" the elder Khan asked. "Where are we?"

"We don't have time for this," Sally said. "Jet: did the others come through with you?"

"I don't know," he said. "No, it was just—just me. You and Mack—"

At that name, Jet watched another something cross her face. Another twitch. Another question, but this one left unanswered.

Jet was about to say something, about to ask what happened after they disappeared through the Atlantean gate (and he suddenly realized that if *this* was the year 2000, almost 70 years had passed since they left the timeline and reemerged), but he didn't get the chance—

A crash of brush and crackle of branch as another pair of mounted psychosaurs shouldered forward into the clearing—already the psychic wall of noise rose up in Jet's head, a cacophony of hateful words prying into his mind and dragging his worst fears out into the light. *You're weak, she never loved you, she's changed, you failed the world, you're no hero.*

But the heroes—well, the heroes and one villain—still knew their roles. In the flick of an eyelash, Sally threw the boomerang as the Conqueror leapt. Jet hit the boost on his jet-wing as the Professor barreled forward.

Jet slammed hard into one of the dino-mounts, knocking it off-balance as Sally's boomerang embedded in the rider's skull—*thwack*! The rider tumbled into the other as both apes dragged the psychosaur to the ground, pummeling the blunt-nosed, needle-mouthed creature with bowling ball fists.

Sally stomped over and reclaimed her weapon from the psychosaur's forehead by planting her boot on its neck and yanking upward. A spray of fluids flecked her cheeks.

"We have to *go*," she said.

And then, without waiting for them, she stormed off into the brush.

CHAPTER THREE

The first thought that struck Benjamin Hu was: *This is not my world.* He fell to the city street and gazed up at skyscrapers buried beneath choking greenery, tangling vines connecting each to each. He saw the bat-like shapes of Pterosaurs orbiting high above, riding heat vectors and shrieking. He smelled nothing of the city: no exhaust, no plumes of burning coal, no perfume or cologne. All his nose could detect were the scents of wildness: the heady odor of jungle tinged with the cloying sour stink of rot, and behind all of it, a lizardy stench like the reptile house at the zoo. Again that thought: *This is not my world.*

That, followed by a question: *Where are all the people?*

And then, down the block toward 7th Street: a cabal of psychosaurs emerged from around the corner, one riding a Tyrannosaur with reins of glowing fungus, the others marching behind in eerie lockstep—

Benjamin knew then that this was not only someone else's world, but this was someone else's fight. His strengths played to the finer points of archaeology, to deciphering occult riddles on old urns or sealed tombs. But this? A world claimed by the psychosaurs? *Lost* to them, even? His was a rapier-touch. He was an elegant weapon for a civilized time.

This was a battle for survival. A brute-force scramble just to stay alive.

He was the wrong weapon for this fight. The wrong *hero*.

He did all he could do: he ran.

But even that plan was short-lived. He took ten steps and another column of psychic saurians turned the corner ahead of him, and suddenly his mind was besieged as if his head were shoved under too-warm waters—his own thoughts, already trending negative, suddenly turned to a deeper darkness: *Die, give up, roll over, you have no weapon, you are no hero, you brought a knife to a dinosaur fight, you are alone and a failure—*

When next he opened his eyes, a glowing orange lash cracked the air just inches from his nose—and another wound around his neck with a searing sting. Everything went electric, then fell numb.

They have Benjamin.

Amelia hid in the shadows of an old café, ducking down behind a window long-shattered, the glass pulverized beneath her knees. The café—meant to look Parisian (a fact that made Amelia suddenly yearn to see Paris again)—was in ruins. Checkerboard floor shattered by bulging roots. Ceiling pulled down, mossy vines dangling from the gaps. A row of brass coffee urns toppled on the floor. The human world was rust and doom; the plant world was alive and eager.

So, too, were the dinosaurs. Outside on the street, a phalanx of psychosaurs marched, sending a spike of anger through Amelia's heart. She knew that in a sense they were just animals, but they possessed a keen and cruel intelligence: they had clearly subverted this world the way any bully could subvert the mind of his victim, the way any dictator might drown a nation in his dread philosophies.

That's when she saw:

They had Benjamin Hu. They dragged him behind them, drawn forth by invisible hands. His body was still.

She didn't know where any of the people in this city were. When she appeared just across the street, dropping out of the space-time-continuum with a rippling burp of air, she spied no bodies—no humans living or dead in this place. Where were all the people? Were they taking Benjamin to the same place everyone else had been taken? Or were they all... dead?

The answers to those questions would come later.

For now, it was time to save her cohort. Her *friend*.

Amelia had no weapons.

And the headband once used to protect her mind from the intrusions of the psychosaurs was nowhere to be found.

She saw the monstrous lot. And heard more in the distance. Plus the screeches of Pterosaurs. The bellows of massive lizards.

The odds were not only against her: they were heaped upon her shoulders, as heavy as the world carried by Atlas himself. This battle was impossible.

But she was a Centurion.

And this was her way.

Amelia leapt into the street, fists cocked and ready to fight.

Atok watched.

He dangled, upside down, from the frozen stone sculpture of a gargoyle made to look as if it were in mid-leap, like a panther. Down below, he watched as the reptilian enemy dragged one of those Uplanders down the ribbon of black asphalt, between the canyon walls of forgotten buildings reclaimed by nature.

Reclaimed by nature. A beautiful thing, in a way: this was the Upland as Atok envisioned it in his dreams. Just as he once hoped he would lead the Neanderthals to take back the above world, he hoped too to let the world be taken back by the environment from whence it arose.

But, in that dream *he* was the warrior-architect of this reclamation. This was a crass perversion of that: saurian beasts from a time long before did not belong here. If any conquering army from beyond was meant to take it all back, it was Atok and his people of the Hollow Earth.

Where were his people?

What had happened to his fellow Neanderthals?

What world *was* this? He was no ape; he knew that they all fell into a rift—a temporal vortex. He *felt* it. Felt time passing them by: the sounds of the world growing, changing, falling prey to saurian claws.

But when? How far forward were they cast?

It made him dizzy to think about it. His people possessed a very simple view of time: everything was *now*. The past remained an ancestor. The future forever unborn. All of life contained in the moment you have, and so this *time travel* business muddied waters once clear. Had he failed his people? Was there a way to—

Wait. What was this?

Down below: a shape moving swiftly. Running from under cover. Ah. One of those other Uplanders. One of the ones who got him into this mess.

He flung himself from the gargoyle's perch, dropping one ledge after the next. Time, perhaps, to get a closer view.

Move fast. Before they can see you coming.

Amelia leapt the curb, bolted for the dozen psychosaurs tromping forward. As she ran, her eyes spied a weapon of opportunity: a dented, rusted hubcap off an old Ford V8. She swept it up, spun it around, and jumped—

The hubcap clanged as she smashed it against the back of one's head, then the other. The two psychosaurs gargled their tongues and dropped, face-forward—Amelia planted her foot on the one's back and launched herself into the mix. *Whongggg.* The flat of the hubcap broke teeth. The edge collapsed a throat. She threw an elbow. Tossed a fist. Launched a boot. All in the span of five seconds.

And that's when it hit her.

It crashed into her like an invisible, mental wave: first a high-pitched frequency in the dark of her mind, like the sound in one's ears after being too close to a gunshot. Then, whispers that turned swiftly to screams: *Stupid woman, so weak, you failed, the world is doomed,* Le Monstre *has won, THE MONSTER HAS WON*—her limbs seized up, the hubcap dropped from her hands.

She felt her back arch as her body fell backwards, her muscles rigid—

All seemed to go slow. A bug caught in pine sap.

The black, dead eyes of the psychosaurs peered toward her. Wormy tongues licking too-sharp teeth.

A pulsing fungal rope wound around her neck—the pressure there, so intense. A deep burning, a foul itch.

Then: a street sign.

The cracked cobalt blue finish, humpbacked in the middle: *5th Avenue.*

It came out of nowhere and bashed a psychosaur's head flat—like a boot stomping on a birthday cake. The sign, wielded by a shirtless, hirsute man. She caught a glimpse of a firm jaw baring yellow teeth, a ridged brow beneath a tangle of dark hair, and a pair of wild, obsidian eyes.

Hands, rough and callused, unwound the spongy rope from her neck— instantly the pressure dissipated, though the cacophony of screams still reverberated in the hollows of her mind. Those same hands swung hard fists, knocking down a pair of onrushing saurians before returning to Amelia's body and lifting her up over his shoulders.

She smelled sweat. And blood. And earth. The view of her world suddenly shifted as she craned her head to see the battle falling farther and farther away. Benjamin Hu was left behind, and suddenly all went vertical as she was carried over something, then up, up, and into bright sun and then, disturbingly, into darkness.

CHAPTER FOUR

Brush cracked beneath Professor Khan's knuckles and feet as he barreled deeper into what was once Central Park. The others fled with him—nearby, Jet Black ducked ropes of vine and gave his wing a boost over a boulder. Sally was ahead. His fath... ahem, the Conqueror Ape was somewhere to his left. And behind them, the snorts and shrieks of the psychic saurians, swift and merciless—and close, too.

But for all the fear of being chased by a battalion of psychosaurs, the Professor couldn't keep his mind from thinking about Sally and the *other* Khan.

Sally had changed: older, yes, obviously, but it was more than that. Most softened as they aged; Khan knew many of the other professors at Oxford whose sharp British edges were rounded over time. They let students get away with more, and were more likely to let a lecture dissolve into a round of personal storytelling.

Sally had not softened. Her edges were whetted—if once she was a pebble, now she was a jagged hunk of lava rock, blasted into a rough, porous palmful. This was not the Sally he remembered. It was hard to imagine what she had gone through to become this person.

And then...

The Conqueror Ape. The original Khan. "Father." The villain responsible—at least in part—for all of this. The sinister, demented ape-lord who went back in time and was the one who brought the psychic saurians from the beginning of all things to what now seemed like the *end* of all things.

Here he was, running alongside them.

The Professor could not abide this. Couldn't even wrap his head around it. And yet, when Sally Slick planned to kill him with her boomerang blade, his first response was what? *To stop her.* Why? He should've let her do it. Matter of fact, he should have *helped her.* Held the old ape's head still while she—

Ahead, to Sally's right—a confetti blast of leaves as a psychosaur on its Ornithomimus mount appeared, racing forward, a whirling lasso of fungus above its head. Sally cried: "Keep running! Do not engage!"

She ducked the lasso, clutched her head, and hurtled forward over a fallen park bench and then a collapsed tree—

Another mounted rider to her left—

Behind them: more of those damned monsters. Khan couldn't even count how many. He could only see the heads of their mounts snapping at branches and open air. Saw too many pairs of those dead eyes catching the gray light of the sun above. Half a dozen riders? Perhaps more? He felt suddenly those psychic tendrils in his mind, whipping about like a lashing tail, looking for purchase—

He tumbled over the park bench and the tree, almost losing his footing.

Knuckles on shattered asphalt. An old walking path? A glimpse of a sign: *Boathouse.* With an arrow pointing.

His muscles began to seize. For that was the true danger of the psychosaur assault: it wasn't their physical presence that could contain you. It was the cage their mind built for you, a cage of fear and regret, bars struck from the raw metals of grief and terror—

You are your father, a monster like him, you're no hero, you're no Centurion, just a foolish ape in a kilt who failed everyone...

The Professor dropped forward, limbs stiff. His shoulder hit the earth—a jagged starburst of pain flared hot and bright.

The psychosaurs had him.

They were done for. Jet was sure of it. They'd dallied too long arguing with Sally, saving the Conqueror Ape from the fate of her blade. And now, as his limbs began to tighten at his side, as a tornado of bad thoughts fast eroded any optimism he felt, he knew they'd truly failed the world.

His jetwing felt suddenly heavy. As he bent forward and fell to the ground, it felt like it was crushing him beneath it—he could barely turn his head to see the dense foliage all around them, the cracked ribbon of a bike path cutting through the trees, the distant shimmer of water—

Then, he saw something else, too.

A pair of eyes. Human eyes. Staring at him from behind a curtain of thick jungle vine. And teeth, too. White teeth. With lips turning up into a mischievous smile.

He wanted to say something, but all that came out through his half-paralyzed mouth was, "Guhh?"

Somewhere up ahead, Sally yelled through gritted teeth:

"Now!"

The eyes and smile emerged from the vines, but the vines didn't move. A pretty girl with big freckles and wild curls of hair literally came *through* the vines as if they were insubstantial—but suddenly Jet saw *she* was the one who was insubstantial. Light shone through her the way it did through a light mist or a suspension of pollen. She giggled as she stepped forward and then floated over his head, airy and free as a child's balloon.

What the—?

Then everything erupted. From somewhere came the crack of a gunshot: a psychosaur spun off its mount and thumped against the dirt. Another woman, this one not a ghost, appeared from under a carpet of moss with what looked to be a mountaineer's axe—an axe she quickly brought against the head of another psychosaur, burying the sawtooth tip in one of the monster's temples.

Then, another psychic wave washed over him.

With this one came a booming voice that sounded familiar, somehow—

YOU'RE FREE NOW. RUN, LITTLE MICE, RUN.

The voice nagged at him but now wasn't the time to think about it: Jet leapt up, his jetwing once more feeling like a natural part of him rather than a boat anchor on his back. He saw Sally ahead, waving him on.

He looked around. The psychosaurs were either being dragged off their ostrich-sized mounts or were instead stiffened up, as if frozen in the grip of their own psychic rigor mortis. Black blood trickled from serpent-like nostrils.

Another gunshot. A rose-bloom wound appeared in the chest of one of those monsters and it fell backward off its beast.

Ahead, past Sally, Jet saw a man in a hard hat with a trencher shovel strapped to his back and an Enfield rifle in his hand.

"You heard the lady!" the man yelled out, his accent clearly Australian. "Move, lads, move!"

Another gunshot split the air.

A voice over his shoulder, almost lost to the high-pitched din of Jet's ringing ears. The Professor. "We'd better move, Jet. I think they have this well in hand."

Bleary, dizzy and more than a little confused, Jet managed to nod and hurry after the erudite ape, with the Conqueror following. Ahead, Sally waved them onto the path—ahead, a pair of unmounted psychosaurs stood stock still and trembling. Sally hurried up on them and—*swish swipe*—took off their heads at the neck.

They hurried forward. And then, suddenly, Sally broke from the pack and darted left—toward the shimmering, mist-covered waters of a lake and boathouse. The Professor shrugged and they hurried after.

Sally ran down a smaller path. Leapt over a fat-knuckled root and hurried onto the moss-slick dock that extended out fifty feet into the lake.

She bolted to the end of the dock.

Then leapt over the edge and into the water.

But there came no splash. She merely disappeared beneath the water's surface as if the water never existed in the first place.

Never existed.

The Conqueror pushed past them, muttering something dismissive as he passed. He, too, did the same as Sally: a cannonball leap over the end of the dock—

And then he too was gone. Whoosh. Silent. No more.

"I suppose it's our turn," the Professor said.

"I admit to thinking I maybe have brain damage," Jet added.

"A logical conclusion, my friend. Shall we?"

Jet nodded, hesitant.

The two of them took a running leap off the end of the dock—

And fell down through a gray layer of mist and tumbled through shadow.

CHAPTER FIVE

Shick.

Shick.

Shick.

Amelia's eyelids fluttered. Her body twitched, then she bolted upright.

All around her: some kind of... hotel suite. Beams of light trapped dust and illuminated plush carpets the color of stomped grapes, bronze wall sconces, marble-topped dark wood furniture, and a massive four-poster bed.

On the bed crouched the hairy, half-naked man.

A butter knife in his hand whittled a broken chair leg—the shattered chair sat nearby on its side—into a clumsy spear.

"You," she said.

"Me," he agreed.

And then, for a little while, silence but for the silver knife slowly winnowing the tip of the chair leg to a splintery point. *Shick. Shick. Shick.* She stood on wobbly legs and looked around the room once more: saw the veneer of fine living ruined by decay. Mice or rats had chewed into the room's corners. Spiders nested in the eaves—spiders big as her hand, unusual for New York City but common for, say, the tropics. On a corner desk she found an old stationary pad: The Sherry-Netherland Hotel.

Shick shick shick.

"You saved me," she said, finally.

"Did. Yes."

"You didn't save my friend."

"Could not. Too many creature."

His speech: primitive, guttural, growled.

Tentatively, she stepped forward. "I need to go save him."

"So. Go."

But she didn't budge. Not yet. Instead she asked, "How? How did they not... mess with your mind? You waltzed in there like it was nothing."

He shrugged. "I'm strong."

"You saying I'm not strong?"

Another shrug.

She balled her hands into fists, assumed a boxing stance.

"Let's go, then."

The hairy caveman—because that's what he looked like, like a damn caveman out of the Natural History Museum displays—offered up a curious smile.

"You woman," is all he said. "Human woman."

That's it.

She ducked in fast, threw a hard punch. He was fast, too—he brought the spear up like a club—

The chair-leg club swished through air—

Her fist slammed into his jaw like a train. *Pow!*

The caveman bowled over the side of the bed, legs akimbo.

He groaned. Stood up. Amelia rubbed her nose with a knuckle and sniffed as she did so. Her fist radiated pain from clocking him so hard in the jaw, but it felt supremely worth it.

The caveman nodded. "You fist good."

"I *hit* good."

"Mm." He grabbed his club-slash-spear off the floor, then sat back down and continued to whittle. "Me Atok."

"Me... er, I'm Amelia."

"A-me-lee-uh." He nodded, then, as if he approved. "We wait. Night. Go down." He pointed to the floor.

"Go down where? I have to leave now. My friend—the one we left behind? I don't know what they're going to do with him."

"No. You no make it."

Anger bloomed anew. "Oh, what, because I'm a woman?" She cocked a fist, tested the air with it. "You want to go again?"

"No. Too many creature."

"I don't know about that." But she did. She'd already been overpowered in that earlier fight. If this city was teeming with them... "How'd we get away, anyway?"

"I climb up. I move fast. They move only together. In group. That make them slow." She thought then about a lone soldier being a lot swifter on his feet than a whole army: it's why scouts traveled alone. "We need ally."

"I have other friends."

"I too. Down." Again he pointed toward the floor.

"In the lobby?"

"Beneath ground. Inside caves."

"Others like you?"

He nodded. "Many."

For all her toughness and bluster, Amelia felt suddenly tired and damnably weak. The psychosaurs played off her weaknesses, but they didn't conjure any thoughts that weren't already there: she had, with the others, failed the world. This was a ruined place. Ruined because they couldn't save it. Just as she couldn't catch her parents' killer, *Le Monstre*, she couldn't save mankind from this fate. Whatever that fate was. A fate Benjamin Hu would soon discover: another fact that proved how she had failed.

It's then she knew she couldn't do this alone.

"We can get their help? Your friends down below?"

"I am war leader." A pause. "This is *war*."

CHAPTER SIX

Benjamin Hu's mind was no longer part of Benjamin Hu's body.

There came the point when he felt the two disconnect, like a wagon unhitched from its tractor. Except his mind was not left behind as the body continued on: rather, it remained inside him, still seeing through his eyes and hearing through his ears and retaining all his other senses. But if his mind was a tractor—or a car, or a plane, or some giant robot like the ancient Hyboreans used to build—then he was no longer the one driving.

The psychosaurs were now the pilots of his flesh.

He was just a passenger inside his own body.

He saw as Amelia came to save him. He could feel them reach out for her mind—and, through it, still her muscles and her bones. He watched in horror as they came for her and in relief as a Neanderthal man descended upon them brandishing a street sign as a weapon.

An inelegant weapon. Nothing so deft as, say, a *rapier*.

(What he wouldn't kill to have a rapier.)

(And control of his hand to swing it.)

He saved her. Took her away. The psychosaurs gave chase but they weren't prepared to go vertical, and the Neanderthal was. More interesting was how they kept trying to find his mind to control it—but he could feel their control slipping off like hands trying to hold an oil-slick tool.

Time seemed to have little meaning. He could see the sky above and also the tilting, towering jungle-taken towers. A tropical heat washed over him. Sweat beaded on his brow.

He saw dinosaurs, too—the long neck of a Brachiosaur shoving his head in and out of shattered skyscraper windows like a bear looking for honey in a broken tree. Pterosaurs orbiting overhead like bat-winged vultures. Little chicken-sized lizards running close to him for a time, cooing and gurgling.

But time felt blurry. Unmoored. Like his journey through the city, dragged behind a pack of psychosaurs, took minutes. Or hours. Or a thousand years times a thousand years.

Eventually, though, his journey came to an end.

The saurians dropped him on a curb, his eyes cast skyward.

Towering above him: the familiar spire of the Empire State Building.

It had changed.

It was a tower of fungus, now: bloated fungal pods and intestine-like tubes wound around it. The pods swelled and deflated like a bladder of air. The tubes pulsed with glowing light. As Benjamin's mind recoiled in shock, his body remained utterly still as a trio of squirming mycological tendrils descended toward him, moving of what appeared to be their own volition— one coiled around his legs, another around his hips, the final under his arms and around his forehead.

They began to lift him up, up, up.

The hot breath of a jungle wind washed over him. The city disappeared beneath him as he was carried story after story. His head lolled and shifted, allowing him to see the side of the building as he was carried up it—

The windows were gone, but some walls had been removed entirely—supported by rubbery struts of gooey fungus. In the building he saw people. Hundreds of them. *Thousands.* Not office workers. *Slaves.* Bedraggled and dirty. Dead-eyed. They worked to harvest the fungus. Scooping glops of wet stuff off of walls, plopping it into bags. Others using crude stone tools to cut harder, more turgid pieces of fungus—like the stems of mushrooms, but big as a child's arm—for harvesting purposes. Slime molds scraped. Spore pods lanced and bagged. All of it offering up a wild, earthy smell: sour and enzymatic.

Eventually, the tendrils slowed and stopped. Then rolled him to the side—a moment of vertigo assailed him and his mind wanted to freak out, take control, make his limbs flail to catch himself, make his legs find balance. But he couldn't. The body rolled off onto one of the top floors of the Empire State Building, and he felt his body stiffen, then stand, then walk and pick up a bag and a piece of bent rebar from an older woman who lay on the floor, still.

She's dead, Benjamin thought.

His mind wept.

The body didn't care.

The body, instead, got to work.

CHAPTER SEVEN

Jet Black fell.

To be honest, he was getting pretty tired of falling. He was a *flier*. That was his thing: he was supposed to go *up into the sky*, not *tumble end over end toward the deadly earth*. As he plunged through shadow, the thought crossed his mind that he was perhaps not as good at this as he wanted to be, that he was not the hero the world needed; but unfortunately, he was the hero they had.

Then, the darkness lit up with the buzzing green glow of mercury-vapor lamps—Jet saw the shape of Professor Khan, and he started to reach out before realizing it was not the Professor at all, but rather the older ape, Khan the Conqueror. He jerked his hand away, troubled by the mistaken association.

Suddenly, his descent slowed preternaturally—almost like he was a magnet coming up against the polar opposite of another magnet—his body buoyed in the air before gently being carried to the ground by invisible hands.

He was in a carved out cavern, the rock walls wet and dripping. More eerie green mercury lamps stuck out of the stone, the phosphorescence balanced out by torches bracketed along the way, too.

Jet got his feet under him and stood up—

And all his hero alarms went off. He reached for his pistols reflexively, but knew none were there. So instead he threw up his fists and assumed a fighter's stance as an old enemy emerged from a side tunnel.

A brine-plumped human brain in a shining bell jar (like a horrible cake under gleaming glass) sat atop a steel platform lined with plush red and purple pillows. The platform moved forward on legs that were not legs at all, but rather hinged mannequin arms that ended in fake hands with palms turned to the ground.

Jared Brain. One of the worst enemies the Centurions ever faced. Similar in his way to the psychosaurs, Brain—aka *The Walking Mind*—was capable of controlling minds and also possessed a grave telekinetic reach. He could stop a bullet from puncturing his mind-jar. He could throw a Centurion around like they were naught but a rag-stuffed dolly.

And suddenly it all made sense. Jet's blood froze as he realized that the Walking Mind was behind it all from the beginning. The psychosaurs made natural allies. And all this: Sally, the ambush above, the illusion of a lake, it was all a trap.

Was Sally even… real?

He hit his jet booster, bursting forward with great speed—

And was bowled back by an invisible fist of air.

STAY YOURSELF, BOY.

That voice came into his mind unbidden: an intrusion like he heard above. Then he realized that familiar voice speaking to him only minutes before (RUN, LITTLE MICE, RUN) had been the Walking Mind. Jet scrambled to stand, cocked his fists once more and—

Sally stepped in front of him.

"He's one of ours," she said.

"Wh…" Jet could barely find his voice. "What?"

"He's an ally," she said, as if it were a foregone conclusion. "Let's keep moving. We have things to discuss and time waits for no one." She turned then, and walked past the brain-jar automaton as if he were anybody else at all.

GO ON, FLYING SQUIRREL. FLIT AND FLUTTER ALONG NOW.

Jet gritted his teeth and hurried after.

War raced across the mind of the Conqueror Ape. A war for who he was, a war for what he wanted. On one side of the battlefield: his hatred of these people, these humans, these (this word thought with the cough of failed cannon fire) *heroes*. On the other side: his desire to appease the hero (that word, again) that was his son, to get close and to teach him what it was to *truly* be ape.

Here he was, in the bowels of the heroes' lair in some distant future where his invasion was a failure for ape-kind but a rousing and unequivocal success for the race of psychic saurian monsters he personally rescued from the brink of extinction some 300,000 years before. It struck him: if ever there was a place or a time to once more pick up from where his invasion left off, it was here and now. He could learn things from these people. He could destroy them from within.

But a battle within the war: was he that kind of conqueror? The kind who sat in the shadows, waiting? He was not. He was the type to snarl and show his teeth, the type to goad his enemies into the arena where he would break them like a bundle of twigs. He was not the *sneaking around* type—that was more in the realm of the dread Doctor Methuselah.

Here, then: an advantage for one side of his internal war over the other.

Because if Khan the Conqueror had a true enemy right now, it was his maker and his betrayer: Methuselah. Methuselah had set him up. Had ruined him. And then, at the very end of his own plans, botched them so badly that the heroes gained a foothold and were able to end it all.

Methuselah was the true enemy.

And his son would be one of those who stood against him.

That gave the Conqueror all he needed. The war waged on, but one side would demolish the other in short order. The jungle drums thudded in his wild heart. His lips curled into a smile as he followed along. As he passed the eerily still form of the Walking Mind's physical shell, he gave a chuff and a nod. An acknowledgment of one kept villain to another.

Jared Brain said nothing in response, but in the hollow of Khan's mind he heard a mechanized, raspy chuckle.

A shared laugh, he assumed.

As if to say, *We are both foxes invited into the henhouse.*

Barbarians given a key to the gate, as it were.

But then, as they turned down one tunnel strung with buzzing lights, he realized that whatever key he thought he had was an illusion.

Men and women stepped out suddenly in front of him from a side passage—and others came up behind him. Separating the Conqueror from his son.

They had weapons. A few held machine guns. Others, pistols.

Sally Slick—she with the one eye and the hard edge, a changed woman since last the Conqueror Ape saw her—came back through the ranks.

"Take him to the cells," she said. "Shackle him first."

The Conqueror snarled, was about to spit and curse, but then—

His son—*bless him, his son!*—stepped up, poised to say something.

She shushed the other ape. "I brought him, as you suggested, Professor. But I am not so foolish that I forget where last we left off with the Ape-Lord. This plague of monsters at our door—the ones who summarily took over the whole of our world—are *his* fault. He is no ally of ours. To the cells he goes."

The Professor said, then: "I was only going to agree with you. Take him away."

Khan the Conqueror stiffened. Guns prodded him in the side and the back. Others pointed at his face. He thought: *I can kill them all. A swipe of the hand. A leap up and over them.* He'd be shot, of course. But it might be survivable. Maybe.

But then, that war, lost.

He wouldn't be shot down like a rabid dog in front of his son.

The Conqueror Ape bowed his head and offered his wrists.

Iron manacles clicked closed. Cold despite his fur.

Sally was already walking again. As if this were all *business as normal.* The tunnels down here seemed to be carved right out of the Manhattan schist— the stone striated in brown and gray. They passed several smaller tunnels, a network of sorts, and down those tunnels Professor Khan saw the industry of men laid bare:

There, a table of weapons, and a tall lean man in ratty suspenders cleaning them. One tunnel over, a pair of tough, ropy women stood tilling soil in old soda bottle boxes, the containers of earth below very bright lights. Khan saw tool closets, a dingy machine shop, and then, be still his fluttering heart, a modest—well, fine, a *very small*—library of books.

None of it was enough to draw his mind away from thoughts of the Conqueror Ape led away in shackles. *Good,* he thought. *Let them take him. He should stew for a while. Pickle in his own guilt-brined juices.*

And yet, something else flickered at the edges of the Professor's emotions, a low *tum-ta-tum* of jungle drums, the echo of said drums reverberating in his ears alongside the river rush of blood...

Professor Khan caught up to Jet, shaking it off. "She's quite severe," the learned ape said to the flyboy hero, his voice low so that Sally Slick—now walking twenty feet ahead of them, marching forward with the ineluctability of a locomotive—would not hear.

Jet adjusted his goggles on the top of his head.

"Gosh, you're not wrong there," he said. "That's not Sally."

"But it is. Or it seems to be."

"This is the future," Jet said. "The future we created. Isn't it?"

Khan held both hands in front of him. "It is. I suspect so. But we should not be so chastened. Time is an imperfect river, I believe—it has no main river but is instead a series of limitless tributaries. Like the roots of the tree or—ah! Or like the mammalian circulatory system. Given to great complexity. Many tiny offshoots and branches. This is one of those branches. We could undo it only if—"

Sally wheeled on them, marched back. Her finger thrust out like a scolding school-marm. "I have one less eye, but still two ears. My answer to that is no. *No.* We made choices back then. What happened, happened. It was we who forked the road that day and this is the one we've been traveling down for the better part of our century. We are the Centurions and it is our dictate to see the world through every crisis, and this is one such crisis." Her swift words and angry tone suddenly softened—if only a little. "Besides. We are assured that the timestream is no longer available to us. Our actions back then closed the gates. All of them. You are stranded here, gentlemen. Keep your eyes on the present and cast forward to the future. The past is gone."

Then she swiveled heel-to-toe and continued to march forward once again.

Khan gave Jet a look and was about to say something, but was afraid he'd again draw the ire of Sally. Jet must've felt the same.

All they could do was share a shrug and continue on.

They were in some kind of meeting room. Big table in the center: a massive piece of wood propped up by boxes, stumps, other found objects. Non-matching chairs ringed the outside. In the center of the table and up on the walls hung various documents: maps, mostly, but some charts whose data made little sense to Jet.

"Sit," Sally said.

Khan and Jet sat.

"We have people looking for Benjamin and Amelia," Sally said.

"I had hoped they would be waiting for us," Khan said.

Jet added: "Do you know where they might be?"

"If we knew," Sally said, "we wouldn't be looking for them. Would we?"

It stung. Jet wasn't used to drawing such a harsh rebuke from Sally—she'd always been gentle with him. Mostly, anyway. What came out of her there felt more like the venom from a spitting cobra.

It was as if she realized that they might not be used to such rancor because then she said: "I assure you, we're doing all we can to find them. They must be close. I expect them to be with us by tomorrow morning. Provided they survive the night."

Survive the night—? Jet was about to say something, but then, a curtain of ratty gingham parted from behind Sally and an old Siamang orangutan tottered out with a tarnished tray of food and beverages. The ape set the rattling tray down in front of them.

Sally said: "Eat. Drink. Hard-tack biscuits. Dehydrated vegetables. And that's a pot of tea if you care to pour some—"

Khan swooned. "Tea! *Tea*. So this future is not completely off the rails, then." He reached for the small chipped china pot with a big hand, and Jet thought how odd it looked—a massive ape mitt holding what looked to be a tiny teapot perched over a delicate little cup-and-saucer. It was out of place. Which was also exactly how Jet felt here: very, very out of place.

The Professor brought the tea to his lips and slurped noisily.

His face twisted up like a wrung-out sock. The mouthful of tea was plainly still in his mouth. His eyes bugged before he finally swallowed it. It looked like it required great effort, as if he were trying to swallow a throatful of pennies.

"That's... that's not tea," he said, wiping his mouth. "That's some kind of crime against humanity."

"I quite like it," Sally said. "It's a fungus. We found it in the jungle. We have the mother patch contained in jars. It's quite energizing."

Jet grabbed for a hard-tack biscuit and nearly cracked his teeth on it. But over time it softened and his stomach suddenly did flips and flops inside him, obviously eager to get some food.

As the orangutan started to wobble away with the empty tray, Khan pointed at him. "Wait. Wait one moment. You." Then, to Sally: "That ape was in Atlantis. Just yester... well, not yesterday, not really, but... *back then*." He cleared his throat, obviously navigating the temporal anomaly with some awkwardness. "Captain Chirrang, wasn't it?"

"Yes," Chirrang said, nodding and smiling. A doddering old ape. "Hello, sir. Son of the Conqueror, if I remember."

"You were once of... the Conqueror's army."

"He helped us escape," Sally said. "If you're concerned about his loyalty, don't be. He's been with us since the beginning."

"Since the beginning of what?" Jet asked.

"The Resistance," Sally said. "I suppose it's time to tell you what happened over the last several decades. I was going to wait for the others, but time is of the essence. They will simply have to catch up. Shall we begin?"

CHAPTER EIGHT

The fungus stank. Some like sour milk. Others like rotting roadkill. Sometimes it glowed, with pulses of light traveling along it like the flicker of fire blooming overtop spilled gasoline. Other times it stayed inert but twitched and belched little spore-burps of musty puffs. As if it were coughing.

The stolen body of Benjamin Hu had already filled a half-dozen sacks with various mycological bits and glops. Some of it was quite resistant; he could feel his muscles aching but could do nothing to ameliorate it.

The body worked alongside dozens of others up here on what must've been one of the Empire State's top floors—rough guess, 80th, 90th floor. Others, crowded and dirty, did just as Benjamin did. Scoop. Cut. Into sacks. Squirming tendrils of fungus then coiled around the sacks and pulled them away, sometimes down over the edge of the shattered walls where the humid jungle wind blew in, sometimes into the hands of nearby psychosaurs who always seemed to stop for a nibble.

The body, obviously on some sort of program, suddenly rounded the corner around a giant metal strut, and as it turned its head, Benjamin saw something unusual through the eyes:

A strange spire. Pushed up through the floor. Delicate-looking, as if made from some kind of wire filament. Flickering tongues of blue electricity coruscated between those filaments—but that wasn't what Benjamin found interesting.

Up the one side of this strange obelisk were symbols.

Atlantean symbols.

It was then that Benjamin realized that maybe this was his fight, after all.

A memory:

Benjamin sat on a fallen log—a half of a *shii* tree—as gray skies drifted above. Rain spat in drips and flecks. Ahead of him, a long forest now felled. All *shii* trees, logs dropped on the moist, dark earth. Mushrooms growing up out of those trees—earthen caps, caps the color of black coffee (though some lighter, as if dabbed with cream).

The old farmer, Riku, sat next to him, sipping cold sake. "These are sacred places, you know."

"I know," Benjamin said in Japanese. "That's why I came."

"It would upset the balance of things if we tried to grow these mushrooms anywhere else. These are *donko shiitake*." In the distance, mist crawled between trees still standing tall. "We chop down the trees. We bring them next to trees already growing the mushrooms. And then they grow them, too."

"I'm not here to talk about mushrooms."

"So impatient. You're young. You have the time. Let an old man speak."

"Of course."

"The best harvests are after storms. Storms with great lightning. The lightning comes. Crackles in the sky and strikes the earth, and the next morning, what mushrooms that were here are suddenly bigger, plumper. And twice as many then grow. It is a gift from the heavens. From the ancestors who cultivated the *shiitake* hundreds of years before."

Ah. Benjamin saw now where this was going.

"It was the lightning that brought Noboru, my grandfather, back to us." The old man set down the sake, then reached behind him and with a groan pulled up a small bamboo cage. A small gray bird flitted in there. The eyes red as blood blisters. The beak crusted and cracked. A serpent's tongue flicked from inside the beak when it opened—no sound came out.

Riku handed Benjamin the cage.

"This is Noboru," Benjamin said.

"Yes. I knew it was him. The lightning came that night and the mushrooms did not grow. They turned black and shriveled. Like the toes of a corpse long-dead and burned in a fire." He paused. Stared out over the fallen logs, into the mist beyond. "My grandfather was a bad man. He trucked with *Yato-no-kami*. The snake people. We banished them but he thought to bring them back..."

"I know the story. I am sorry."

"You will remove this blight from my lineage."

"I will."

"Thank you, Mister Hu. I was right to call on you."

"Good luck with your harvest."

He chuckled; the sound of dry leaves underfoot. "Now that Noboru is gone, I need no luck."

Benjamin disposed of the evil ancestor. That was a journey that took half a year out of his life. A journey that took him to meet the snake people, that caused him to grow feathers out of his elbows for a short time, and that first put him on the map as a man who knew things about the other side. And, more importantly, who could *do* something about it.

But right now, that wasn't what mattered. The serpent people, the possessed bird, the ancestor-demon—that was of no help to him here.

What Riku told him about mushroom farming, however...

Lightning. After a lightning strike, mushrooms grew.

The spire thrust up through the floor of the Empire State Building. It was an Atlantean artifact. A generator of power, like something out of Tesla's laboratory, but far older. That suggested to him two things: one, that the psychosaurs pilfered the Atlantean technology before—or during—their takeover. Two, that this massive tower of fungus was here because of that electric spire. An electro-culture like that from Japan.

As Benjamin worked, he stayed alive and awake behind his own eyes. He found that he could tune out, could pull back his gaze and retreat into his own mind—the work remained drudgery enough that the temptation to do so was strong. But instead he held fast to the present moment. Looking for something, anything—some opportunity to get close to that spire.

Again, time passed. He couldn't be sure how long, but it must've been hours—hours of scooping fungal slurry into a sack which tendrils then grabbed and dragged away. Hours of hacking off mushroom stems and dropping fetid mushroom caps into a different sack—that, again, squirming tendrils came and took. His hands ached. His knees throbbed.

Across from him stood a woman using an old metal ruler to shave a desktop coated in twitching pink cilia into a sack—the woman was young but looked old. Once, he imagined, she was tough and vibrant; she wasn't a secretary but maybe someone who worked down at the docks. Pretty as a sunset, but tough as a bull. Or, Benjamin believed, she was *once*. Now she looked haggard, thinned out, her face ashen, her hands trembling. How long had she been here?

Suddenly, the ruler scraped across the edge of the desk and slipped—the edge stuttered and slashed across her palm, opening a fast cut.

Benjamin's world went upside-down.

He felt the hand-pain. Felt the sharp slash, the wet blood gushing. His consciousness went loop-de-loop, then barrel-rolled hard to the left and his mind was swiftly plunged into a dark field with pinprick lights getting closer and closer and closer—

The lights grew and suddenly he saw they were people, people whose faces were clear but whose bodies drifted into non-corporeal mist toward their legs and feet. Like ghosts hovering over a dark plain. Benjamin heard the cacophony of voices: *help us who are you how long have I been here everything hurts EVERYTHING HURTS* and he realized then some of them were talking to him, *who are you we don't know you help us can you help us WHY WON'T YOU HELP US* and then the world dipped sideways and turned topsy-turvy once more—

Benjamin rushed back to his body.

And the body got back to work.

But a lingering realization remained.

One of the faces in the crowd?

He recognized that person, and that person was his ticket out of here.

CHAPTER NINE

Sally stood pensive.

Then she paced in front of them. Then she stood still again.

Stop frittering about, you... you dumb girl.

The tale caught in her throat was not an easy one—how could you encapsulate almost seven decades of struggle and apocalypse? Was it even worth it? And to an audience of two. Not exactly Carnegie Hall.

Khan was smarter than she. Always was, always would be. And Jet... well. She didn't want to think about Jet. She needed him. But she also needed that veneer of naïveté to come crumbling away. This was not a world for the weak. Gee-shucks-golly optimism would get him killed. Or all of them.

With that in mind, she began to talk.

"That day. Atlantis. The last time we saw each other was there, above the gateway. I realized that the Atlantean weapon in my hand wasn't intended to be a weapon, but rather a tool. Like a screwdriver with a screw. I used the tool and... the platform dropped away. Methuselah fell into the vortex. As did you all."

Deep breath. *This is in the past. Don't relive it. Just retell it.*

"Methuselah's ray left me... debilitated. A broken doll on a shattered elevator. I don't know how long I was there. I lost consciousness. But later I awoke as I felt a heavy pressure make the elevator platform dip. And there was Captain Chirrang. He said he came down to find his master, the Conqueror Ape, but I said that he was gone. He fell through the hole, I said, but the hole was already closed up. Chirrang mistook me for an ally of Khan's and grabbed me with one of his big gangly arms and... carried me back up the elevator shaft.

"Chirrang carried me to the wreckage of Lucy. There, outside the plane, was... Mack. Mack was..."

Jet leaned forward. Brow knitted in concern.

She was about to finish her story, but then a voice boomed from across the war-room: "Mack was *what*?"

Dammit.

She barked: "Mack was supposed to be asleep."

"Well, Mack *was* asleep," said Mack Silver, coming into the room, "but Mack had to take a squirt and then *Mack* heard voices and then—"

Mack's eyes landed on Jet Black and Professor Khan.

Those eyes went wide. His sneer spread suddenly into a big white-toothed smile. "Jet! Talking Ape!" He guffawed like a drunken donkey (which was a description not far from the truth) and hobbled toward the table.

A flash of anger flared hot in Sally's gut.

Damn that husband of hers. Damn him all to hell.

Jet stood, saw Mack Silver coming over to him.

Time had not been kind to the man. He hobbled, his one leg stiff as a broomstick, giving him a sloppy, crooked lean. His face was hard lines and peppery stubble. His hair, once black and slicked back by a pomade, was now a snowy gray and mussed up in a tangle that called to mind an overturned mop—his hair truly was the color necessary to earn him the name *Silver Fox*, except now he'd lost the other part of the equation. Jet was no dame, but Mack was no fox.

Still! Still. It was good to see him. He had to remind himself: *I just saw Mack Silver yesterday. Mack hasn't seen me in the better part of a century.*

Mack threw his arms around Jet, then pulled Khan into the middle of the hug. He continued braying with laughter, but then stopped short and said, "Ooh, watch the hip, watch the leg—little brittle, little brittle." But then the braying started anew.

Somewhere in there, the laughing dissolved into crying.

When that happened, Mack coughed loud into his fist and pulled away, blinking quickly. "Been a while. Fella'll get a little nostalgic. Don't think that means I like you, kid."

He thumped his finger hard against Jet's chest.

But then Mack winked. Jet offered a very real smile. He was about to ask Mack how he was doing—

Sally slammed her fist down on the table.

The table shook. The room quieted.

Out of the side of his mouth, Mack said, "Uh-oh. The old ball-and-chain's rattling again, better watch out."

Old ball-and-chain.

Sally barked: "Mack, close your yap and sit down."

"Yes, dear," Mack said, clearly mocking. "Light of my life, love of my heart, splinter in my paw, fly in my soup." He pulled a chair and sat next to Jet.

Jet looked to him and said in a low voice: "You two are... married?"

"We were married at the Koloa chapter house," Sally said. "I would've gotten there soon enough had my story not been interrupted."

Mack rolled his eyes. "Marital bliss, kid, marital bliss."

"Mack, cut the commentary, would you?" Sally said, tone sharp as an axe.

"Yes, boss."

Sally sighed. Rubbed her temples. Jet could see that this encounter had already worn her down.

"Forget the whole story," she said suddenly. "I'm just going to cut to the quick. Mack and I escaped Atlantis on a small Atlantean submarine. Chirrang manned the helm. By the time we made it back to the East Coast of America, the psychosaur invasion was already in full swing. Khan the Conqueror's army was leaderless and thinned by the invading Neanderthals—"

"What jerks," Mack said with a sniff.

"And the Neanderthals were thinned, too. Suffice to say, we fought the war against the dinosaurs. And we lost."

"No, no, no," Mack said, waving his hands about. "That's short-shrifting the story, *dear*. We fought a *twenty-year* war against the psychosaurs. We gave good as we got for a time. And there was a point we thought we could really win it. I mean, hell, the psychosaurs had limited numbers. The time gates were closed. They couldn't keep coming through, wave after wave. And even though most of us Centurions were sidelined, this world was a world of *people*. Ingenuity and a go-get-em spirit. Plus: boats and planes and Tommy guns."

He suddenly looked only to Jet and the Professor and his voice got low like he was telling a ghost story. "But there was something we missed, see? We thought we were crushing their numbers. And maybe we were. But they had a secret weapon. A volcanic island. Middle of the Pacific nowhere. Lush jungle. Perfect for what they needed: a breeding ground. And for the better part of five years all those bastards did was *make more of themselves*. And the more of them there were, the stronger their *mind powers* became. Came a point when all they had to do was swim to us, and once they reached the shoreline, their psychic power swept over us like a wave. They'd gotten stronger. They'd *evolved*. Those little tinfoil doohickeys for the temples—they were done for. About as useful as wings on a pig." He gave Sally a look. "Sorry, sweetheart."

Professor Khan spoke up: "How did you survive the onslaught, then? If they could not be contained and their powers were so severe..."

Sally answered: "Like I said, the Koloa chapter house. That was where we managed to bring all the remaining Centurions. Not many of us left. Just a few dozen heroes left behind."

"But here you are," Khan said. "Not in Hawaii. How?"

Sally looked about to answer, but it was Mack who spoke up: "We danced with the devil, Professor. The world of men was almost over. Our enemies— the Shadows of our century—were just as done as we were."

Suddenly, Jet got it.

"The Walking Mind," he said. "That's how you do it."

Mack snapped his fingers. "Give the kid some cotton candy."

"Of course." The Professor nodded. "The Mind has his own psychic powers. He can... presumably create an impermeable bubble? That's how we're protected right now. That's how they won't find us."

"And," Sally continued, "in part how we maintain the illusion of the lake above our heads even though no such lake exists. A little physical trickery thanks to the Great Carlini coupled with the mind powers of Jared Brain and we were able to carve out a space in Manhattan from which to lead the Resistance."

"The Resistance," Jet said. "You aim to still stop them."

"Of course we do," Sally said. "We're taking back New York City first. Then America. Then the world. And we're doing it with your help."

Mack clapped a heavy hand on Jet's head, then mussed his hair.

"*Viva la Revolución*," he said, chuckling. "But first, let's get some grub. I'm buying."

CHAPTER TEN

Atok stifled a cry. He dared not bleat in weakness with this human woman at his side. It would do no good to have her see him like a mournful child, but that was suddenly how he felt: like a child whose parents were taken away, whose world was ripped asunder.

He stared out over the wreckage of his world.

The city above their heads, the one called New York and now claimed by the lizard people, was where Atok had staged the Neanderthal invasion of the Upland. The membrane here was thin between the human world and the civilization of his warrior-people, and so climbing down through tunnels and boltholes took only the better part of a day.

He expected to return home, to be greeted by a pair of guards at one of the tunnels, guards armed with tusk-maces or saw-tooth swords. But the passage was empty and unguarded. Cobwebs fluttered in the breath of the underground, and a few fat millipedes scurried into crevices.

They descended further and now, before them...

Empty homes, the stone walls scratched with claw marks. Bones of Neanderthals, the skeletons hidden beneath the desiccated leather of what was once the flesh of the body. Everything, empty. And silent. No children playing. No warriors practicing battle. Just death and doom and stillness.

They had a myth that says a Neanderthal's death is just him losing a battle against the Ghost Beast—a creature that's part bear, part tiger, but with the heart of a Neanderthal warrior beating in its chest. All succumb to the Beast eventually—one can never truly defeat the specter. But to have so many fall to the Beast—and, in this case, a literal beast with claws and fangs in plenty— struck Atok in the heart like an arrow. He had no vision of the battle, but to die at the hands of these atrocities was honorless and crass.

The human, Amelia, said nothing. She wandered off, perhaps to explore, perhaps to give him a moment.

In the time he was alone, Atok felt his rage bubble over.

He grabbed a rock and smashed it into a wall. He snarled and stormed about, gnashing his teeth and pounding his chest.

He wailed for a time, and then, with no eyes on him, he wept.

Some time later, Amelia returned to him. She placed a steadying hand on his shoulder as he sat, crouched, his head low, his greasy hair in front of his face.

"I found something," she said.

It was a map. Carved into the wall of a Neanderthal temple. She drew Atok past the pillars, past the paintings on the wall of men and women like him hunting monstrous prey: giant insects, hairless albino tigers, stags thrice as tall as a man. At the back, though, what stood carved was, to her mind, a map.

Atok hurried over to it. Studied it. Said, "This is our kingdom. Part of it." He began pointing out locations on the map. "This us. Temple of Krong the Hunter. Here, the White River. This testing ground of Night Cricket assassins. Down here, unspeakable place. Rift in earth where Gods of the Dark hide."

"Yeah," she said. "But what's this?"

At the top of the map was what looked to be a new carving. Different from the rest. Atok frowned. "Someone defile map."

The addition looked like an offshoot—a smaller passage that led... well, that was the question, wasn't it? Right now it seemed to lead nowhere. In the space beyond someone had carved a strange symbol like a broken axe.

"The symbol—" Amelia was about to ask, but Atok stiffened.

"Retreat," he said. "Means place of retreat."

"That's good news, isn't it?"

He cast his eyes downward. "Retreat is never good news."

Atok reeled. They exited the temple, a place devoted to one of the first among them, the ancient worm-hunter, Krong.

Some of his people may yet be alive.

But that news sat sour in his gut. Because that meant they did not fight to the last. It meant they gave up.

It meant they fled like sick dogs. It wasn't just that they fled, either—they abandoned their home. They left this, their ancestral place below the surface world of the Uplanders, to wither and rot.

The joy that came with knowing some may yet live was then tempered by the thought of them... retreating. Surrendering. It was worse than rolling over and letting the Beast take you; it was sidestepping your duty to die well in the face of one's enemy.

He drew a deep breath. Smelled the mineral air of the Hollow Earth. Amelia looked to him: "They may be alive. That's good news. Why so grim?"

Atok wanted to say, *Because that means they are no longer my people*, but he could not find the proper words in her guttural human tongue. He was about to say something, anything to cease her inquiry, but then—

A roar split the air, echoing through the underground chambers. From somewhere beyond their city. But not far. Not far at all.

Then came by a second bellow. And a third. Then a whole cacophony.

"Attack," Atok hissed, and hurried forward, teeth bared.

CHAPTER ELEVEN

Jet sat at a table made from an old carnival prize wheel, the chair beneath him a half of a barrel turned upside down. Before him sat a chipped china dinner plate (mismatched to all the other plates he saw around the room on similar cobbled-together tables), and on that dinner plate, an odd mix: a gray kind of gruel paste, but then also: some sliced banana, a cut up mango, a little kindling of charred carrots and mushrooms.

All around the room, a rag-tag mish-mash of heroes and workers, each belonging to the other like an unmatched left sock. A man sipped from a coffee mug with a normal hand while a fist ten times the size rested next to him, giving his table a little lean. A tall woman with a domino mask sat writing in a little book that hung from a chain around her neck. A fancy fella in a black cape and with a crumpled top hat entertained a small crew of onlookers by juggling what looked to be metal playing cards—the cards flipping up and around and behind his back before he finally dispatched them all like throwing knives into the shaft of a broomhandle leaning against the wall thirty feet away.

Jet didn't see the Professor anywhere. Where did Khan go?

Across from him, Mack sat, empty plate in front of him. He fished in his jacket, withdrew a dinged-up flask. His thumb spun the top and he took a pull.

He offered it to Jet. "You drinking yet?"

"We just saw each other yesterday."

"Oh. Right, right." He took another quaff. His face twisted up into a wince that turned fast into a toothy smile. "Hey, listen, kid, I wanna talk to you about—"

Suddenly, Mack's eyes flitted over Jet's shoulder and he interrupted himself to shout and bellow and laugh.

"Hey! You guys, get the heck on over here, c'mon, c'mon," he said, waving his hands, his laugh dissolving into a throaty chuckle. He coughed into his hand and Jet found himself surrounded by a handful of familiar faces.

Here, then, stood the ghost girl with the freckles and the wild tangle of hair. Next to her was the redhead with the mountaineering axe. And coming up behind, the Australian with the Enfield slung over his shoulder and a plate of steaming gruel in his hands. Mack started the introductions.

"The sometimes see-through girl is Lily-Belle Atkins. The strapping lad is Colin, the Aussie Digger. And this saucy minx—" He reached to pat the redhead's hip. With a fast motion she tilted the pick-axe hanging at her belt forward so the very tip of the front-facing blade bit Mack on the back of the hand. He yelped and withdrew his mitt. "Ehhh. That's Shepersky."

"Tara," she said, and offered her hand. Her voice was strong and lyrical. Jet took the hand and gave it a shake.

"Good to meet you, mate," the Digger said, eschewing a hand-shake and instead clapping Jet hard on the back.

Lily-Belle just said: "Hope I didn't scare you too much back there." And before Jet could summon up a proper answer (because, actually, she *did* scare him), she drifted up through the rocky ceiling like it was naught but a layer of fog.

The other two headed off to sit down across the room.

"Good people," Mack said, still rubbing the back of his hand.

Jet frowned at him. "You're married to Sally."

"Hm?" Mack sucked down another sip of whatever was in the flask. "Yeah. Yes. That's true, kiddo. See, and now I can call you kiddo for real because I've got about... sixty-some years on you. I am officially *your elder*."

"Then act like it."

"What?"

"Clean yourself up. And flirting with that lady? Tara? *You're married*."

"Our marriage is..." His words drifted off and suddenly his eyes narrowed in anger. He thrust a finger up under Jet's chin. "You listen to me, you little bumblebee. You don't know what went on. You don't know what we've seen. You punks popped out of our reality like folks leaving a party, leaving us around to handle all the damn *clean-up*. I'm tired. I *hurt*. My leg's about as worthless as a short-sleeved straitjacket. So you best not judge."

"I'm allowed to judge. You're a Centurion and so am I. You're better than this."

"Better." Mack leaned back, snorted. "See, kid, there comes this moment in every person's life that they realize their parents aren't as smart or as *adult* as they figured—your parents are supposed to be the ones with the brains. But they're not. They're not our heroes. They're just dum-dums like the rest of us. Just humans. Stupid, broken humans. Fumbling their way through life. That's the thing about the Centurions. We're imperfect, too. We're not heroes. Not really." His voice went quiet all of a sudden. "If we were heroes, we would've saved the world."

"Mack—"

Mack launched himself onto his feet into a wobbly stance. "C'mon, kid, let's go talk somewhere private."

Jet stood as Mack started to hobble off. "Mack, wait—"

"I said, *c'mon*."

The Professor crept down the rocky corridor where he saw the guards take his fath... progenitor. His heart thudded dully in his chest: *lub-dub, lub-dub, lub-dub*, fast turning into those jungle drums that sometimes plagued him now during times of duress: *ba-doom, ba-doom, ba-doom*.

There. A room shaped like a teardrop. At the far end, a cage like you'd use for a wild animal at the zoo: iron bars fixed to the rock above and below. A door welded together and locked with several loops of chain and a handful of die-cast padlocks. In the darkness beyond the bars, a pair of gleaming eyes.

A breathy nostril snort broke the silence.

"Son."

"Don't," the Professor warned. "I'm not your son."

"Would you rather that I remind you that *you* are actually *me*?"

"Were that true, then I would be *like* you. But I am not." Khan stammered as he continued: "I'm... an Oxford professor. And a hero of the Century Club. Whatever is inside you is not inside me. We are most certainly not the same."

A rheumy, rumbling laugh. "You *are* like me. That's why you're here right now. You want to ask about your wild heart. About the drumbeat you hear."

Lub-dub, lub-dub.

"I wanted to gaze upon a false Conqueror," the younger Khan bit back. "A fallen idol whose sense of self-importance defeated him in the end. A classic story, isn't it? Phaethon thinking he could control his father's solar chariot. Narcissus falling so in love with his own image that he couldn't look away from his watery reflection. If we recall our Proverbs, *Pride goeth—*"

"'Pride goeth before destruction, and a haughty spirit before the fall.'" The Conqueror grinned. "See? I read."

Ba-doom, ba-doom.

"As they say, the Devil can quote scripture."

"Let me also remind you that the story of Phaethon is the story of a child who thought he could equal the father."

BA-DOOM.

The Professor raced up against the cage, teeth bared, fists pounding on the bars: "I am not your son! *Say it again and I'll tear you apart.*"

His ape fists curled around the bars. His chest rose and fell like a great surging tide. His heart calmed. The blood river in his ears dulled its roar.

The Conqueror applauded. A slow-clap of ape mitts.

"The wildness within wants to come out," the elder Khan said. "You had best let it. It wants to dominate. It wants to take *ownership* of this world. These people around you are not your friends. They are fools who would die for imaginary ideas—false notions of heroism and other *pap*. Be the conqueror. Take control. Leash them and own them. Let me out of this cage and together—"

"We can rule the world?" the Professor asked.

"Yes! *Yes*."

"I don't want that."

The Professor pulled away, sure he meant those words. But a tiny part of him thought how glorious it would be: away from the books, from the classroom, no longer wearing a suit jacket or a pair of little eyeglasses made to pinch his flaring gorilla's nose. Out there. In the world. Decked in armor. Or in nothing at all. Roaring and charging and crushing anything that stood in his way.

No.

That was not him. That was just this old foolish ape showing his true colors: the Conqueror was no gorilla, but rather a worm. A worm crawling inside the Professor's mind. The younger Khan turned and began to walk out of the room.

"You'll be back."

"I won't."

"You'll need me. I know things. You said it yourself. About the psychosaurs. I can help you. Together we can—"

"Together, we do nothing." A pause. "Alone you can rot."

And with that, Khan hurried out of the chamber.

Jared Brain stalked the subterranean passageway ahead of them, the mannequin arms forming the herky-jerky legs that carried him forward. No mechanism was necessary to animate them: his telekinetic powers handled it fine.

Jet and Mack pushed ahead.

Inside Jet's mind:

HELLO, LITTLE MOUSE. OR IS IT, LITTLE FLY?

Jet scowled at the brain floating beneath the giant bell jar. Mack pulled Jet down a side-passage.

"I don't like that guy," Jet whispered.

I CAN HEAR YOU.

"He can hear you," Mack said, a half-second too late.

Mack spun Jet around, pushed him into a small enclave, then sat down on a rusted cabinet that rattled.

"She wants to take the city back," Mack said.

"Sally."

"Yeah, Sally. Who you think we're talking about? Mother Goose?" He popped the cap on his flask, took another pull.

"I know Sally wants to do that. She told us as much."

"She wants your help in doing it."

"I know."

"And how do you feel about that?"

"I..." Jet stopped. Tried *not* to think about it. "I'm tired. It's been a helluva day. I just need to stop, get my head around everything—"

"We'll get you to your bunk soon enough. But don't lie to me, kid. I saw that... twitch. That little *moment of hesitation*. Chase that spark. Capture that firefly. I want to know. How do you feel about reclaiming the city?"

He didn't want to say it but—

"I feel like it's too late," Jet said.

There. Those words. The sting of pessimism. Rare for Jet Black. He was always the *go-get-em* type, the one who even in the face of a thousand enemies thought he had a way forward. A way to *thread the needle*. But he couldn't summon that kind of spirit now. It felt... forbidden. It felt final.

"Thought so," Mack said. His face, crestfallen rather than relishing in it. "The optimistic one doesn't even think it's a good idea."

Another pull of the flask—back, back, back until it was empty.

"Mack, it's not like that—"

"It *is* like that. And I agree with you. This isn't worth saving. None of it."

"But you and Sally—"

"Should've never gotten together. You were right back then, kid. She and I, we don't mix. She's a puddle of jet fuel and I'm a spark from the engine and—" He clapped his hands together. "*Voosh*. It was always you and her, kid. Always."

Jet didn't know what to say.

His body knew what it wanted to do, though.

He threw a fist. Punched Mack Silver right in the jaw.

The flask dropped to the floor with a rattle.

Mack's tongue snaked out, tasted a bead of blood rising up on his split lip.

"I deserve that," Mack said.

"All this time," Jet seethed. "And you don't even love her."

"Jet," Mack said, suddenly sounding tired and drunk and, strangest of all, sad. "I love her. I do. But I don't think she loves me. And love ain't enough. All the storybooks say it is but it's more than that. Love'll get you through the first ten years but the next ten, twenty, *fifty* years... you gotta have bigger logs on that fire to keep it crackling. Sally needs you. And not this Sally. But the Sally from back then. You see what I'm saying?"

"We can't go backward. We're here. Now."

"Kid, you're only here because you time traveled here."

"Well. Yeah. Okay, fine, but those time gates are all closed—"

"I say we find a way to open them again."

"And how do you propose that?"

"I don't know. I don't have much going on up here." He tapped his head. "But I know someone who does. C'mon."

CHAPTER TWELVE

Another memory:

Baalbek. Once known as Heliopolis, the City of the Sun.

Benjamin ran. Not above it—not within the ruins of the Temple of Venus, no. Rather, far beneath it. He hurried through the twisting knot-like catacombs—tunnels once carved by the hands of man. Soon they broke apart, revealing a hole into a far greater, far older labyrinth. This labyrinth was also an unnatural one, but too smooth, too perfect to have been carved by the hands of mortal man. Not, at least, without some help.

On the smooth-sculpted walls, Benjamin saw images of the ones who may have helped shape these twisting channels: glyphs of huge humanoids in bell-helmets with what looked to be antennae rising from their heads.

The Ancient Astronauts. Figures who came from space—or, as Benjamin believed, from another dimension altogether—to deliver wisdom to the human species. To "uplift" them with knowledge and science. A controversial theory, one that suggested that mankind wasn't responsible for its own advances and was instead handed a gift by powerful beings. (Not far, Benjamin thought, from the notion of gods and goddesses. Why would one reject the idea of Ancient Knowledge-givers but embrace the idea of a Sky Father delivering wisdom?)

It didn't matter. The old texts and glyphs didn't show a successful "uplift"—the Astronauts had judged us able, but we proved that we were still a species of warriors, unready for a boost to the *next level*. Glyphs deeper in chambers like this one ended inevitably the same: with the large helmeted humanoids being cast to the ground and torn asunder, or stabbed with spears, or crushed with rocks.

Benjamin believed that humanity just wasn't ready.

But we've come a long way, he thought, boots echoing on sculpted stone.

Just the same: the Astronauts left behind gifts. *Devices*. In this case, a powerful occult battery that—if it matched the one beneath the ground at Catal Hayuk—absorbed the energies of the dead and turned them into *actual* energy.

In this case, electricity.

Just as he thought that, a coruscating ripple of dancing purple lightning flickered down the smooth-bore tunnel, washing over Benjamin. His body seized for a moment and he almost tumbled forward—everything numb, stars behind his eyes, tongues of electricity still licking up the blade of his rapier.

But he found his footing. Kept running. If he was already too late...

Benjamin burst into a wide-open chamber, the walls smooth but for the scalloped furrows starting in the center and running up the walls like ribs.

In the center of the room stood a platform.

On that platform was an object that looked not unlike a small stone fountain—the edges sharper, and inlaid with pearl and copper. What poured forth from the fountain was not water, but rather—

Lightning.

The room strobed with blue light as crackling fingers of electricity came off the fountain, searching the air.

Behind the device stood a man in a metal suit, a massive helmet on his head that looked not unlike one of the Mayan helmets seen on carved figures at Tikal (itself a place where Benjamin believed the Ancient Astronauts visited). But this helmet was made of coiled wire and jagged spires.

Lightning climbed off the fountain and crawled up to the man's helmet, electricity bridging the two spires rising off his helmet.

"You come too late, Detective!" Der Blitzmann yelled, cackling.

"Friedrich," Benjamin shouted over the snap-hiss of electricity. "You're a scientist. Not a scholar of history!" He thought, but did not add, *And you're mad as an oracle, to boot.* "You're messing with forces you could not possibly understand!"

"This is electricity! This is the *only* force I understand, Detective!"

Blitzmann tilted his head forward and from the twin spires atop his metal helmet fired two searing white bolts of lightning.

The room lit up as they struck the ground only ten feet in front of Benjamin. He smelled ozone. His legs tingled and itched. All the world was washed away in a bright tide of pure white—

When his eyes adjusted again, he saw them.

Two tall figures. Like the Ancient Astronauts.

But made entirely of electricity.

The electric elementals charged forward, hands out, threads of lightning wrapping around Benjamin's chest and then head. Everything buzzed and the world shrieked and he knew then that all was lost.

It wasn't all lost, of course.

That was ten years ago. Funny how then everything seemed like a crisis. It was, in a way. But now, with the world fallen to the psychosaurs, all of that turned out to be just a precursor to a much bigger, scarier cataclysm.

Regardless, what mattered now was that Friedrich Blitzmann was here. *Here.* In the Empire State Building. Working the fungus as a slave to the psychosaurs.

Blitzmann was insane. A formidable threat not necessarily because of his skills with electricity (which were well-practiced and dangerous, indeed), but most certainly because his actions were always unpredictable. Other villains had motivations that made sense: they wanted a great deal of money, or they hoped to control the world, or it was a matter of vengeance, so on and so forth.

Blitzmann—or, rather, Der Blitzmann, his practicing name as one of the world's deadliest malefactors—only wanted electricity. He loved it like most people loved a spouse: he wore the suit only so he could get close to it.

"My lightning embrace!" he would sometimes cry as he called electricity to him. He spoke to it. He claimed it was his *friend*.

Somehow, in some way, Friedrich Blitzmann was going to help him escape this place. And maybe, *just maybe*, bring it all to the ground.

The woman cut her hand. That's what did it. That's what brought Benjamin roaring out of his body and into the collected hive-mind of all the fungal workers.

As for the woman—

It was as if the pain of her hand freed her. Benjamin watched as her eyes went clear, losing that ignorant cultist shine all of them had, that *thousand-yard stare*. And she suddenly looked left, looked right, made a cry in the back of her throat like a wounded animal, then took one step—

And vine-like tendrils of pulsing fungus swung down from above, coiling around her arms, her midsection, her legs. She shrieked as they hauled her upward through a gap in the ceiling fringed with finger-like spore-blooms.

Then she was gone.

And that's it, Benjamin thought. One more piece of the puzzle slotted into place. The electro-culture of the fungus. The presence of the villain known as Der Blitzmann. The freedom brought on by a moment of real pain.

Only one more piece of that puzzle remained, and it too lingered in the deep of Benjamin Hu's memories.

CHAPTER THIRTEEN

Before Amelia even knew what was happening, Atok launched himself forward, running back down through the ruins of his own civilization.

Toward the danger, if she figured it right. *Toward* the shrieking monsters.

This wasn't heroics. This wasn't a man defending his kingdom from intruders no matter the cost. This was personal. Some axe he was grinding in the dark of his mind—he had something to prove and it was going to get him killed.

She understood it, of course. She'd been in his position many times before. Leaping into danger with nothing but your fists because of some principle, some stupid idea lodged in your craw like a piece of meat between your teeth.

Amelia knew it well.

Didn't make it smart. And she'd always been lucky to have people pull her feet out of the fire just as she was about to get them burned off.

Besides, until she found her friends—if her friends were even here—Atok was her only shot of getting Benjamin back from those monsters.

So, just as Atok ran, she ran after.

He was fast. Faster than she was. He clambered up over earthen rooftops, using ridges of stone and shelves of clay pots as ladders and as springboards—she found herself sticking to the ground only, watching him dart along walls and up rocky outcroppings with the same combination of might and finesse found in Khan the Conqueror or any of his primate-kin.

There came a point when she lost him.

But then she heard his barbaric yawp ahead—

Coupled with a howling saurian roar.

Oh, dammit.

She launched herself forward, legs burning with the extra oomph she gave them—she damn near lost her footing and went tail over teakettle when she tripped on a root popping up out of the cracked ground, but managed to recover and skid down a short slope. Just in time to see Atok thrown from twenty feet away, his body a tumbling boulder that she had to sidestep lest he knock her down, too.

And there, ahead, stood a trio of massive beasts. Amelia didn't know dinosaurs from door-knockers, but what she *did* know was that these so-called thunder lizards were big as a city bus with massive spiked sail-fins atop their backs, sails that were as tall as the beasts were long. One of them raised a blunt-nosed head—a head like a damn wrecking ball torn off its chain—and bellowed, revealing a mouthful of yellow teeth.

Teeth big as Amelia's arm.

"Atok" she growled. "We gotta go—"

But Atok was already gone. He sprang up and was already bolting back toward the three beasts.

I will not retreat, Atok thought.

Then the thunder-beast's head collided with him like a giant fist and sent him hurtling backward into a stone shelf. Pain ignited in his spine, a torch-bloom of misery. But there, that thought again, clinging to him like a burr.

I will not retreat.

His people were cowards.

Anger and disappointment were two snakes that coiled together in his belly. He set them on fire and jumped back into the action.

One of the sail-fin beasts charged to meet him. But he was faster. More agile. He planted a bare foot on the thing's nose and launched himself up over its tree-trunk neck and toward its sail-fin.

Upon reaching the fin, he ducked to one side, then pressed his back against the sail-fin...

It was like a sling-shot. The sail-fin, pushed to its limit, catapulted him off the one rampaging lizard and into another: fist first. His coiled fist popped one of the creatures in its scale-ridged eye, and suddenly the creature shuffled backward, shrieking and blinking and shaking its head like a snow-stung wolf.

Atok whooped and pounded his chest.

A half-second later, the third beast's tail crashed into his legs. He fell, his back hitting the ground, the air blasting free of his lungs. As he gasped and tried to suck air into his chest, he saw the massive maw of one of the lizards open above him—all broken yellow teeth and foamy gray-pink tongue. He kicked out, snapped off a tooth, but the creature was undeterred. It plunged its mouth toward him.

A rock rebounded off its leathery snout.

The lizard's head recoiled. A low growl rumbled in the back of its throat.

Hands grabbed under Atok's arms, dragged him backward. Amelia. The human. Good. Yes. She would help him defeat these intruders. She would help him complete what his own weak whelp people could not. *Would not.*

But then she stepped in front of him, a rock in her hand.

"My turn," she said.

Then brained him with it, knocking Atok into darkness.

CHAPTER FOURTEEN

Mack hurried fast as he could, what with his lame leg and all. The kid, Jet, came behind him—still so eager, with bright eyes like shining quarters and a heart that wouldn't quit. Mack envied him for that. Loved him for it, too.

And maybe hated him a little.

He was a good kid, though. He deserved better than this world.

Which is why Mack wanted to destroy it.

"C'mon," Mack said, waving the kid down a small passage. Ahead, there was a metal door in the rock. Two guards standing outside: Smythe and ehh—what was the other guy's name? Jenkins? Johnson?

"Silver, whadda you want?" Smythe said, all that eye-rolling head-shaking. They didn't respect him around here. He heard the way they talked about him. *Gone to pasture. Useless as a bump on a frog's behind. When was the last time he did anything worth talking about?* They'd know soon enough.

"Smythe," Mack said, smiling big and holding out his hands. "Old buddy, old pal. How you been? How's your wife, my kids?" Smythe scowled. "And you, Johnson—"

"Jameson."

"That's what I said. Jameson. Hey, you guys, did you meet Jet Black—"

Mack grabbed Jet and shoved him hard into Smythe. As the other guard, Johnson—Jameson!—was distracted, Silver threw a hard punch across the man's jowly jaw, knocking his lights out.

Smythe pushed Jet back and Silver hollered, "Get him, kid!"

But Jet just spun his head toward Jameson, then toward Mack.

"What the heck, Mack?" Jet said, incredulous.

Smythe scrambled backward into the door, reaching at his belt for a Webley revolver hanging there—but Mack slammed into Smythe with a hard shoulder, once, then twice, catching the guard's wrist in his hands and bringing it hard against his knee. The pistol dropped.

Mack headbutted Smythe in the nose.

The man's eyes rolled back in his head and he slumped to the floor.

Mack rubbed his forehead.

"I gave you the signal!" Mack said.

"Signal? What signal? What's going on?"

"It's fine, it's fine, it's just been some years. We've forgotten how to work *properly* together is all."

"I saw you just yesterday!"

"Right, uh-huh, yeah, let's stop with the jawbreaking and get on with it." Mack stepped over the bodies of the two guards and opened the door.

Together, they entered the chamber of Doctor Methuselah.

Professor Khan fretted.

He paced the passageways of this subterranean place, noting how different it looked from the Century Club he was used to. Was this even the Century Club anymore? They didn't have any of the symbology. None of the mottos. This was a place of rock and dust and grease. He smelled sweat and toil mixed with the mineral stink of subterrestrial air.

Khan was used to the smell of wood oil. Of soap and hair pomade. Of books and the dust that collects upon them.

Of course, his fretting had only a little to do with all that—mostly his disorientation in this place was serving only to heighten the tensions he felt about being in a place like this with that ugly villain with whom he shared genetic material. He knew that the sinister ape was right: at some point they'd have to go to the elder Khan and find out just what he knew about the psychosaurs.

The Professor just didn't want to be there when that happened. The Conqueror Ape had a kind of... power over him. Nothing supernatural, of course. But the Professor couldn't deny the connection, and in the Conqueror's presence he felt the jungle drums beating louder and louder—not just in a way that demanded he step into the world as a two-fisted hero of the Century Club, but in a way that relished in the potential violence of those two fists. A tiny voice inside said, *With your brains and his brawn, there is no land you couldn't conquer.*

He protested that voice, of course, but the voice was as seductive as the snake in Eden: *But you could do it for the good of mankind. You could conquer the psychosaurs. You could conquer mankind, too—not to destroy them or hurt them, but to be a benevolent leader, of course! They are so often the architects of their own misery. Look at this place, look at how far civilization has fallen. They need someone like you to step up and remind them of their glory by presenting your own in full display...*

No! What the—? That wasn't him. That had *never* been him. The most he'd ever led was a classroom full of Oxford girls. The most he'd ever conquered was a bevy of dead languages (the Eyak of the Na-Dene still gave him the sweats).

Khan's mind wandered back a few steps, to the smells that appeased him: wood oil, soap, pomade, and—

Books. Yes! Books.

He felt suddenly naked without *books*.

Books were his armor! His weapons!

And hadn't he seen books on his way into the headquarters?

To the library!

Mack spoke, but Jet barely heard him.

"...last thing Sally built was this contraption..."

Jet staggered into the chamber. His entire body tensed up. Hands into fists. Teeth pressed against teeth.

Along the back wall of the earthen chamber stood two pylons that were fed by various wires and pipes. Next to each was a phonograph, both were playing different records simultaneously and at great volume—one, Glen Miller's *In the Mood*, the other, Mozart's *Requiem in D Minor*. The resultant song was one of noise—aural chaos that set Jet's nerves on edge. Carved in the walls of the chamber were symbols that made no sense at all to Jet: squiggles and angles, starbursts and alien ampersands. All of it the alphabet of another world.

And in the middle of it all stood Doctor Methuselah.

The old man looked frail. Thin and without much substance hanging on his bony frame. His body was propped up between the pylons: wires hooked him to each, and his eyes roamed in his head without any sense of pattern, gaze drifting over the symbols as if he were trying to parse them without any success at all.

Once again Jet tuned back into Mack's voice:

"...found him ten years ago in Columbus Circle. He dropped out of the time-space continuum earlier than anybody figured. He was doddering and deranged. Harmless as a fly with his wings plucked. The other body, the one he'd given part of his mind to, that handsome gentleman thief, Spears—yeah, we found that about 50 yards away, deader than dirt. So, we captured him and brought him here. Hooked him up to this rigmarole. Sally built it with the help of the Brain. It's meant to make sure Methuselah's mathy-magic doesn't come back to him. The chaos confuses him. Or that's what they say."

"Methuselah," Jet said.

The old man's eyes suddenly stopped rolling in his sockets.

His stare fell swiftly to Jet.

"Jet Black."

Methuselah's voice: like a door creaking open. Dry mouth. Ragged throat.

"This looks like torture," Jet said to Mack.

"It is," Methuselah answered. "I... could use a drink of water."

Mack scowled. "Not my job to wet your whistle, you old codger."

Quieter now, Jet said, "Mack, I don't like this."

"It is what it is, kid. This is the mad monster who caused all this in the first place." Mack's glare was like hot irons. "And I think he's the one who can help us undo it all."

"You come seeking advice," Methuselah said.

Mack nodded. "Yeah. We do."

"Mack—"

"Mister Black," Methuselah said. "Is this the world you hoped for?"

"...No."

"It is not the world I hoped for, either."

"It's the world you made. This is your fault."

Methuselah chuckled. "Yes. It is. I thought I was a perfect creature. That my understanding of the cosmic equation was flawless. But the gem was cracked. I am imperfect. A terrible revelation for one's self-esteem, but there it is."

"You're a megalomaniac."

"Ah. A megalomaniac who has realized he will always fail."

"So what?"

"I'm a neutered wolf. A gelded bull. The best I can hope for is to unravel the tapestry I've made. And you can help me do that."

Mack stepped to Jet, put his hand on Jet's shoulder. "See, kid? This is what I'm talking about."

Jet asked the old man, "But what do you get out of it?"

"A return to ignorance. The me that is now will... well, who can say? I can no longer see the patterns. I do not know what will become of me or how this timeline will fare given its unwriting. I only know that somewhere back there lives a Methuselah who goes on in great ignorance. And I miss him the way I miss my childhood, a childhood of math on blackboards, a childhood of popping the heads off mice to see what waits within. A childhood of stars and books and death. I miss it. I want it back. And so I concede to help you. That is why you're here, isn't it?"

Jet said nothing. He felt paralyzed. Part of him wanted to run. Part of him wanted to free the old man. Another worse part wanted to kill him—both as an act of mercy and of vengeance. An unusual feeling for Jet. Maybe Mack was right. Maybe this world was bad for him. Bad for everybody. *A poisoned timeline.*

"Somebody needs to go back in time," Mack said. "But the time portals are all closed."

"Yes. You made sure of that, didn't you?" Methuselah chuckled. "Though, what if I told you one still existed? A time portal that did not close? Then what would you say?"

It was Jet who spoke.

"Then I'd say we're interested in making a deal."

Khan tottered into the library. Though, calling it a "library" was a crass exaggeration: it was a closet with books piled onto ramshackle shelves.

"Let's see, let's see... what wisdom lies within..." For that was what books were to the Professor: each a little treasure chest piled with the shiniest gold of all, *the gold of knowledge.*

Grapes of Wrath. Okay. *Ulysses.* Khan always struggled with Joyce, though he appreciated the man's mythic Irish underpinnings if not his style. *Bullfinch's Mythology*, a few of the Hercule Poirot mysteries, the *King James Bible...*

"Egads," Khan said, crestfallen. "None of these will—"

A scuff of a heel behind him.

Khan turned to see who had come upon him in this cramped claustrophobic space, half-expecting Jet or Mack or anybody—

But when he turned, his breath caught in his chest.

Psychosaur!

The creature lurched toward him, hissing, reaching out with clawed hand. *We are under attack!*

"My Arctic lair," Methuselah said. "I opened a portal there—this was no natural portal, no gateway connected to the other gateways as was the Atlantean chasm. No, this one I ripped open like a child cutting holes in his mother's bedsheets to wear as a costume. This gateway will not be so easily closed and so I am sure it still exists—though, I can no longer feel it for my connection to the cosmic equation has been snipped, as if with a pair of magical scissors."

Mack smirked. "Then I guess we'll have to find your lair, then. Thanks, old man. I'll send somebody in with a damp sponge that you can suck on."

"Wait!" Methuselah rasped. "You will never find the lair. Not without my help. It is protected by a dozen equations of stealth and misdirection. You will lose yourself trying to find it. You will freeze to death in the icy wastes."

"What are you, Santa Claus?"

"I am no Spirit of Giving," Methuselah said with a chuckle.

"Mack," Jet said, grabbing Silver's elbow. "Maybe we do need him."

"Kid, we got what we came for—"

Suddenly, the door to the room flung open.

And there stood Sally Slick, flanked by the Walking Mind and the pair of guards—Smythe and Jameson.

Sally stormed in, silent as a snow squall. Jared Brain's herky-jerky automaton body followed after, mannequin hands clicking on the wood-plank floor. She marched up, ignoring Jet, and stood nose to nose with Mack.

"Sally—" Mack started to say.

Her fist pumped into his gut.

Mack doubled over with an *ooff*.

"Sally!" Jet cried.

She wheeled on him. "Don't. You're already on ice so thin that one more word from your fool mouth will melt it. I thought you were better than this. Getting roped into some harebrained scheme by *him*, of all people."

"He's... your husband." Those words pained Jet, but there they were.

"He is. And I know him well. I know that he's lost his courage. Which means he's lost his way. My husband he may be, but he is no longer one of us. The century is over. We're all on the way out and he's the first among us."

"Sally, this world, this timeline—"

"It isn't a *timeline*," she barked. "It's now. It's where we are. It's *when* we are. There are no other timelines. There's you and me and this place and a mankind that needs saving. Not yesterday. Not in 100 years. *Today*, Jet Black. The call is out. We need a hero. Are you the hero of today? Or will you forsake today— will you forsake all I've accomplished here—for some foolish whim planted in your ear by a drunken old pilot and one of the century's worst Shadows?"

Jet had no answer.

But before he could even muster a sound of uncertainty, a voice boomed through his head—and by the look of it, through everyone's head.

The Walking Mind spoke to them all:

WE ARE UNDER ATTACK.

The Professor chuffed in alarm, grabbed a copy of Joyce's *Ulysses*—no small book, weighing in at 1000 pages—and swung it hard against the psychosaur's half-lizard, half-humanoid head. The book clubbed the creature, knocking it back out of the library closet. The creature's arms pinwheeled and its legs gave out as it collapsed to the ground.

Khan leapt, baring teeth, the book raised high like a boulder.

"No hurt Steve!" the psychosaur hissed.

Khan pinned the creature with two prodigious ape legs, but held the book aloft without letting it drop.

"Wh... what?"

The psychosaur winced, turning its head away.

"Steve just want read new book! *No hit Steve with book.*"

Well. That was certainly curious.

A contingent of guards followed Sally, Jet, and the Walking Mind as they stormed through the winding passages of the Central Park HQ, Tommy guns and pistols at the ready. Jet asked for a couple pistols, but Sally just gave him a look.

Mack Silver followed, hobbling and shaking his head.

Jet felt bewildered. Marching into what may be battle with the evil Jared Brain jogging alongside him in his four-legged automated housing just showed him what a topsy-turvy world this was. He was half-surprised Sally Slick didn't have a sinister-looking Van Dyke goatee that she stroked as she conjured her malevolent plans.

Still. No time for any of that now. *Get your head in the game, Jet.*

They rounded a bend and gazed suddenly down a long tunnel, a tunnel whose lights faded in the middle. Darkness waiting at the end.

Sally held up a hand and they all stopped.

"That way's been closed off," she said in a whisper. "Someone breached."

"Psychosaurs," Jet hissed.

She gave him a look that said, *Must be.*

In the distance—the sound of footsteps. Plodding. Slow.

The men raised their guns.

Jet cocked his hips, held up a pair of fists.

A shadow emerged. From out of darkness and toward the light.

LOOKY-LOOKY came the psychic voice of the Walking Mind.

"Oh, gosh," Jet said, suddenly bursting from the pack and running down the tunnel. Sally called after him but she stopped when she saw:

It was Amelia. Carrying the slumped body of a Neanderthal man.

CHAPTER FIFTEEN

Doctor Methuselah hung amidst the bundle of wires and tubes, the alternating sounds of Miller and Mozart competing in his ears. All around him, the symbols of nonsense meant to muddle his mind and disturb any chance he had of reclaiming his hold on the equations that bound the universe together—the same equations that could, in the right hands, tear it all apart.

But the symbols were not nonsense. Obscure, yes. Occulted, true. But they were by no means without value. And the two competing records playing on the phonographs did indeed create aural chaos, but the resultant chaos was a beautiful thing: a fractal flower of auditory possibilities, synced up *just so*.

In just such a way that the soundwaves were like a key.

Slowly unlocking his mind. *Click-clack.* Tumblers falling.

It still hadn't trained his magic back.

The equations remained outside his grip. Like butterflies flitting just beyond the mouth of one's swooping net.

But they were closer now. Just a little bit... closer.

He whispered aloud: "Are we in any danger?"

A voice returned inside his mind: NO, GOOD DOCTOR, NOT YET.

"They have not yet found Benjamin Hu?"

THEY HAVE NOT, BUT WITH THE WOMAN AND THE NEANDERTHAL THEY ARE THAT MUCH CLOSER.

"For now, we are safe. But we must not let Hu near this place."

I AM WELL AWARE OF OUR NEEDS AND VULNERABILITIES, DOCTOR. TUT-TUT. LET'S NOT PRETEND THAT YOU ARE THE ONE IN CONTROL OF THIS OPERATION.

Methuselah chuckled. "Of course, Jared. I doff my cap to you—ahh, metaphorically, of course—and your wisdom in this great plan."

PART TWO:
FIGHT THE FUTURE!

CHAPTER SIXTEEN

Night.

Sally took out an unlabeled bottle, poured a draught of amber liquor into a tin cup, then slid it across her desk to Jet. She poured one, two, three generous splashes into her own tin cup, then held it aloft.

He scrambled to toast her, but she didn't wait: Sally's head tilted back and she drank it all in one quaff.

Jet set his own cup back down without drinking any.

Sally's office had none of the organization that her old workshop used to have: she used to label every tool, clean them religiously, hang them in their place (and every tool had a place). This desk had maps strewn about. A journal tented on each cover stood at the corner. On the other side: an Enfield revolver with a half-circle of bullet casings around it.

It wasn't just that her tools didn't have a place. It was that there were no tools at all.

She must've caught him staring. "Not like my old workshop," she said.

"No. This is different."

"I'm leader, here. I'm not expected to be some kind of greasemonkey."

"Sure. Yeah. Of course."

"I don't really do much of... that anymore."

"Making stuff, you mean."

She poured another shot for herself, then gestured toward him with the neck of the bottle. Jet shook his head.

"Yes. Making stuff. Or fixing it. No time for that."

"But it's what you were good at."

"Oh, I see." There, a signal flare of red, raw anger. "You don't think I'm a good leader. You think I'm just some... *farm-girl* who's real good with a tractor motor, that it? That was a long time ago."

"It wasn't that long ago for me."

She ignored that and talked over him: "So is that why you were trailing after Mack like a puppy dog? Listening to his schemes and conspiracies?"

"No—I... how did you even know about that?"

Sally rolled her eyes. "We have Jared, remember? The Walking Mind?"

Right. Of course. *Him.* Even now, Jet realized the old villain could be inside his mind, a presence standing unseen in the psychic shadows. That was powerful surveillance, indeed. A chill ran up his spine. It was the same fear he had whenever he saw one of the psychosaurs: that sense of invasion, of being ripped open like a book with all your pages torn out so they could be read under an unforgiving light.

He asked, because he had to: "How is any of this worth it?"

Sally's eyes narrowed. "What does *that* mean?"

"It means, in order to fight the psychosaurs you've lost who you were. The Century Club has given up so much of itself to win this battle."

"No, we've given up what we had to in order to *survive*, Jet. This isn't us winning any battles. This is us *just on the edge of losing*. See, and that's what you don't get." She pointed at him with the bottle again, this time not as an offer for more but rather as a glass finger making silent accusations. "We're what's left. The world has been taken over. Most of humanity is enslaved or dead. They work people to the bone. They breed them like we used to breed cows. The slaves farm the fungal towers. They clean the psychosaur hives. When they fall, they get eaten because those dino-bastards love a good meal. So *forgive me* if my loss of naïveté offends you. *Apologies* if me being a hardcase offends your tender sensibilities."

"Do you remember growing up on the farm?" he asked, suddenly.

"The farm for you was a couple decades ago. But it was almost a hundred years for me, Jet. I'm at the end of my century. Time is starting to wear me down to a nub. One day soon I'll just be broken or dead." Jet blanched. He hadn't even thought of that. She continued: "And that's fine. I've made my peace with it. But I'm not going out without taking this city back. And that's where you come in."

"Sally—"

"Zip it, flyboy. Here's the news: you brought your jet-wing from the past into the future. We're going to use that as a template to build an armada of Jet Blacks. A sky full of flyboys to bring the fight to the monsters. They have dominance on the ground but the skies can still be ours."

"But why didn't you build the jet-wings before—"

Sally stood suddenly, knocking maps and papers off her desk. She growled: "I told you, I don't *do* that anymore."

"I—I'm sorry—"

"I'm not going to be building these, either. That's why having the jet-wing as a template is essential—it's basically like tracing a sketch from one drawing to another. I just need you and the others to copy."

"I... okay."

Sally came around the side of the desk. Stood over Jet and put her hand on his shoulder and squeezed. A gentle touch. Even now in this poisoned future he felt a shiver go up his spine.

"You're my ace," she said. Her touch suddenly turned rough as her hand clamped down on his shoulder, squeezing tight. "But if you betray me, I'll do what I did to Mack: I'll lock you in your room and throw the key down a dark hole." Suddenly, she let go and offered a smile that seemed forced. "Now: go get some sleep. Busy day tomorrow."

And with that, their meeting was over.

Sally stalked the halls. The whiskey—if it could be called that, and it really couldn't—was a campfire in her belly. She'd been drinking a lot more, lately. A little voice asked: *Who are you—Mack?*

She'd been having that little voice a lot, lately, too.

And so, the chicken and the egg: which gave way to which? Was she trying to drown the little voice with the whiskey? Or did the whiskey summon the little voice? No matter, now. She tamped all of it down into a dark corner because there was work to do. Even now, at night, work. Not sleep. *Work.*

(That little voice: *When was the last time you slept, Sally?*)

(Her own big-girl voice in response: *Shut up, already.*)

Back in the meeting room she found the Professor sitting there, playing a game of chess—ah, no, checkers—with Saurian Steve. The psychosaur plucked a red puck and jumped it across one of Khan's black pieces.

The psychosaur screeched in delight and Khan shushed him while chuckling. It was then the Professor noted her presence.

"Ah! Miss Slick."

"I see you've met Steve," she said.

"He knows checkers."

"Steve knows checkers!" Steve said, fangs clicking together as he spoke.

"Steve is one of our secret weapons," Sally said, coming up behind the dinosaur. He smelled... well, reptilian. She once knew a hero of the Mexico City chapter house—El Lizardo Loco—who raised reptiles, and Steve smelled like Lizardo's terrariums. That little voice reminded her: *El Lizardo is dead, most likely. At the very least, his mind's thrown backward through time. Trapped.*

"Weapon?" Khan asked, looking suddenly concerned. "How so?"

"We raised Steve from an egg. Well, Jared did. His own psychic powers interfered with Steve bonding with the psychic hive-mind of the other saurians. Just the same, he must... psychically *smell* like they do, because they don't even notice his presence. We've done tests. He can traipse about the city like he's invisible. As such, we intend to use that to our advantage. We just don't know how, yet."

"Steve is weapon, Steve is weapon!" chanted the reptile.

"If you'll excuse me," Sally said, pulling away from the table.

Khan nodded. "Of course, Miss Slick." She noted the look of concern on his face, not a look aimed at the dinosaur, but rather at her. As if a giant kilted Oxford-taught ape was one to judge. As she left the room, she heard Khan continue: "I think it's time to teach you chess..."

She took ten steps toward the Brain's chambers before Amelia stepped in her way.

"Sally," Amelia said.

"Miss Stone."

"You're... different."

"I'm older."

"You are."

"How is the Neanderthal?"

Amelia stuffed her hands into her pockets. "Sleeping it off."

"Will he be a problem for us?"

"I don't think so. He saved me. I saved him. Plus, some of his people are here, so..."

"Yes, we have a handful of the Hollow Earthers working with us here." Sally tried to sidestep Amelia, but the woman matched her step and continued standing in her way. "What is it? There's more?"

"We need to find Benjamin."

Ah. This. Not the best time for this conversation. She told Amelia as much.

"Best time or no," Amelia said, "I want to have it now."

"Fine. We will not... at present be expending any efforts toward rescuing Benjamin Hu from the psychosaurs."

Amelia looked gut-shot. "Wh... what?"

"I feel I was quite clear."

Now, the woman looked angry. Flinty eyes staring burnholes clean through Sally's own. "You gotta be kidding me. Why would you say that? He's one of *us*."

"It's simple, if unpleasant, math. Benjamin's own abilities are not in line with our needs. He is a scholar of a time that no longer exists. His strength is in weapons of finesse and we have none of those. Solving occult riddles and curious puzzles from antiquity will be a distraction, not an asset."

"Something happened to you," Amelia said, thrusting her finger against Sally's chest. "Something changed you."

"Time happened, Miss Stone. Time and war and defeat." She cleared her throat. "Now, if you'll excuse me?"

Amelia stepped aside, rage wearing etches into her face.

Good. She'd need that fire if they were going to win this war.

The chamber of the Walking Mind was a horror show. Sally asked him time and time again to change it, but he was intractable. Jared Brain made it very clear that his role in the resistance was essential, and he would not be denied.

It was the brains on the walls that troubled her the most. Jar after jar of psychosaur brain. Each eerily the same. Bubbling in some kind of pink fluid.

The Walking Mind stood—if that's the word when you travel about on a moving dais with psycho-animated mannequin hand-legs—toward the far end of the chamber, telekinetically dissecting yet another brain. Scalpels and slicing wire floated about in mid-air. Jared's jar gurgled as bubbles fluttered to the top of the bell.

"Mister Brain," Sally said, begrudging that twinge of deference she put into her voice.

WELL, HELLO, MRS. SILVER.

"I still go by Slick," she said. And she added, knowing he could hear her: *Which you well know.*

I AM HAVING A BIT OF FUN.

"Yes. Well."

YOUR INSURGENCY HAS BEEN TAMPED DOWN, I SEE. THOUGH THAT FLYING SQUIRREL OF YOURS IS STILL A TAD... TWITCHY.

Flying squirrel. He meant Jet.

"He's under control."

HE LOVES YOU, YOU KNOW. OR DID, ONCE.

"That isn't a relevant topic of discussion."

ANY STRONG HUMAN EMOTION IS RELEVANT TO THIS SCENARIO, MISS SLICK. BECAUSE THEY CAN BE USED.

EVERY EMOTION IS A NAIL. YOU CAN BE THE HAMMER THAT PLUCKS THE NAIL FROM THE BOARD OR HAMMERS IT DEEPER, INSTEAD.

She bristled at that.

THIS IS HOW IT IS, SALLY. YOU WANT MANKIND SAVED, YES?

"You know I do."

THEN THIS IS THE WAY FORWARD. IT FEELS LIKE YOU HAVE LOST SOMETHING BUT THAT IS UNTRUE. YOU HAVE GIVEN IT UP. SACRIFICED IT. SACRIFICE IS A NOBLE THING. YOU GIVE SO THAT OTHERS WILL NOT HAVE TO. IS THAT NOT THE ROLE OF HEROISM?

She didn't care to examine this any further. Instead, Sally jumped ahead: "Tomorrow we attack the junkyard. Parts for the jet-wings. As much as we can gather for as many as we can make."

"WE" CAN MAKE? WILL YOU PUT YOURSELF BACK IN THE WORKSHOP?

At that, the blood-roar of anxiety rushed swiftly to her ears. Her memories were yanked backward through time to that moment when they lost it all—*it's not a weapon, it's a tool, gate open, Methuselah blasting her, platform dropping, they've fallen, they're lost, the gate closes...* Sweat beaded on her brow. It lined the creases in her palms. Mouth, dry.

"No," she said, her voice an unexpected croak. "I mean... the others."

OF COURSE, MISS SLICK. AS YOU SEE FIT. BE ADVISED, MY DEAR, THAT I WILL NOT BE ACCOMPANYING THE RAID TOMORROW.

"Wait, what? Why?"

I WILL BE SENDING STEVEN ALONG.

"But we need—"

ME? NO. STEVEN'S RADIUS OF PSYCHOACTIVE DEFENSE IS STRONG ENOUGH FOR A SMALL CELL OF SOLDIERS. BESIDES, AS I HAVE SAID ALL ALONG, IT IS A RISK FOR ME TO LEAVE THIS PLACE. IT EXPOSES US IN MY ABSENCE. YOU DON'T WANT TO LOSE IT ALL OVER A TRIP TO THE JUNKYARD... DO YOU?

She did not.

EXCELLENT! THEN IT IS DECIDED.

"Of course," she said.

HAVE A NICE NIGHT, MISS SLICK.

"And you as well, Mister Brain."

Jared Brain chuckled in her mind as she retreated through the metal door.

CHAPTER SEVENTEEN

Atok sat, bleary-eyed, head throbbing, sipping a cup of something they called "coffee" but that tasted like a cup of volcanic silt stirred around a cup of hot spring water. Still, it was bracing, and muscled his headache back into its bag.

Others milled about this room—a room for "eating," it seemed, a puzzling inclusion but perhaps appropriate for a species of creature so fond of keeping everything in its clean little boxes—talking and shoving food in their mouths.

I am in the wrong place, he thought. *I retreated—no, I was* forced *to retreat, and now here I am.* He remembered very little of his journey here; only fits and starts as consciousness flitted past like a startled bird. Amelia woke him up this morning and brought him here and told him that she'd be back, and now...

I could fight all of them, he thought. And then he stood up, dropping his cup. He picked up the chair beneath him, earning startled looks. Then he thrashed the chair into the back of some clod-headed pink-skinned Uplander—the attack was on. His foot. His head. His fingers. His teeth. He was a weapon and...

All a delusion. A fantasy. As the others continued milling about, ignorant to the thoughts of war sweeping across his mind like a grass-field set aflame, he caught movement to his right. There. Amelia. And then—

Now he truly did stand.

Two of his people stood behind her. A young man with sandy hair pulled back in a clumsy braid, and an older woman with lush hips and a wild mane-tangle on her head. *My people.*

He gasped. Gaped. Nearly knocked over a table crossing toward them.

Amelia said, "They came here. The remnants of your people."

"They retreat here," he said in Amelia's guttural tongue. Suddenly, a reminder of their shame.

"No," Amelia said. "They were *brought* here. Just like I brought your shaggy behind—Sally's people found them under siege. They made them come. They didn't retreat. Do you understand me?"

Atok turned.

"Brother, sister," he said. Then he clasped both their hands at once and laughed so hard he almost cried.

Sally unfurled the map. Jet stood around the table with the others who were embarking on this trip: Tara (the redhead with the ice-axe), Colin (the Aussie with the Enfield rifle), Lily-Belle (the ghost girl), Steve (the *psychosaur*?!), Amelia Stone, Professor Khan, and a trio of Neanderthals (!), including the one called Atok that gave him and Mack so much trouble back... well, for Jet it was just a few days ago. Atok, who hit like a freight train. *Atok the Horrible.*

This is our crew, he thought.

A rag-tag scraped-together cabal of heroes.

Er, maybe that should be "heroes."

Sally laid out the details:

"The world has been claimed by the psychosaurs. Few pockets of humanity remain. Mankind has been diminished. Some are slaves, but just as many have died—either in attacks, or as workers for the saurian horde, or killed for food.

"This city is no different. Except here, we are the last pocket of humanity unclaimed by the invading monsters. With the saurian invasion came not only psychosaurs but also flora and fauna from before time: mosquitos as big as your fist and with a helluva bite; small raptors that alone are no danger but in packs are like vicious dogs; carnivorous plants with beautiful flowers and acid within their stalks and leaves. The city is their home now."

She began tracing different locations with her finger. "The Brooklyn Bridge is a nesting ground for Pterosaurs. Washington Heights is, too. The harbor and rivers are where the sea monsters swim." Sally began listing off breeding ground after breeding ground: Oviraptors, Ornithomimus, T-rex, Sinosauropteryx.

"And here," she said. "These are the two fungal towers."

Jet blinked. "The two tallest buildings in town. The Chrysler and the Empire State Buildings. What is a... fungal tower?"

"A colony, hive, I don't know. The strange fungus they use grows here in massive quantities. Humans are brought there to... farm it, I suppose you could say. We're not sure of the purpose. But those are not our focus. I just wanted you to be aware of them. What matters to us right now is..."

She stabbed her finger down on a red circle at the south end of Manhattan, not far from the start of the Brooklyn Bridge.

"This is the Hentz Brothers scrapyard. It's been in commission since the Great War. Or was, at least, before everything went to hell."

"I know the place," Jet said. They'd gone there during their fight against the Cult of the Lotus Engine when Sally jury-rigged a transmission tower that—

Well. Those were different times.

But just before Sally began to speak again, Jet asked: "Are you coming with us, Sally?"

"No," she said, the already short word made curt and clipped.

"But you'll know more than we do—"

"Colin knows enough. I've given him specs." She seemed tense, all of a sudden. "It's not math. It's just scrap."

She kept talking before Jet could speak up, and began to outline their path through the city.

"The Sandhogs dug this," Colin said, voice echoing throughout the tubular tunnel in which they all walked. This was the Eighth Avenue Line, part of Manhattan's Independent Subway System. Their feet clomped on broken brick. Toward the back, Steve, Khan, and the Neanderthals pulled carts for bringing scrap home. Colin continued: "Same gents who dug the caissons for the Brooklyn Bridge. Whole union of these guys. Amazing diggers. Many of 'em died down here in these tunnels, digging just the same because that's how progress is made. One inch at a time. A man a mile. Bloody amazing."

Tara snerked an ill-stifled laugh. "Here the Aussie's the one giving the New York City history lesson."

"Pretty recent history," Jet said. "They just built it..."

But his voice trailed off.

"Pretty *ancient* history for us," Tara corrected. Which explained, of course, why the top ceiling of the tunnel was already starting to crumble—tree roots and snaking vines pushed through the stone and brick.

It was hot down here. Humid. Flies buzzed.

In the distance: a sharp screech. Jet skidded to a halt, drew the two mismatched pistols Sally had seen fit to allow him—a bulky Mauser and a Colt M1911, both with magazines only half-full. Lily-Belle chuckled and Tara made a gentle gesture for him to lower the pistols.

"*Nemocolopterus crypticus,*" Tara said with a small laugh.

"Is that bad?" Jet asked.

Colin put his hands less than a foot apart. "My right foot is longer than one of those little bloke's wingspans. Tiny buggers. They nest down here. You get a swarm of them they're a bit of a pain the keister, but they scare easy."

"Oh." Jet felt suddenly foolish. He holstered the pistols.

They kept walking. Jet lagged back toward Amelia. Atok and the other two Neanderthals passed him, giving him dismissive looks. Atok grunted and scowled.

Jet had always felt like he was in good company. Always felt like part of a team. This felt like... like he didn't belong. Not with this group. Not in this place. Certainly not in this time.

Toward the back, Amelia and Khan walked.

Amelia looked troubled. Haunted, even.

"What's wrong?" Jet asked.

"Your girlfriend is what's wrong," Amelia said.

"Amelia..." Khan cautioned, but she shot him a silencing look.

"Sally's not my..." Jet shook his head. "What's the problem?"

"It's Benjamin," Amelia said. "Sally won't go after him."

Jet stammered, his tongue tumbling over words. "I... I didn't know—" He felt a sharp spike of anger. Anger at Sally. That anger was new to Jet—this was a kind of bitter rage, a resentment unnatural to him. "We can't leave Ben behind."

"Perhaps you misunderstood her," Khan said.

Amelia stared. "I didn't misunderstand. She made it clear: he's not of value to us. So, we ditch him. Done deal." She gritted her teeth. "*Dammit.*"

"I don't like this place," Jet said. "I don't like what's become of the world." He was about to say something else, but then—

A slight cough from the back of Khan's cart.

The rest kept on ahead, but Jet, Amelia, and Khan stopped.

"Did you—?" Khan started to say, but Amelia silenced him with a finger against her lips. She made a gesture to Jet. He went around the one side, she around the other. Together they found a blanket in the back, but this blanket was more than a little lumpy—

They both reached down and whipped the sheet off.

Mack Silver reclined underneath. Smirking.

"Hey, kids," he said with a wink and a blast of booze breath.

CHAPTER EIGHTEEN

This final memory, this last piece of the puzzle fitted in:

Benjamin sat shirtless on the mat of reeds, dark wooden beams above his head. His body trembled and ached. Every blink of his eyes burned like he had sand grit coating each eyeball. The fever was eating him up.

"The sickness is in you," Ji Quan said with the tenor and wisdom of an old man, despite being a boy of only 12 years. "You opened the Box of Peng. You saved the village. But you took the sickness within you and now the ghostly parasite is consuming you from the inside. Your body now. Your mind after. Your emotions as its final meal."

Benjamin moaned and whimpered. Sweat poured down his brow. It tasted salty. Smelled sour. "I..." Even speaking was difficult: even the slightest vibration in his vocal cords felt like he was swallowing razors.

"But there is hope," Ji Quan said. "There is hope in the strength of your mind. Is your mind strong enough?"

"I... don't... know..."

"If you do not know, then it is not strong enough."

"Please..."

"If you *beg*, then it is not strong enough."

In the distance, thunder rumbled like logs tumbling.

Benjamin willed his body to still. For just a moment. Breathe in. Breathe out. The cool air from the coming rain washed over him.

It felt good.

"I am..." He swallowed knives, lightning, sand. "Strong."

"Good," Ji Quan said. "Now it is time to starve the ghost. We must deny the sickness its second meal. Your mind must detach now, Benjamin Hu. It must be unmoored from your flesh and be allowed to drift out to sea. Not too far, or it will be lost forever. Are you ready to say goodbye?"

"Hello, hello," Mack greeted again, this time toward Amelia specifically. "Been a while, sweetheart. You are a spoonful of sugar in this bitter cuppa joe."

Jet pulled Mack out of the cart. The man was loaded down with an ammo strap over one shoulder and a grenade belt over the other.

The others heard the commotion and were suddenly all around—Colin with his rifle up, Tara with her axe in hand. Lily-Belle floated in the back and the Neanderthals thumped their chests and bared their sharp caveman teeth.

"Mack?" Colin asked. "Aw, what the heck?"

Tara made an *ugh* sound and lowered her axe.

"Good to see you, too," Silver said, hopping up out of the cart on his one good foot. "Oh, but not you." He pointed at Atok. "I remember you. You smelly dirt-farming mongrel." He turned to Jet, cocked an eyebrow. "I feel I could've come up with a better insult. I'm off my game."

"You're drunk," Jet said.

"*Mildly pickled*," Mack corrected.

Atok sneered.

"What are you doing here?" Jet hissed.

Mack laughed. Held up a finger to all the others, started to pull Jet back by ten feet or so. He whispered: "I escaped."

"Yeah, I see that."

"Brainface back at HQ isn't here."

"So?"

"So he's not—" Mack tapped his temple. "*Listening in*."

"Again I ask: so?"

"Kid! This is our shot! To plan. To *scheme*. There's an airfield just south of the scrapyard—hell, it's not even an airfield, it's just a, a, *landing pad* on top of a warehouse, and they have an untouched Cierva C.19 there—"

"Mack, I don't know what that is—"

"An autogyro! It's like, a... a plane but it gets lift from this big floppy rotor on top. Doesn't need a runway because—" He made a sound with his mouth and lifted his finger in the air. "*Shoosh*, it rises straight up."

"I hate to repeat myself but... *so what?*"

"We're gonna steal it, kid!"

It was, in a way, like stealing his own mind off a shelf while the shopkeeper looked elsewhere—he concentrated like he did back then on that reed mat, the wind against his skin, this time hot and breathy, not the breeze of a coming storm but the whispered heat of a jungle damp, and he pulled away from his working body, the hands scraping fungus with a metal sheet, the feet rooted to the eyebeam beneath him, the mind drifting, drifting—

And when he saw his chance, Benjamin withdrew his mind entirely.

This was where it got tricky.

He just needed a moment. That single moment where the mind would detach from the flesh and the control over his body would be lost—but if he missed the window, if the mind fell too far and too fast off the shelf, he'd never get it back. The body would collapse. Or the fungus would claim it in its entirety.

Mind oozing, slipping, a smooth pebble on a frozen pond, away, away...

There—the moment—

He tried to grab for it. Found it slick beneath him. Impossible to hold. This was different from when the fever took him, from when the Box of Peng had him in its diseased thrall. He realized it too late: *I've made a terrible error.*

But then, his body jerked. A myoclonic twitch.

A second's worth of freedom.

It would have to be enough.

Benamin threw his mind back into his body—a psychic truck slamming into an invisible wall. He already felt the clamps of telepathic control locking back down, but he raised his arm up—

And brought the sharp scraping blade against his own chest.

Jet pushed past Mack. "No, uh-uh, not doing this." He reached Amelia and the Professor and waved them to continue walking down the long decrepit subway tunnel. "Come on. We have work to do."

Mack hobbled after. "Wait, kid. Dammit, hold up! I got a gimpy leg here—"

"All the more reason I'm not listening to your insane plan," Jet called after.

Tara and Colin gave him—and each other—looks.

"Plan?" Khan asked.

"What plan?" Amelia said, jumping in.

"Nothing," Jet said.

"We're gonna undo this timeline," Mack said with a drunken eagerness that Jet found more than off-putting. "Unravel it like a cat playing with a ball of yarn."

"Ohh," Khan said. The erudite ape looked suddenly concerned—but Jet knew the look. His intellectual side would soon take over and... "It is theoretically possible, I suppose." *Yep. There it is.* "It depends on your perspective on time, really, though the larger problem is that I'm to understand the time gates have all snapped shut—or worse, ceased to exist entirely..."

"We have a way around that," Mack said.

"I'm in," Amelia said, unbidden.

"No," Jet said, thrusting up a finger and waggling it about. "No, none of you are *in*. None of this is *theoretically possible*. This is a bad plan."

"This is a bad place," Amelia said, simply.

Now it was Atok's turn: the feral-looking Neanderthal lifted his head and muttered: "This future. Is bad like rotten fruit."

Jet couldn't help it. He felt the mercury rise inside his own emotional thermometer—he wasn't the type to yell, but here the words came bolting out of him like horses past an ill-closed gate.

"You don't *get* it! You undo this timeline and you undo *all the people in it*. You know what that is? You know what *I* call that? I call it murder. We're heroes. We take the hand we're dealt and we play it as well as we can. We don't try to get a Mulligan. We don't use our abilities to enforce our will. That's called *being a villain*." He finally found control and quieted himself. He took a deep breath. "We're not killing off the people in this timeline."

"Kill who now?" Tara said, finally popping over.

"Mack," Jet said. Mack watched from beneath the brim of his askew pilot's hat, idly scratching at the gray-flecked stubble on his face. "That means we undo you, too. Because our past has a Mack. A Mack with most of the century still ahead of him. You'd..."

"Be dead. Or made to never exist. Yeah. I get that, kid. I want that. Because I don't like who I am. I don't like what this world made me. And I'm willing to throw myself on the chopping block because to me, *that's* what heroes do. They make the... hard-as-hell decisions so that others don't have to. I'm willing to unravel. I'm willing to let it all go."

Jet felt a chill go up his spine. In that moment, he'd never cared for—and at the same time feared and even despised—Mack more.

Khan interjected with a gruff throat-clearing: "As I said, though, a lot of this depends on your perspective of time and space. I am of course no expert, but recent theory—er, the theory of our age, not this one—suggests that time, and thus the space that fills each moment, is not precisely a linear progression but rather one that looks like the capillary system of the human body. Offshoots and tributaries, whole new arterial flows—the question becomes, if you break one such artery off, does it die? In the human body metaphor, it would. But if we looked at it as one looks at plants, a clipping from a plant survives and sometimes even flourishes..."

"I say," Colin offered. "What are you all talking about again?"

"Nothing," Jet said. "We're not talking about anything. We're not... unwriting anybody. And we're not abandoning them, either. We're sweeping up the mess at our feet, not stepping over it and pretending it never existed."

"Your call, kid," Mack said.

"It is my call because I'm the one leading this expedition. Now let's get to the surface and get some scrap. I have a jet-wing army to build."

Everything shifted. It was like falling horizontally down a hallway of light—the inescapable whoosh of air, the dizzying vertigo, the jarring moment when his mind slammed back into his body and reclaimed it as his own.

Benjamin blinked.

He'd done it.

He didn't have long.

A lashing fungal tendril whipped toward his feet—Benjamin hopped over it, or tried to; his body was stiff and underfed. The tendril coiled around his ankle and dropped him to the ground. His buttbone slammed against the floor. His head racked back and suddenly he saw stars.

The ground slid beneath him. The tendril began dragging him.

Others reached for him, too.

No.

He grabbed one, twisted it, ripped it off with the sound of a starving man tearing into a lobster claw. Then used it like a whip—*kerrack!*—to wrap around a nearby eyebeam, ending his journey. The tendril coiled around his ankle yanked harder—his leg burned at the hip, felt like it was going to rip out of the socket. He took the heel of his boot and slammed it against the puffy fungal lash, kicking hard against his own shinbone until it released him.

Others reached for him—Benjamin ducked one, swatted another away.

I need a better weapon. The whip is not my weapon.

There!

A broken shelf, a pair of rusted metal brackets still in the wall.

Benjamin pirouetted over, grabbed each, wrenched them out of the wall and spun back around just in time to slice a seeking tendril in twain.

And so began his dance—as the tendrils sought him out, he ducked, ran, cut, spun, leapt, all with one goal in mind: to find the villain known as Der Blitzmann. The good news: he knew where Friedrich was. His psychic connection told him that, lit him up like a bulb on a switchboard. The better news: no psychosaurs were here in the tower. The psychic control was not *from* them, but rather from the fungus: once broken, it could not be reclaimed.

It made him wonder just what the connection was between the saurian race and the fungal hive—but no time for that now. And there were heroes better equipped with the knowledge to answer that challenge.

For now:

He found a torn apart elevator shaft and leapt into the open space.

The tunnel, surprisingly, opened up right into the junkyard. As they clambered up a makeshift ladder through carved space, Colin noted with some pride: "I dug this."

Tara clarified: "We used the scrapyard to help build some of the HQ."

Colin cracked the massive lid—a metal plate spot-welded to a couple cranky hinges that complained as it opened—and they all clambered out into the white-bright light of day. Immediately after, Jet, Tara, and Colin began setting up a pulley in order to lower scrap into the hole. The Neanderthals stayed down below to help load carts.

Khan followed the rest of them up. His mind, though, was elsewhere, mental fingers searching through the possibilities of time travel—and, more to the point, what would happen should they attempt to undo this reality. Was that even possible? If they went back and changed the course of events, would they do so back on that day in Atlantis? Would they have to first encounter themselves?

Would that cause a paradox? Could all of reality unravel then like—as Mack put it—a ball of yarn? They would have to go back much farther, of course. Before they were born. To the beginning of it all.

And then, what would happen? Would time flop about like a fire hose until all the water ran out and it corrected itself? Or would everything simply fragment? Would there be a Sally Slick with an eyepatch in this world, and a Sally Slick with two eyes in a reality where the psychosaurs never claimed this world as their own?

"You coming?" Jet asked. Khan snapped back to reality. Found himself in a scrapyard—junk piled high all around him. Moldering chairs and heaps of tin and aluminum. Wound around the mounds and walls were tangled vines and jungle trees whose pleached branches filtered the sunlight above into bright spears.

"Puzzling," Khan said, hurrying along after the others.

"What's that?"

"This city is... hot. Humid. Half of it seems like a rainforest jungle. Seventy years is not enough time to create these conditions. The climate of Manhattan now should be the same as it was 200 years ago." He paused. "They're terraforming. Keeping it hot. Optimal conditions." *Of course.* "It makes sense! They're reptiles. Cold-blooded. You don't see snakes in Alaska, do you?"

"What's that mean for us?"

"I don't know yet," Khan said. And he didn't.

They rounded a bend in the labyrinthine scrapyard.

"Bingo," Tara said.

Colin chuckled. "Stevie, old mate. We good with your psychic voodoo?"

Steve stared blankly. "I know not what that means!" Khan touched the saurian's shoulder.

"I think, Steven, that he's asking if your connection with the hive-mind is keeping us safe? Are we safe, Steven?"

The psychosaur nodded, grinning through needle teeth.

It was quite unsettling, Khan thought. Making allies with one such as this. But he'd rather have one on his side than none at all.

"Then let's get to work," Colin said, clapping his hands.

I could save them one by one, Benjamin thought as he swung down through an elevator door blasted open with the super-slow-motion explosion of a fungal bloom. He raced past victim after victim, thin-middled, sallow-cheeked workers cutting and scraping and harvesting fungus. All it would take would be a small moment of pain—a bruise, a cut, a shove—to free them from their bonds.

But then he'd be left to protect them, wouldn't he? The tendrils would come. Take them away. They weren't Centurions. Not like him.

For better or for worse, right now they were protected as they were not an enemy to this place. Which meant they needed to stay where they were.

The time will come to save them, he thought.

That time was not now.

Now he had one target, and that target was 50 feet away.

Friedrich Blitzmann.

Enemy to the Century Club. Madman. Electro-obsessed. A dangerous, self-made, self-proclaimed "scientist" whose only goal was to spread the gospel of lightning. And now, Benjamin's only hope.

He ducked a lashing thread of pink-orange fungus—

Launched himself past the sparkling electro-obelisk that was thrust up through the center of the Empire State Building—

Fell to his knees, slid forward—

Then slammed into Der Blitzmann and punched the poor sucker right in the chops. *Wham.* The villain went down, heels over head, a line of blood running from a freshly split lip. The man's eyes focused and his gaze fell to Benjamin.

"*Ich kenne dich,*" Der Blitzmann said. "I... know you."

"Hello, Friedrich. Have you made friends with the lightning today?"

"I think some of this stuff's been moved," Tara said from behind Jet.

"You might be right, Shepersky," the Aussie Digger called from behind. He planted his boot on the ground and began to lift a steel plate.

Jet was barely listening. His mind was elsewhere: Sally, Mack, this world, that world, Methuselah, Jared Brain. So much swirling around. So many conflicted feelings: optimism clashing with pessimism, two bulls locking horns, one light, one dark. He got his fingers underneath a massive eyebeam and braced his legs—he gave his jet-wing a little juice. It still was busted enough not to carry him high up into the sky but it was enough to let him lift the beam up, up, up—

He cried out.

There, beneath the eyebeam: a trio of psychosaur faces. Small, puckered, each behind a fleshy membranous bubble. Pink fluid sloshed around. Dead black eyes stared up, as if dreaming.

"Bloody hell!" Colin barked, backing away and mirroring Jet's own surprise. "I'll be stuffed. Look at this!"

He, too, had uncovered a small pocket of what looked to be gestating psychosaur children.

"I've got some here, too."

Khan gasped. "When was the last time you were here?"

"Five, six months ago," Tara said, gaping at what had been revealed.

"Then in that time," Khan said, "they chose this as a new nest."

"Babies!" Steve cried out with no small amount of glee. Jet watched as Khan steadied the saurian with the flat of his gorilla mitt, shaking his head just slightly. "What? No babies?"

"I suspect," Khan said, "that we are in grave—"

A clang of metal.

A psychosaur head rose over the metal walls as the creature crawled on all fours before finally standing atop an old overturned clawfoot washtub.

Others emerged, too. Two more. Five more.

Then, the floodgates opened: dozens of psychosaurs rose up all around them.

Hissing. Clacking their teeth together.

Jet could feel them trying to enter his mind, but their grip was slippery and kept sliding off. Thanks to Steve for that. It was a small favor.

Colin reached for his Enfield.

Tara twirled her axe.

Khan raised his fists, Amelia unslung the Thompson machine gun she'd been given, and Jet unholstered both pistols just as the psychosaurs screamed and rushed forward. As they swept over them, Jet suddenly realized:

Where the heck is Mack Silver?

Friedrich Blitzmann had always loved electricity.

He dreamt of it even as a child, even before he knew what it was, before the world understood its power or saw its implementation. He dreamt of himself as one who could ride lightning. As a man in a cage that burned and crackled with white hot fire. Dancing with elementals of electricity. Leaping with licking tongues of the sky-spears of searing voltage.

He wanted to feel the lightning inside of him.

Then came the day when his parents sent him out to pick bushels of *Birne*—pears from the pear trees in the orchard that did not belong to them. The skies had darkened and he climbed the trees and waited, thinking, *This will be the day*, and it was, but not for him. Lightning struck his home while he was away. It burned the house down. His parents with it.

They are so lucky, he thought at the time.

His jealousy only deepened with time.

The dreams came to him in great fits and starts—in much the same way that fickle lightning broke from the storm clouds. He dreamt of diagrams and blueprints for cages that captured the lightning and soon he began to build. He made mad little devices that moved when they were powered by lightning, he created gloves from which crackling capillaries of electricity leapt, finger to finger to finger. They said he was a genius. They called him an inventor.

Many companies wanted him to work for them. To help them bring electricity to the world. They wanted to bring lightning to the home, controlled, made *safe*—and they wanted to charge for the privilege.

Friedrich just wanted lightning to be free.

The chaos of it was beautiful.

They were trying to make it ugly.

The first place he worked, he burned it all down.

And in the ashes of the workshop, he built two devices that would stay with him for decades (if in upgraded form year after year). First, his electro-gloves—no longer only letting voltage fleck from fingertip to fingertip, now they could fire massive root systems of fulminating fire as if from the grip of Zeus himself. Second, his Helmet of Tlaloc, named after the Aztec thunder god—a helmet that could store lightning charges and power any of the glorious devices he chose to wear on his body or plug himself into as a conduit.

All of that, a memory that was just now returning—rushing back into him like a great thunderclap, *boom*.

He stared into the face of...

Yes. Benjamin Hu. An old... enemy, was it? One of those pesky people who always stood in the way of communing with the lightning (and, in his greater plans, helping the *whole world* commune with lightning—a gift, not a curse!). But here he was, helping him stand, freeing him from the mental shackles that had pinned him to this place for years, and now he was asking him about the lightning—

Benjamin pointed toward the center of this place, this skyscraper, and there stood the crackling obelisk he'd gazed upon with painful envy for so long now, a spire that caused in him a great and mighty ache that would not subside.

And now, he was free.

Friedrich giggled like a schoolboy on the first day of summer.

He sprang forth, past Benjamin, his legs almost betraying him (they felt like the legs of a newborn fawn, gangly and tangled) before finally getting underneath him and propelling him forward. Past tentacles of fungus, over whip-cords of mycological opposition, until he stood there, before it, his face bathed in the blue-white of the lightning spire and then—

Der Blitzmann plunged his hands into the spire and felt all the lightning course through him. He became the lightning. He shone like a star.

Amelia thought for a little while that they had a chance. The psychosaurs came over the scrapyard walls with a vengeance, obviously intent on protecting their awful little spawn in their horrible little egg-sacs—

But even now, even with uncertain heroes at hand, they worked like a machine. Her Tommy gun spat bullets, tearing through psychosaurs. Jet had mastered the stuttering propulsion of his half-ruined jet-wing, using it to blast himself up on top of the walls, then over the psychosaurs, then back down ahead, all the while popping off shots from his pistols.

Khan's fists swung. Atok's skull crashed into the heads of the saurian invaders. The Enfield barked. The tooth of the ice-axe bit hard.

They were managing this. They would *win* this.

But then, a dread realization:

That was just the first wave.

The next bunch swept over the scrapyard walls on every side like an all-encompassing tide pushing past a weak seawall—already she felt tired, and she saw that others were losing it, too. Khan fell first—he wasn't a fighter, not really, not yet, and though he managed to crawl free and lope forward with his fists against the earth, she knew he wouldn't last.

Then her gun jammed. *Click click click.*

Psychosaur claws tore into her shoulder from behind. Knocked her down, face first in the spongy earth—she kicked out, caught a psychosaur in the gut. Propped herself up on her gun, stood, swung it like a bat—*crack*. Another psychosaur down, and as the hissing serpent-man fell, she saw Atok break two saurian heads together like eggs. But then he too was dragged to the earth by two monsters leaping upon him from above.

Jet spun, firing blindly, psychosaurs racing around him.

Khan bounded from scrap wall to scrap wall, a furry wrecking ball shuddering each heap of wood and metal, just trying to stay one step ahead of the trio of psychosaurs on his tail.

Colin's Enfield was out—he grabbed the shovel off his back, starting swinging in wide arcs.

Tara went down—disappearing beneath a pile of claws and teeth. Her axe spun away and clipped part of an old ice box.

And more kept coming. Shrieking like banshees. Hissing, spitting, claws clicking. Her heart sank. The weight of all of it came crashing down on her: the loss of the past, this questionable future, the now near-certainty that they were not going to leave this scrapyard of their own volition—maybe not even *alive*.

She was supposed to be better than this. *You're a hero, girl, start acting like it.* But the fire in her belly had burned to smoldering ash and in its wake were the smoke wisps of fear: hollow and hot and acrid, eating her up from the inside.

The psychosaurs were everywhere.

She couldn't see Jet.

She swung a fist—the thing captured her arm, bit down—

Pain—

Amelia thrust her knee up—

It only imbalanced her. She fell to the ground.

The thought struck her: *We thought they were dangerous for what they did to our minds. But they're still vicious creatures in the flesh.* It explained why humanity never regained its foothold. These creatures bred. And dominated. An unstoppable force no heroes could diminish...

Amelia's head hit the ground—a fireworks display popped in the dark behind her eyes. Above and around she saw the walls of the scrapyard, and beyond them the tall buildings, skyscrapers of the fallen city, buildings reclaimed by a nature that was itself somehow unnatural, vines and roots and trees, colorful birds and flying lizards and fat flies as big as a baby's fist and—

And that's when she knew the fight was over.

She was right, of course. This battle was, indeed, over.

Just not for the heroes.

The sharp hiss-crackle of a storm cloud arose and then came a loud rumbling thunderclap that split the air like cannon fire—

Beyond the scrapyard, into the sky rose a blazing blue arc of lightning, bigger than any bolt of electricity she'd ever seen. It smeared across her vision, burning itself into her eyes and then she saw that it came from the top spire of the Empire State Building...

The psychosaurs ceased their assault. They howled, clutching at their heads, backs arching so hard Amelia could hear their bones crack.

They fell to the ground, writhing.

The heroes took their opportunity. Shovel lopping off heads. Ice axe puncturing their broad, ridged foreheads. Amelia stood and reclaimed the Tommy gun, then used the butt of the weapon to collapse their throats.

Jet said: "We need to figure out what that was, and we need to figure it out *now*. Amelia, Khan, Steve—you're with me. The rest of you: get some scrap and head back to the tunnels. We'll return for more later. Chop-chop, people! Let's move."

CHAPTER NINETEEN

Sally stood in front of the cage.

The Conqueror Ape's nostrils flared. Lips curled back to expose teeth—the way the lips shifted, sometimes it was a scowl, other times a smile. Always feral.

"It's your fault, you know," Khan the Conqueror said.

"We're not here to talk about that," Sally said. From behind her back she pulled a wooden baton. At the end were two metal probes. Sparking. Snapping.

"Everything rested on you in that moment. Didn't it? I didn't see it myself but even here in my cage I hear the others talking. Our return to this world has stirred conversation about how you made a choice, a choice that directly led to the world that has poisoned you so completely—"

She thrust the baton in between the bars. The probes connected with the ape's gut. He stiffened, screamed—when she pulled the baton away he fell backwards onto his rump, panting, whimpering.

"Torture," he said, gasping. "...is not your style. Or wasn't, once."

"I want to know about the psychosaurs. At the dawn of time you managed to corral them. Control them. How?"

"A hero doesn't torture. And if you're not a hero, that must make you a—"

The baton, again.

Bzzt. Khan the Conqueror fell onto his side. Into a black, feral ball. His shoulder rose and fell with shuddering breaths.

Sally had answers to get and no time to worry about her methods.

"I asked you a question: *how?*"

"The fungus," the ape gasped. "That's what you never understood. They have a..." He coughed, tried to sit up against the cage bars. "They have a bond with the fungus. They eat it. It controls them as much as they control it. I controlled the fungus. Which means I controlled them."

"And how did you control the fungus?"

He chuckled: a raspy, throaty growl of a laugh.

"That is a secret from prehistory, and I shall not share it with the likes of you."

You'll pay for that and then you'll tell me, she thought as she lurched forward with the baton once again—

But this time he caught the baton, pulling it forward. Her forehead slammed into the iron bars and suddenly she smelled the gamy, wild breath of the ape as he gripped the back of her neck with hands strong enough to pop her head off her shoulders.

"You can't control the fungus because you're not *strong* enough," he hissed. "You're weak. Worse, you're a pawn. A pawn in Methuselah's game. I don't know his game but I know he's playing one. And I know that the Walking Mind must be a part of it, you dumb little girl."

She spat in his eye.

He robbed her of the baton and slammed it, probe-first, into her midsection. Her world lit up like a thousand Christmas trees and when it went dark he shoved her backward—but not before she caught the glint of the keys he *also* robbed from her belt.

Sally lay on her back, trying desperately to crab-walk backward, but her limbs felt disconnected—the arms and legs of a doll hanging by a meager thread, a numbness spreading from the electroshock.

The rattle of keys in a lock.

The squeak of hinges.

The Conqueror Ape was free.

Khan stepped out of the cage and stretched.

His left eye still twitched. Thanks to the woman with the baton.

Sally Slick. Who would have thought a woman like that could have fallen so far? She was not a proper villain yet, no—but this change, so late in the century, certainly suggested she wasn't much of a hero, was she?

He stepped over her, standing astride atop her still-shuddering body.

The Conqueror stooped. "How did you lose that eye, Miss Slick? When last I left you, two of those... *peepers* still sat in your pretty head."

She craned her head to speak, teeth chattering—

Just then: the ground shuddered. The lights of the underground compound flickered and buzzed and streamers of dust poured like tiny dry waterfalls from the craggy rock ceiling above their heads.

Tectonic plates moving? A small earthquake? Or something... else?

When the lights stopped flickering, Khan looked up, saw movement:

The Walking Mind.

Silent. Still. Implacable. A brain bubbling in a jar on a four-legged platform. There at the door to the room. Almost like a piece of truly bizarre furniture.

"Jared," Khan said.

HELLO, GORILLA KHAN.

"Prove your villainy. Stand aside and let me free." He thought but did not say: *I have to go after my son, unburdened by the iron bars of this cage.*

I CANNOT DO THAT, CONQUEROR.

"Then perhaps we can work together."

I DO NOT THINK THAT LIKELY, APE LORD.

Suddenly what felt like a psychic hammer crashed into Khan's mind—everything inside his skull was noise and light and swarms of wasps and coruscating lightning and then his body saw fit to follow as an invisible locomotive hit him square in the chest. He felt speed, wind in his fur, and—

When he opened his eyes, the cage door clanged shut.

Whonnnng.

And the lock crumpled like an origami crane in a child's crushing hand.

Khan roared. Slammed against the cage. Hooted. Shrieked.

THIS, A MESSAGE ONLY FOR YOU, came the thought intruding upon his mind. WE HAVE NO ROOM FOR YOU HERE. YOU ARE A FAILURE. THIS WORLD IS THE RESULT OF YOUR GRAVE INADEQUACY. YOU WILL ROT IN THIS CAGE EVEN AS THE FUTURE FALLS DOWN AROUND YOUR SIMPERING SIMIAN EARS.

"I'll crush your jar, I'll smash your brain—!"

Another invisible fist hit him. This one, in his throat.

He gurgled. Clutched at his neck.

SHHHHHH. SILLY MONKEY.

I'm not a m...

He coughed into his hands.

Sally stood on trembling legs. Backed out of the room, her eyes never leaving Khan's. Her mouth twisted into a scornful sneer.

CHAPTER TWENTY

One minute, Friedrich Blitzmann was there, face lit up like a child's smile on Christmas morning. Then he thrust his hands into the intricate wire-work of the electro-spire and—

Then he was *truly* lit up: the man was gone in the snap-hiss of lightning. A flash of light came and all the world was washed out, and when it ceased, and when Benjamin's own eyes adjusted...

All that was left were Der Blitzmann's dirty shoes. Still smoldering.

Tongues of electricity still licked up and down the fungal walls.

The fungus had been orange and pink and red—

But now, it was drying up. Blackening like paper over a campfire. Flaking away in much the same manner. A snow of brittle ash. The smell of burning.

All around Benjamin, he saw them: the workers, dozens of them on this floor alone, they were pulling away from their work, blinking and confused. One woman in a mechanic's jumpsuit fell to her knees and wept. A bald man in a filthy soda jerk uniform held both hands together in fists and began to cackle almost madly. Somewhere below, on another floor, Benjamin heard someone yell: "Freedom!"

He'd done it.

Now he needed to get these people to safety.

But where? Where was safe in this ruined world?

Right now: only one direction mattered.

Down.

The Empire State Building, Jet thought. That's the building that erupted in lightning. The last time he was there, he fought Atok and saved Mack. The time before, he'd fallen off the observation deck after a psychosaur attack left him reeling and crumpled his original jet-pack like a tin can in a lion's mouth, and then—

Again, he returned to his only thought on that day and most days since:

Sally.

No time to think about her now. They rushed into the streets and for a moment he was certain they'd made a terrible error: psychosaurs were everywhere, clambering down out of building windows, climbing from trees and vines, swooping on the backs of Pterosaurs and riding their thunder-lizard mounts—

But it was like Jet, Khan, Amelia, and Steve weren't even there.

They were heading in a single direction like a swarm of rats.

They were heading toward the Empire State.

"Where they go, we go?" Amelia asked.

"Oh my," Khan said.

"Oh my," Steve said, clearly trying to mimic the Professor.

Jet took a deep breath. "Into the fray. Let's find out what's going on."

The stairwells of the Empire State Building remained intact—all 100-plus floors. Benjamin charged down, floor by floor, gathering what stragglers he could find, pulling them into the stairs and sending others down ahead of him as the fungal ash swirled around him in gray whorls.

But then, down below: screaming.

Oh, no.

Footsteps that had been echoing downward were suddenly echoing upward—in a great stampeding mass.

A shriek: "They're coming!"

The tide of freed humans hit him like a tide, panicked as cats trying to escape a housefire—he grabbed a boy, a reedy teen with ginger-sand hair, and asked him what was happening.

"They're comin' up the stairs, mister! A holy storm of 'em!"

Benjamin circled his hands in a lasso gesture: "Up the stairs! Up, up, up!"

But he knew that up was a dead-end. Tallest building in the world and the only hope of escape up there was to leap to their deaths—

Right now, he had to hope that some other solution presented itself. *I got us this far.* He could only hope that the other Centurions—if they were even alive or had their own minds intact—saw the light show and would come to their aid.

The anthill had been kicked over.

Amelia stood shoulder-to-shoulder with the others, watching psycho-saurs stream toward the Empire State Building, pouring in through doors and windows like so many ants—a gray flaky snow rained down from the massive structure. She saw that the fungus that clung to the inside and out-side of the skyscraper was drying up before their eyes: from bright pink to blood red and finally to a char.

"It's like the fungus took over the whole damn tower," Amelia said, star-ing upward. She had to yell: the steady stampede of psychic saurians made a mighty clamor.

"It's all dying," Khan said. "And the monsters are none too pleased."

Steve bared his teeth in a crass facsimile of a smile. "I sense anger! They are most angry! And *weak*."

In Amelia's heart she felt a moment of proxy triumph—she had nothing to do with whatever was going on here, but to see these monsters all stirred up and then to hear that they're ticked off and maybe even weakened because of it? It gave her heart a mighty horse-kick, made her think, *Maybe we can really do this.*

But then a surge of frustration arose, too: they didn't do this. They didn't even know what was going on. Worst of all, they were powerless to capitalize upon it—it was happening outside them, beyond them, *without* them.

Suddenly, Jet nodded, like he made some sort of decision. He grabbed Steve and spun him around so that both their faces were pointed in the same direction, then Jet pulled Steve's back against his chest as he began undoing the straps of his jet-wing.

Amelia gave them a look. "Boys, I don't know what this is..."

Jet rolled his eyes, then re-connected the buckles of his jet-wing straps, this time around Steve's chest.

"Steve and I are going for a ride. We're going to the top."

Khan placed a steadying hand on Jet's shoulder:

"Your jet-wing is damaged. It can't sustain that kind of flight."

"Doesn't have to. I'm going to use it to boost myself a few floors at a time, kind of... half-climb, half-rocketboost myself to the top." Amelia saw a flash of concern on his face. "At least, that's the idea."

"What do you want from us?" Amelia asked.

"The subway station is right over there, under that... big tangle of vines. Things go akimbo, you head back to the subway. Now, remember, without Steve here, you don't have..." He tapped his head. "You don't have any way to keep them out."

That sent a chill up Amelia's spine. To again be subject to their psychic invasion...

But she stiffened her shoulders and stood straight, giving Jet a nod.

"Go get 'em, Jet," she said.

And he did.

The observation deck at the Empire State Building had been taken over by thick green creepers with fat fern-curl leaves—out here, the fungus had already gone all the way black and was breaking off the surface of the building like flakes of wall paint bubbled up in a desert heat.

Wind swept over Benjamin and the others—a hundred other survivors with more pouring onto the deck, cramming shoulder to shoulder. Soon it'd be too crowded; they wouldn't be able to sustain it. It'd be a riot. He had to calm these people down, so he climbed up a wall of creepers against the flat of the building and called out to the people:

"I need everyone to stay calm, my name is Benjamin Hu and I'm a member of the Century Club—"

A voice from the crowd: "The Century Club is here!"

And a cold thought inserted itself in his mind: *Not the Club. Just me.*

Then, before he could say anything more:

Screams from inside the building. Terror contained in each shriek. Benjamin knew what that meant: *They're here.* The psychosaurs had come to quash this little revolution—yellow jackets mounting to defend the hive from their own prey.

Benjamin leapt down away from the vines and instantly through the shattered doors of the observation deck he saw: human bodies panicking, running, then suddenly dropping to the ground as they were dragged away, one by one.

The psychosaurs had come to reclaim what was theirs.

The wave of energy crashed over him: their hive-mind fell over him like an avalanche, asserting psychic control, plunging his mind beneath a rockslide of awful feelings: *You failed to save these people you failed everything you are alone nobody is here to help you Blitzmann didn't deserve to die—*

His body fell backward.

The psychosaurs raged onto the deck. Flashing claws and gnashing fangs. Black eyes fixing people to the spot until they were dragged backward, inside the building, toward the stairwell and elevator shaft—

But then:

It was like a blanket lifted off of him.

The psychic avalanche turned to dust, blew away.

He didn't understand it. They no longer had his mind.

Nor the minds of any here. People were getting back up. He saw a man in rags throw a punch, knock a psychosaur backward. A woman with her hair in a dirt-caked bandana began to flail and kick, earning herself a small radius of freedom. All around, the humans began to shake free their captors' control.

And they began to fight.

A surge of hope rose up in Benjamin just as the psychosaurs descended upon him to crush it. He concentrated. Stilled himself. Steadied his mind for the fight—

They leapt.

Pop! Pop!

Black goo erupted from two of them as they fell. The other two dashed forward as Benjamin stepped aside, slamming them into the wall behind him—

There, at the far end of the observation deck, stood Jet Black.

A mismatched pistol in each hand.

And, apparently, a grinning psychosaur swaddled to his chest like a baby.

Benjamin would have to ask about that one later.

For now: the fight was on.

"Benjamin!" Jet called, planting his feet on the observation deck.

Steve craned his head around. "My name Steve!"

Jet ignored him—Benjamin, the actual Benjamin Hu, gave a small salute—two fingers skyward and thumb downward, a hand sign of the Century Club, often accompanied by the Latin cry: "*Doctius*! *Audacius*! *Fortius*!" meaning, "Wiser! Bolder! Braver!" A motto suggesting optimism and a Centurion's ability to stand steadfast in the face of danger, to take risks none other would take, and to have the wisdom to know when they should succeed and when they would fail.

Jet suddenly felt it was a cry for a better world.

The surge of good feelings at seeing Benjamin again crashed hard against the rocks of reality as he saw what they were up against—even as he spun around, letting his pistols pop off shots, taking down psychosaurs one by one, they kept coming. And he knew they *would* keep coming; he and the others saw how they streamed in the doors and windows of the building at street-level.

Here stood Benjamin, fighting alongside him wielding, at present, some kind of antenna broken off the observation deck—he used it as one would use a fencing foil ("*En Garde!*" Benjamin cried, stabbing through a psychosaur throat with the tip of the antenna). And here were dozens of humans, each up and swinging and kicking and...

It wasn't enough. One by one, the humans began to drop. The psychic countermeasures of the psychosaur swaddled around Jet's chest were not enough—these people weren't fighters. Worse, even if they were, they looked weak and filthy and even wounded—raw skin, blistery feet, ribs showing.

The enormity of the problem was suddenly clear as a hard wind swept over the deck. Jet had been here before. He knew what it was to fall.

All these people couldn't fall.

They wouldn't survive.

He barely survived *his* fall from the Empire State Building.

He had a jet-wing that hardly worked. And that was all he had to save them.

His heart was suddenly dragged beneath dark waters by an anchor of dread.

Then, as if it couldn't get any worse—

Pterosaurs. A sudden pair of them, shrieking an unholy din, their saurian riders staring down with black eyes glinting in the hot sun—

It suddenly occurred to Jet. *Pterosaurs have wings. If we could harness them, and maybe get more, maybe, just maybe we could—*

Suddenly, one of the flying dinosaurs shrieked and crashed into the observation deck face first, its head craning back at an unnatural angle, blood pooling. Jet stood, flummoxed.

A loud sound—an echoing report—and the other one fell on top of it. Also dead.

No. No!

That was their one chance—

A new surge of psychosaurs pushed forward from within the observation deck. The humans inside had been taken—the remaining two dozen others stood with their backs against the edge wall of the deck, that wall the only thing separating them from *psychosaur slaves* or *the sweet oblivion of falling.*

Psychosaurs hissed. Swiped at the air. Their collective screams were deafening. Jet heard a sound, a *thump thump thump* that must've been his own heart on overdrive—

The psychosaurs began their rush forward—

Jet saw something spin through the air. A dark shape—small, no bigger than a shoe.

It was on fire.

Glass shattered against the deck with a *pop*. A bloom of bright fire emerged from that tiny dark shape, droplets cast skyward and suddenly burning—the air a smeary heat haze, and behind it, psychosaurs shrieking.

What the—?

Jet turned, saw something hovering in the air—

A plane. But not a plane. A wireframe almost-plane with a big rotor atop it, spinning wildly.

Mack pointed at Jet and winked.

Then he threw another petrol bomb.

Another bloom of fire.

Jet clambered up onto the fence surrounding the deck, using the vines as handholds. Mack lowered the plane-copter... thing (what had he called it? An *autogyro*!) and called out to Jet.

"I'm gonna get you outta here, kid."

"We need to get them *all* outta here! That thing can't hold everybody!"

But then Mack licked his lips and gave a thumb's up.

He told Jet the plan.

It was certainly bold. Definitely brave.

Probably not wise.

But it was all they had. Jet gave a curt nod and began to rally the troops.

This would never work. And yet, it *had* to.

CHAPTER TWENTY-ONE

The Walking Mind told Sally Slick:

SOMETHING HAS HAPPENED.

The human acted predictably. Were you to tell them something vague, something with the promise of more information, they wanted to know more. Even if it was of no value to them, that deepest human urge of curiosity was greater than all other forces combined. Greater than hate and love and fear. Curiosity. The urge to know. The obsessive desire to have answers no matter what it would take—it was like the habit of biting your fingernails down to the cuticle or combing your hair again and again until you got it right.

Not that the Walking Mind had fingernails or cuticles or even hair anymore.

(Though once he'd tried to put a wig atop his bell jar. A long time ago.)

But Jared understood curiosity. He, ironically enough, *embodied* it. 'Twas curiosity that drove him to be who he was. Once facing down a terminal disease, a disease of the body but not of the brain, he wondered: *Could I continue living? Could I free my brain and thus my mind, from this collapsing prison of flesh, from these soon-to-be-ruins?* He was already psychic... capable of some feats and powers of the mind. But they were parlor tricks, mostly. Levitate some playing cards. Bend a spoon. Glean surface thoughts, an act so simple and brutal it was like scraping mud from the sole of a boot.

But when he freed his body thanks to the driving urge of curiosity, his powers grew tenfold. Then tenfold again.

Unfettered by the walls of skin and meat, he was made anew.

Forged in the fires of curiosity.

Curiosity, after all, was what gave stories their power. It was the nature of those old dimestore serials, wasn't it? Cliffhanger after cliffhanger, each chapter book ending with some new peril, those silly dumb-bucket heroes' lives like the cat in that experiment by that young upstart, Schrödinger: undecided until you looked upon the first page of the next installment.

So: telling Sally Slick that *something* had happened, well—

Predictably, her heart jumped. A surge of adrenalin and dopamine. *Oh how the mind loved an unsolved puzzle.* She was a fish on a hook. His hook.

"What? What is it?" she asked. Always the question to seek the answer.

He considered telling her: *What has happened, my cyclopean idiot, is that you've fallen prey to a terrible ruse. Once I truly did think to help you, not because it is my inclination to help but rather because I am inclined to survive, and further, I am inclined to control, and what good is my extended life if I am left to wander the jungle wasteland with nobody to control?*

Things changed, of course.

They found Methuselah. And that added a far greater dimension to Jared's plans. But that train of thought could be ridden to its conclusion at any time.

For now, he told Sally, venturing into her mind with his own—

ONE OF THE FUNGAL HIVES HAS FALLEN.

"What? How can that be?"

I CANNOT SAY PRECISELY, BUT AT THE EDGES OF MY AWARENESS I SENSE THE PRESENCE OF JET BLACK AND THE OTHERS. INCLUDING MACK SILVER AND—here Jared's roving psychic fingers picked up another face out of the crowd, the face of Benjamin Hu, and quickly he shut his (metaphorical) mouth lest he tell Sally that piece of information. Benjamin Hu could not be allowed in here. It was too risky.

"Mack Silver?" Sally said, jaw clenched. He felt the fires of anger stoked in her belly, but there, too, another feeling in competition: the feeling of love for him *and* for Jet Black, and there too a kind of triumph that, in destroying that hive, someone had managed to do what she had long hoped.

And behind that, a feeling of jealousy: envy that *they* had perhaps won the day, and that *she* was no part of it.

Jared had watched her perspective darken over these last fifteen years.

It warmed him the way a hearth-fire would once warm his flesh.

He barely even needed to nudge her toward that darkness. Mostly, she did it all on her own, the poor doe.

"We need to... rally the troops," she said. "We need to help."

THE TOWER OF FUNGUS HAS ALREADY FALLEN.

"But we have people out there. Are they in danger?"

AREN'T WE ALL?

He neglected to mention the exact sort of danger they were in, which, unlike in a pulp serial cliffhanger, was a danger of *certain doom*. They had no way out of their predicament.

Which, it suddenly occurred to Jared, was not ideal.

He'd been so delighted by the fact they were probably going to die (the death of a hero was, after all, like a taste of wine or a warm bath, two things he could no longer experience except through the minds of others) that he forgot he actually *needed* those wool-headed hero-types.

So, he amended his somewhat *sardonic* reply with:

YOU'RE RIGHT, MISS SLICK. THEY ARE IN GRAVE DANGER. MOUNT THE COUNTERATTACK!

He imagined this was the joy of a dog owner, once upon a time: fling the stick, watch the insipid beast pounce after it, yapping and drooling.

Sally fled to rally her people.

His mind then drifted to Methuselah's chamber and wrapped his own mind around the old man's. Like a hug. A cold, evil, psychic hug.

It was the only manner of hug Jared Brain knew.

HELLO, DOCTOR.

Yes, Jared. Tell me good news.

I CANNOT. THE NEWS IS UNCERTAIN. He explained to Methuselah the situation at hand: heroes in danger, Sally marshaling the troops, *their plans* suddenly plunged into peril much like the heroes of the serial chapbooks.

WE REQUIRE THE HEROES TO LIVE. IF THEY PERISH—

Then we will find another way. We have all the time in the world. And in time, we will have all the world. Patience, my fleshless friend. Patience.

CHAPTER TWENTY-TWO

"They're trapped up there," Amelia said. Her finger itched to pull the trigger of the Tommy gun as she and Professor Khan stood in the shadows of a small alleyway overgrown with a dense tangle of jungle foliage. Above their heads hung upside-down flowers, plump as a piglet and breathing a heady perfume that Amelia found cloying (to her, all perfume was that way—why some women refused to accept their own natural smells was beyond her).

Meanwhile, the saurian throng continued to pour into the Empire State Building. Some even started to climb up the building, leaping from ledge to ledge and scrabbling up the stone like reptilian spiders.

"They are," Khan said. In his voice she heard fear. But a wild something danced in his eyes, too. "It's up to us to help."

"A distraction," she said. "A big damn distraction."

"Look!" Khan said. Up above, it looked almost like a mosquito hovering—but it was no such thing. Amelia stared: it looked like a gyrocopter— an *autogyro*. She knew they were building them in France at Lioré-et-Olivier (she knew because her nemesis, *Le Monstre*, wanted to steal an army of them, a plot she herself foiled), but they were notoriously unreliable. "Who do you think is flying it?"

Amelia parroted the question right back at him:

"Who do *you* think is flying it?"

Khan snorted. His lips curled into a smile. "One suspects it is the Silver Fox himself, wouldn't you say?"

"Sounds right to me," she said. "Let's give them that distraction."

Ashen fungal snow whirled about Jet's head as the wind whipped.

They had to move fast.

Already Jet was at the base of the Empire State's famous spire—the piercing tip like the sharp pointy end of one of Benjamin's rapiers, built to be a mooring mast for dirigibles, with the 102nd floor acting as a landing platform. But it was deemed impractical and nobody—well, nobody but Khan the Conqueror during his takeover of New York—tried to use it for that purpose.

Nor would that be its purpose today.

A foot stepped onto Jet's head, and he winced, craning his neck until the foot disappeared. Above him were two, maybe three dozen people. Victims and workers of the fungal hive. All of them climbing onto the spire. They hooked their elbows and knees around the narrow beams that made up the spire.

This was as dangerous as anything they'd ever done.

But it had to *be* done, just the same.

Steve looked up at Jet with a horrible, toothy smile and blank eyes.

It still creeped Jet out. Having a psychosaur lashed to his chest like a toddler.

But they needed his radius of psychic control. They fled the observation deck when the fire died back, and Jet and Benjamin blocked the lower stairwell as they sent everyone up, up, up, to the 102nd landing deck—and then, onto the spire itself. The only thing keeping the psychosaurs at bay right now was the curtain of fire cracking in the stairwell—another petrol bomb, thanks to Mack.

Benjamin leapt up onto the spire. Next to Jet.

"This is classifiably insane!" Benjamin yelled over the sound of the wind. Jet could hear the tremors of fear and weariness in his voice: rare for Benjamin, who always sounded so calm, so collected.

"It's our only shot!" Jet said. "You planted the packages?"

Benjamin nodded. "I did. I hope you made peace with your ancestors."

Jet gave a thumbs-up to the autogyro hovering nearby.

A grenade—without its pin—sailed through the air. Past Jet and Benjamin. Down another twenty feet to the base of the spire.

One moment. A small one stretched out like a string of melting cheese—Jet thought about the past, the future, about Sally, about if she could be turned back into the woman he remembered, about what it would be like to kiss her—

Boom.

The one grenade exploded.

And in a half-second, so did the others. The "packages" laid at the base of the spire. All of the grenades from Mack's chest belt.

They went off like a series of cannon fire.

The spire, now unmoored from the building, began to tilt and fall—

People screamed.

Jet heard a sound from his own throat—a low, keening wail that refused to be contained behind clenched teeth and mashed lips.

The spire fell.

And then, ceased its fall in mid-air.

It hovered. It swung.

Above, the autogyro chugged along, a long length of chain secured to the top of the spire by a steel hook secured around a beam.

Jet felt weightless. And scared. And excited.

If only because: *I'm flying!*

Beneath him, the city lay splayed out—he'd never thought he'd see Manhattan looking like this. Mist crawled between stone canyons formed of buildings that were now fuzzy with green. Broadway was no street, but rather a slow-moving river. Some buildings had fallen, reclaimed and pulled back to the earth by the hands of flora. Colorful birds—not parrots, but something else, something that might've been the link between the thunder lizards and birds—flew below them, squawking and diving.

It was beautiful.

"Incoming!" Benjamin said.

Jet turned his head, and saw just *what* was incoming.

Flying dinosaurs.

But not like the Pterodactyls he'd fought before.

These were bigger.

Much bigger.

Wingspan: the size of a city bus. Lean needle-shaped heads on long necks. Massive claws. Not a high-pitched shriek, but rather a warbling scream.

Ten of them. With two psychosaur riders on each, lashing the dinosaurs with reins of pulsing fungus.

They were there in the blink of an eye, barely enough time for Jet to draw a single pistol and begin firing. He clipped one rider and sent the saurian plummeting like a sack of potatoes to the city below.

Then: *crash*.

One of the beasts slammed into the bottom of the spire—now a twisted base of steel beams blasted apart thanks to the grenades—and suddenly the whole thing was swaying wildly. Above their heads, the people screamed.

Jet quickly gave his jet-wing a few blasts so that when the spire swung one way he gave an equal and opposite force through the rocket booster.

It stayed the spire from swinging.

But it wasn't enough.

A young woman with bent eyeglasses and a ratty lemon blouse cried out— And fell.

She fell past Jet and Benjamin, reaching for them.

Benjamin's eyes went wide with horror.

"I can't lose anybody else," he said.

And Jet knew what would happen next.

Benjamin jumped.

"Quetzlcoatl," Khan said, with no small amount of awe.

"What?" Amelia asked, looking back at the erudite ape, who had stopped in the middle of the moss-covered street to stare up. She followed his gaze, found the sky filled not only with the gyrocopter and what now seemed to be the broken spire of the Empire State Building, but also a sky full of massive flying things.

"The largest Pterosaur that we know of," Khan said. "Huge beasts. Gliders more than fliers." He stiffened, suddenly. "They're going to need that distraction."

Ahead, the Chrysler Building stood tall—an art deco spire thought to be one of the finest buildings in the world. It remained tall, but was now impressive only in what had been done to it. Its pale architecture stood cracked and shot through with bulging, coiling vines. The front arch lay crumbled on the sidewalk. Windows shattered. Doors gone. Everything was orange fungus. Ropes of the stuff hanging like vines. Choking the building the way ivy chokes an oak tree.

"Ready?" Amelia said.

"Do it."

She raised the Tommy gun and began to fire at the building.

The first thought that struck Benjamin, even before he landed, was: *I can ride a horse.* He had, many a time. Riding across the Mongolian Steppe in search of the spoor of the Death Worm. Or the Sonoran desert tracking one of the world's most notorious art thieves, the Crimson Coyote. Or riding with the Bolivian *gauchos* in the hopes of finding an entrance to the secret passage that would take him to the Tiwanaku's secret golden pyramid.

He landed on top of one of the massive flying creatures with a thud.

A fast elbow clipped one psychosaur in the jaw, sent the monster tumbling. The other saurian—the one holding the reins—shrieked and reached for him. He ducked it, grabbed the creature on one side, and *shoved.*

Suddenly, he was alone.

He grabbed the reins.

I can ride a horse.

Of course, he'd never ridden a sky-horse capable of moving in directions besides left, right, and forward.

Benjamin took a deep breath, yanked down on the reins.

The beast plunged through the sky, and Benjamin tried not to scream.

The drums, the drums, the jungle drums.

It was like in slow-motion. Amelia firing the weapon. *Chuff chuff chuff.* Little golden shells hitting the cracked asphalt, rolling towards spongy puffs of moss and mushroom. Bullets clipping the building. Chipping away. Cutting into the fleshy fungus—*squit squit squit.*

It was only a moment before the psychosaurs emerged.

None of them came from the Chrysler Building itself. It was as if they refused to stay there. But from all the neighboring buildings—that's where they lurked. They climbed out of windows and doors and craters. Swarming toward them.

Khan wanted to tear them all apart.

A strange thought, that. He'd never felt quite *so* violent and angry before, but there it was. Almost as if he were experiencing it from outside himself.

Amelia was saying something. Pulling on his arm.

Trying to get him to run.

His only thought was: *No run. Conquer.*

Absurd. But he found himself baring his teeth. Knuckles on the ground.

But then: *whap.*

Amelia backhanded him.

A moment's surge of rage toward her—*Tear her apart, rend her limbs from her body and beat her with them, no human should dare to tell you—*

But this was Amelia.

A hero. A friend.

"I said, *run!*" she screamed.

"Oh, bother," Khan said, feeling suddenly himself.

The psychosaurs were almost upon them. Already that sense of a psychic wave about to crash on the shores of their minds.

Together, they turned tail and ran.

The woman's name was Mary Elise.

She was, once upon a time, one of the steno pool at the Mayor's Office—one of a rotating group of girls who could, at any time, perform secretarial duties for the mayor or his aides. It was a good job. She didn't have much to say about the city or its politics, though she wasn't ignorant of them, either. They just weren't where her mind was. Mary Elise wanted to be a writer.

A poet, actually.

She didn't know what kind of poet she wanted to be, not really. Would she aspire to one of the slots on Ted Malone's CBS radio show? Could she write Christmas poems, which she could sell to those companies interested in marketing the holiday with a little swipe of light literary esteem? Or would she write about her life? The troubles of growing up poor in upstate New York? The troubles of being a woman in a world made for men?

It mattered little.

Because then the city was invaded.

Taken over by monsters: angry apes, cavemen, monsters out of schoolbooks. And then the apes and cavemen went away and one day there were only the monsters, and the monsters took over.

She didn't know how long ago that was. She only knew that time had passed. Too much time. *So* much that she felt she should be dead. And now, in free-fall, she thought: *Here, then, after all this time, the death I deserve.* Emily Dickinson's poem suddenly flashed before her: *Because I could not stop for Death, he kindly stopped for me...*

For her death had long been kept from her. She and the others taken. She lived in the hollows of her own mind. Her body worked. Then when it was exhausted, they walked the body to another building—a building that looked like it was once a sewing factory, rows after rows of machines and tattered fabric and unspooled thread—and there they sealed them into the walls with a spackling of fungus and all went dark, dark like death but not death. Sleep. Coma. Nothing.

Then she'd awake and go back to the greasy, rubbery fungus. What glimpses she saw of her body—her face reflected in a shard of glass, her hands scraping fungus—never looked older. Even though time had clearly passed outside: trees thrusting up out of tented asphalt, strange and unfamiliar birds and bugs roosting in broken windows. The city drifting toward collapse in fits and starts.

All the while she worked, she just wanted to be free. At any cost. Her flesh stood rooted to the floor when all she wanted to do was fly away.

And now, she was falling.

Poetic, in a way.

She closed her eyes and willed the ground to come and meet her.

But then—

A warbling screech above. A heavy rippling sound cut the air—

And suddenly, arms wrapped around her, and she was snatched from the air like a leaf caught in a child's hand.

A roguish chap—Asian, she thought, though it was hard to tell with the wind whipping in her eyes and stirring tears that blurred her vision—with a look of consternation and concentration on his face.

It occurred to her, in a flash:

I'm riding on the back of a flying dinosaur.

She almost fainted.

That's when the spire of the Empire State Building—the one that mere moments ago she was clinging to like a koala on a tree—dropped out of the sky, plummeting toward the earth.

The screams of the people reverberated—distant to loud and back to distant again—as they fell.

"Hold on," the man piloting the winged thing said. Then suddenly her stomach was left behind as the beast dove.

One minute, there they were—swinging and swaying, Jet using pulses from his boosters to keep them as balanced as he could manage. All around them: the massive thunderbird dinosaurs. Then, Benjamin dove and leapt on a passing beast and suddenly it was as if all the beasts were properly dissuaded; they began to fly away, ducking and diving in a whole other direction.

Jet cast his eyes that way and saw the Chrysler Building, its sculpted, scalloped art deco peak no longer shiny and glinting in the sun, but rather it was corroded and shot through with holes and, worst of all, covered in a shellacking of fungus.

They're racing toward the other fungal tower, he thought.

And then:

Wham.

One of the last winged beasts clipped not the dangling spire, but rather the chain that held it to the autogyro. The gyrocopter dipped and Jet saw Mack clutching the stick just before everything dropped out from under him: the chain above looked like a half-bitten vine of licorice and, with a metal groan followed by a sharp snap, the chain link broke.

Then: free-fall.

Jet Black—and a whole lot of innocent people—fell.

Khan and Amelia raced down unfamiliar streets, canyons of cracked concrete and shattered asphalt that were as much *jungle* as they were *city*—a trickle of water ran from one building to another, fat flies buzzed about and thwacked into their heads like bumblebees at windowglass, and massive fern fronds cut their visibility in thirds.

Behind them, they heard the thrashing of brush. The sound of claws clicking on macadam. Khan's heart felt suddenly like it belonged to this place, like these trees and vine-choked buildings were *home* in a way, and before he even realized it he was leaping up, bounding off one tree to another and to another after that.

Amelia ran below him—she was a stallion, a fast-runner, a bullet tumbling from the barrel of a gun. But suddenly she pitched forward, landing hard on her shoulder. Khan grabbed a netting of vines and started to swing down, calling out to her—but it was too late.

The psychic wave washed over him. The psychosaurs emerged from in front of them as well as from behind, hissing and spitting. The horrible voices rose up in a malevolent chorus inside his mind: *You are your father's son, but you're weak too, child of the conqueror, the jungle is within you, you can't control it—*

They had him. And they had Amelia, too.

He hoped their distraction made a difference.

(That poisonous voice: *It didn't.*)

The spire fell.

The city rushed up to meet them.

They were all going to die. Jet knew that, now. Knew that they had failed to save these people. The only cold comfort was that maybe, just maybe, the fall of the fungal tower would buy Sally and the Resistance some small advantage in the war to take back the world from the monsters.

The people clung to the metal framework. Below, the Manhattan jungle zoomed towards them—or so it felt.

Their screams haunted Jet. Failure had never before been an option.

But now it seemed the only one.

He needed a miracle.

And a miracle—if a troubled, uncomfortable one—is what he got.

The spire's fall suddenly slowed in mid-air, as if buoyed by an updraft of wind or held aloft by an unspooling rope. The spire drifted slower and slower until it eventually settled into the boughs of a massive banyan tree, the spidery branches making a perfect cradle for the spire and its riders.

Jet didn't understand. Not at first. But when he rolled off the spire (trying not to crush poor Steve in the process, who'd seemed largely oblivious the whole time to the doom that was rushing to meet them), he felt the thought in his mind:

I SAVED YOU, LITTLE MOUSE.

Then, beneath the branches and on the ground, Jet saw:

The Walking Mind. Not staring up because, of course, Jared Brain had no eyes, no face, nothing but a platform and a jar and the pulsing organ of thought.

Which made it all the creepier.

Others rushed past the Walking Mind: men and women of the subterranean Century Club chapter house. The crackle of rifle-fire punctuated the air like the *rat-tat-tat* of a snare drum. Dinosaur shrieks. Neanderthal war-whoops.

Time, then, to fight.

Pow. A hard slap across Khan's gorilla mug.

Clarity came rushing back: a dam breaking.

The Neanderthal man—Atok—crouched in front of him, hand poised to deliver another slap. Amelia stood next to him, and behind them, Colin the Aussie Digger raised his Enfield and popped off shots.

"Wake up, ape-man," Atok growled.

"I'm... I'm here." Khan blinked.

"You look like father."

"He's not my—!"

Atok shushed him. "Rescue time, ape-man."

They pushed back toward the subway—for that now-decrepit tunnel system would be their escape. The Walking Mind flung whole packs of psychosaurs left and right as if they were gripped in a giant invisible hand. Atok returned with Khan and Amelia—the ape threw fists, Amelia let her Tommy gun do all the talking. Atok was himself a wild man, literally and figuratively, hurling himself into the fight with the rage reserved for a rabid animal.

The fight went on like this for a while—they all stayed behind to help those rescued from the fungal towers, shepherding them down into the tunnels. Jet remained shoulder to shoulder with the others, two pistols firing as Steve was finally allowed to unmoor from his chest straps.

A glint from a razor boomerang grabbed his attention.

It cut the legs out from under a pair of psychosaurs rushing up from a blind spot at his side. They dropped, flailing and screeching as the boomerang returned to its wielder.

Sally stepped up next to him. Boomerang in hand.

"Saving your tin can again," she said. At first it made him feel small, but then she gave him a sly smile and there was a glimpse of the old Sally Slick—she was always serious, sure, but she had that other side to her, too. The flash of it was gone quick as she flung the boomerang again—

But its existence, brief as it was, gave Jet hope.

A shadow passed overhead.

Sally knew the rescue attempt was a risky one, but they were winning this battle—the psychosaurs seemed disorganized, unable to muster the fight with the same kind of coordination they were usually capable of rallying.

It gave her a little hope. A blossom of triumph blooming on the vine.

Then: the shadow. A saline rush injected into her bloodstream.

A warbling shriek from above.

They're attacking from the skies.

A massive beast, one of the Quetzlcoatls—"Thunderbirds," they called them—landed on the ground ahead of them.

And one of the riders stepped off.

It was Benjamin Hu.

Sally's heart leapt. A feeling of joy erupted—*he's alive!*—that fell quickly as she realized his survival was not her doing. She'd dismissed him. Left him to the monsters because of his value. That tiny voice again inside her:

Sally Slick, what have you become?

Who are you?

Are you even a hero anymore?

Benjamin hopped off the beast and helped a woman—another rescue by the look of it—down off the Thunderbird.

She turned to say something to Jet, some acknowledgment of their victory that she knew would sound as half-hearted as she suddenly felt—

But Jet was gone.

CHAPTER TWENTY-THREE

One minute he was standing there, the next minute—hands grabbed him and pulled him into an alleyway. Jet spun around, pistols up—

And into the face of Mack Silver.

"Whoa, whoa, whoa," Mack said. "Pull back the reins, kid, you're working up a froth."

"Mack!" Jet hissed.

"C'mon, kid. Let's go. I got the gyro waiting up on one of these apartment buildings. While they're all distracted—" He made a sound like a whistle and clapped his hands together. "We're gonna hit the skies and find a real plane."

"There's a fight out there. Join it or leave me be."

"Jet. *Jet.* This world..."

"This world is our world. It's the one we made. It's the one we helped break. And now it's the one where I want to pitch in fixing it."

Mack stiffened. "It's Sally, isn't it." A statement, not a question.

"She's your *wife*, Mack."

"And I love her. But I loved the old Sally better. And like I said—"

"It wasn't *meant to be*, and yet it was, and—" Jet suddenly waved Mack off in a hand-flip of frustration. "It's an excuse! It's a pile of... *it's a pile of horse-apples is what it is.*"

Mack offered a dry chuckle. "Whoa, kid, watch that language, geez."

"Shut up, Mack! You just want the excuse to be a terrible husband. To keep acting like a loosey-goosey boozer, to... explain away your limp and your failures. Maybe Sally's the way she is because you didn't love her enough. Maybe if you had been a better husband—a *better man*—I would've appeared in this timeline to find a Century Club that had already saved the city."

Mack suddenly grabbed Jet and jacked him up against the wall. Little startled monkeys bounded away between tree branches and fire escapes above.

"You're laying this at my feet?" Mack seethed.

Suddenly, like a balloon with the air cut out of it, he dropped Jet and stepped away. His eyes lost focus, like he was staring at an unfixed point—a sign somewhere in the distance that advertised his guilt and shame.

"I'm gonna go," Mack said, suddenly.

"Mack, wait. Come back. This isn't over. The fight's just getting started. We need you."

"The world needs me, but not like you want it," Mack said. "I'll see you later, kid. I'm sorry. I really am."

Mack hobbled over to one of the fire escapes and swung his stiff leg up onto it, then pulled himself the rest of the way. Jet moved to follow after, but he heard Sally calling for him, a call joined by Khan and Benjamin and Amelia.

It was time to go home.

PART THREE:
FIGHT FOR
THE FUTURE!

CHAPTER TWENTY-FOUR

The rubber mallet slipped; instead of hammering the sheet of tin into shape, it smacked Jet's thumb. He winced and shook the hand like he was trying to get a crab to stop pinching his fingers and chucked the mallet to the ground.

"You okay?" Amelia asked. She was better at this than he was. Amelia took to things the way a duck waddled on ground, waded into water, and flew up into the sky. She was competent and didn't complain.

All around them stood the makeshift jet-wings.

Two dozen of them, so far. Others worked at the margins of the workshop chamber, fitting in portable engines and boosters, attaching the collapsible wings. These devices wouldn't be as capable or as complex as the one Jet himself wore, but it gave them an opportunity to claim supremacy over the skies: one area where the psychosaurs had found only marginal dominance.

"I'm fine," Jet said. "Just... clumsy is all. Once upon a time I had to open up the spouts at the grain elevator with a rubber mallet and sure enough I used to bash myself in the hands then, too."

"I didn't mean about that."

He gave her a look. He knew what she was talking about but he didn't want to admit it. Hence, the look. That was a small act of duplicitousness that Jet wasn't sure he would've been comfortable with a month ago when he first arrived here out of the time portal, but already this place had started to eat away at him.

"Jet. I'm talking about Sally."

"Sally's good. Fine. She's leading this group best as she can."

Even he could hear the concern in his voice, though. He thought after the daring escape and retreat from the Empire State Building that things would be different. That the pendulum would swing the other way. *And that look Sally gave him, that little smirk...* And things really *were* on an uptick, at least in terms of strategy and capability. But the mood around here had darkened.

"Jet, she's not the Sally you remember. Time hasn't been kind to her. This whole *world* hasn't been kind to anybody—"

"Oh, no," Jet said, standing up. He snatched the mallet and shook it at her—not a threat or a warning, but a gesture of dismissal. "We're not talking about this."

"Khan said—"

"I don't care what Khan said."

"We may have a chance. Just talk to him."

"I'm not gonna talk to him, I've got work to do."

"We're almost done here."

He scowled. "But then we have tests and—"

"Not much time for tests. Sally wants them ready in five days."

"Five days!" He scoffed and stammered. "*Five. Days?* Just because they're built doesn't mean they're, they're... *safe* to use. I haven't even tested the fix we've done to mine! If she thinks..." *If she thinks what?* His voice trailed off.

Amelia stepped over to him. Held him with both hands. "Sally should be in here. She should be leading *this* charge. The workshop is her home. And all this time the most she does is... creep in here, arms folded over like she might catch some kind of disease. Can you even *think* of Sally without a wrench in her hand?"

He couldn't. Even when thinking of *this* Sally, the one with the eyepatch and the razor boomerang, he couldn't envision her without a wrench hanging at her hip. And yet, that's who this Sally was. No wrench. No time in a workshop.

So much anger.

"I don't want to talk about this," he said, returning to his overturned bucket and resuming the hammering of tin.

"Go see Khan."

"I'm *not* seeing Khan."

Khan looked at himself in the cracked shard of a mirror he'd taped to the wall in his bunk. He licked his fingers, ran them across his eyebrows. He picked lint and dirt off his tweed suit, smoothed out his kilt.

He was dirty. And looked older. No way around that. They had working showers, but you only got one every week and the shower water was so hot it almost charred the hair off his body.

He'd never heard himself yelp like that before.

Still. Today he had to look good. Clean. Presentable.

At the door, Steve—Khan thought of him more properly as *Steven*—the psychosaur watched.

"Chess!" Steven said.

"Not today, Steven," Khan said, "I have things to do."

"More drawings?" the saurian asked, pointing a claw-tipped finger toward the chalkboard on the wall, a chalkboard crammed to the edges with calculations and drawings of vortices and funnels.

"No, I think my calculations are complete."

The creature blinked. Not like man or mammal blinked. A clear curtain of skin—a nictitating membrane—slid over his eyeball like a tongue. "Okay!"

Steven tottered off.

Then Khan exited his chambers and ran bodily into Jet Black.

The two of them looked at one another. Jet offered a smile, but it seemed strained and uncomfortable. Khan felt no such discomfort and grabbed Jet's hand and shook it vigorously.

"Ooh ow," Jet said, pulling his hand out of the gorilla's grip.

"Oh my. Did I... grip too strong?"

"No," Jet said, shaking his head, "I just hit my darn fool hand with a mallet."

"Nothing's broken."

"No. Just smarts is all."

"Jet, it's been a while since we talked—"

"I have work to do, we're on a tight schedule."

"I feel like you're mad at me, somehow."

"Not mad, Professor, just... really busy." But the look on Jet's face betrayed that statement.

"I'd like to talk. About what you and Mack were discussing that day in the tunnel. I've done some calculations and—"

Jet tried to juke left and right, but Khan stood in the way. "Not now, Khan."

"Oh. Okay." The erudite ape paused. "Still nobody's heard from Mack."

"...I know."

"Sally never sent anyone, Jet."

"It was his decision to leave like that. Can't afford to waste the man-power—the *lives of people*—just to go find that cowardly fox."

Khan felt himself bristle. "Now you sound like her."

"Get out of my way, Professor." Jet squeezed past with a shove.

And then was gone.

The Professor drew a deep breath. Tried to center himself. Today wasn't supposed to go like this. It was already a complex and upsetting day and...

He straightened his back. Dusted off his jacket one last time.

It was time to visit the Conqueror.

Benjamin wandered with Mary Elise through the maze-like chambers of the subterranean Century Club chapter house. If it could even be called that. A chapter house used to be a thing of some elegance: recovered artifacts and beautiful art, libraries packed with books from all eras of man. This was like a war bunker. A twisting, labyrinthine bunker.

He didn't feel very much at home here.

They had no Atlantean symbols that required deciphering. No items of antiquity that needed to be disarmed or deweaponized or *re*weaponized. No mysteries of translation, no murders where the dead bodies had strange symbols freshly tattooed on every inch of the corpse's skin.

Nothing. Nada. He wasn't a man without a country so much as he was a man without any purpose at all. He knew when the time came he'd be out there on the front lines—someone had found him not a rapier, but a nicked-and-chipped scimitar and that would have to serve him. But for now, he felt like a moo-cow idly wandering the pasture, wondering which patch of clover to munch on next.

Mary Elise helped all that.

She locked her arm in his. "You seem troubled."

"I'm fine," he said, offering a stiff smile that melted as soon as he saw her own. He was hesitant to say that he was in love. He'd been in love before. Or thought he was. This was better, somehow. Different. Deeper. Stranger. It wasn't even that they were romantic—though they were—but that he felt like a man out of time, and she felt like a woman out of time and together...

Well, once in a while he came across an artifact that had two pieces. Dangerous occult statuaries, for example, were often separated into two pieces with each half taken around the world so that they couldn't be used as the weapons they were. And when you brought those two halves together, it *clicked*. And frequently glowed. And sometimes killed everybody in the room.

This wasn't like that, obviously—nobody was dead. But the *clicking* and the *glowing*—? Yes. This was that.

Maybe this is love, he thought suddenly.

Time to change the subject.

As they wandered past the mess hall and deeper into the chapter house, he asked her: "So, how are the other survivors doing?"

"Happy to be here," she said. "Some of them are already working on the jet-wings. You know, they're all hungry and tired and more than a little scared but... they were inside their bodies all that time. They saw some people not make it. They—*we* know how lucky we are. Well, you understand."

He did. He was a captive mind in a stolen body, too.

"Though I wasn't captive as long as you," he said.

He clasped her hand and gave it a squeeze.

Suddenly, before he even realized it, they were at their destination. Well. Not *their* destination. But his.

There. Down a crooked hallway. A pair of guards. Gregory Smythe and Delbert Jameson now. Next shift: Anita Nix and George Malmon.

A constantly guarded door.

The *only* constantly guarded door in this place.

He realized then that Mary Elise was speaking to him: "...and so I thought maybe we could... pretty up the place a little, it's so drab down here, all the rock and stone, dripping and damp. Metal and rust and... well, one of the others was a ticket-taker at Coney Island but she's also handy with murals and... you're not exactly listening to me."

"I am," he said. "I'm sorry. I'm just... lost in thought."

"It's okay," she said, but he wondered if she was a bit stung.

Still, he asked: "What do you think is through that door?"

"I don't know," she said. A mischievous smile emerged like a mouse creeping from a bolthole. "Something *secret*."

"I don't like secrets," he said, quite serious, no smile.

"Oh."

"No, it's just..." He turned to her. "The Century Club doesn't do well with secrets kept from one another. Our chapter houses have always been open places. Once in a while it happens—or, happened—that someone kept a secret from another. An affair. A stolen artifact kept close. A betrayal, however small." He paused to consider his words. "Secrets are like seeds. They grow twisting trees and darken those beneath them. Trees with heavy branches and hungry roots that will tear everything apart. That's why I don't like secrets."

What he did not say was that the other day he saw one of the guards leave the post, go get a meal from the mess hall, and carry it back through that door.

A meal. As if someone were on the other side.

Then, he added, nodding toward that door: "That's why I don't like *this* secret. Stay here. I'm going to have a look."

Atok crashed into another Neanderthal, a young bull named Gorak—shoulders meeting shoulders, foreheads smashing together, teeth bared in the way of the tiger. Atok snarled: "You will not take my scepter."

Gorak was all corded rope and hard bone with a head as hard as an uncracked geode. He was slippery. Every grapple, he contorted his body and escaped. His hands found the scepter. Held it tight with both hands.

The young Gorak stared at it and smiled.

And his want would be his downfall. Atok was able to flick the scepter forward as Gorak stared at it—

The tip of the scepter bashed Gorak in the nose. He staggered backward, pawing at his face, eyes welling with tears.

Atok pulled the scepter away, set it on the ground, and shoved Gorak over.

The scepter was an old chair leg topped with a tin-can held fast by a bundle of rusty wire. It was, of course, no scepter at all. But this was one of the old games they played to train: Atok knew that battle was coming and he had to help these surviving Neanderthals harness their warrior instincts and fight with him.

Gorak looked stung.

"You will do better next time," Atok said. "Maybe one day you will take the scepter from me." His mouth twisted into a smile. "But probably not."

The smile faded quickly. Atok felt restless. Agitated. He wanted to *fight*. Not... sit here and train and practice. He was a war leader. He was Atok the Horrible. He was already battle-hardened even if his companions were not.

The one called "Sally" told him that she mirrored his eagerness but the time was not now. It was *coming*. That's what she told him. She said others of his kind were taken and enslaved much the same way hers were and that one day very soon they would go to war and she would need him to be ready.

But he was ready *now*, by the deepest gods.

"My god," the Professor said.

"Gaze upon me in my glory," the Conqueror croaked.

The warrior-ape was a pale shade of what he once was. His muscles had atrophied. His face sagged. His eyes were jaundiced and shot through with dark, spidery veins. He shuffled to the fore of the cage, pressed his nose through the bars and took a long sniff, baring his teeth after.

"What have they done to you?"

The Conqueror did not answer the question. Instead he said: "What is it you call me? When you to speak about me to others, how do you refer to me? Khan? But you are Khan. Conqueror? You wouldn't dare to speak of me with such deference unless you said it with a glib curl of the lip. Father? Hah. Not likely. I'd sooner believe that time-traveling pigs had taken over the world."

"I don't call you anything. I just refer to you as... him. Or, 'the other ape.'"

"Ah. Barely deeming to recognize me at all. Sensible." His voice was rheumy and wet. "They have Chirrang bring me what few meals they allow me. It's salt in the wound. That's what this is all about, you see. Punishment. Not just for what I did but also because I won't tell them what they want to know."

"What do you mean?"

"They thought to pluck my thoughts from my brain but the Walking Mind is only so gifted. I long ago learned techniques to keep people out of my head. Methuselah. The psychosaurs. Jared Brain. The drums you and I hear? I let them play. Glorious, pounding drums. None can get past them when I allow them control. My mind stays my own.

"So, they cannot take what they want and I will not give it and so they punish me. I waste away. I'm a shadow of the Conqueror." He snorted. "I can barely 'conquer' my own waste bucket."

"I'm... sorry."

"Do not apologize." That, a snarl, but a weak one. As if his heart just wasn't in it. "Apologizing is an act of weakness. You are Khan. You are strong."

The Professor bit his tongue. No argument would do any good.

"What is it they wanted to know?"

"They want to know what the relationship is between the strange fungus and the race of dinosaurs. They want to know how I did it. How I made them my own. They want to know how I keep them out of my *head*. And I won't tell them."

He laughed, then. The laugh of a madman: a warbling cackle.

"Just... tell them," the Professor said. "Why hold it back?"

"Because it's all I have left!" the Conqueror spat. "I have *nothing* else. I give that away and they either murder me in my cage with a spear through the heart or they give me a place at the table, and I want neither of those things." He let his fingers dance in the air. "So I fade away. Conquering silence, if nothing else."

"I have to go."

"Yes. Go. Pretend you didn't see me. Do you know why I'm here?"

"They captured you—"

"Don't be an ass. You're smarter than that. I didn't even have to come through the portal. I was coming for you. I wanted my son by my side. It's why I came here. Why I let them take me. For you. All for you."

"I can't be... I can't be responsible for that. The burden isn't mine."

"No, you're right. It's mine. Because I was wrong, son. Wrong all along. Wrong that you were like me. You aren't. Ultimately, you're weak. You are neither villain, nor hero. You're a primped professor, a proper whipping boy stuffed with the hay of academia. A villain would've joined me. A hero would've saved me. You do neither. You stand back. You merely... *abide*."

Khan fled the room. The Conqueror's cackles faded, but he could still hear them in the hollows of his heart.

CHAPTER TWENTY-FIVE

Sally swept everything off her desk.

Map tubes rolled. An old coffee mug didn't shatter but spun on its edge before falling and *then* shattering. Sally stood at the desk, chest heaving.

YOU SEEM TROUBLED.

She looked up. There stood the Walking Mind on his platform. Implacable and emotionless. Still and silent as a hat rack. A hat rack with a brain.

"You don't need to come in here to talk to me. You can just..." She let her hands fritter in the air like the legs of a spider spinning a web.

PEOPLE FIND IT LESS JARRING IF I AM STANDING IN FRONT OF THEM, PHYSICALLY PRESENT. I WANT TO PROJECT AN AURA OF COMFORT. I WOULD NOT WANT TO... IMBALANCE YOU FURTHER.

"Don't be condescending."

YOU SEEM UPSET.

"Every day that passes that we don't secure the city..." She didn't need to say it. She just let her mind wander over the events: they mounted a very fast and frankly *very effective* rescue effort. The one fungal hive was lost. It was, by all reports, a huge win for them. But now she was saddled with feeding and clothing a few dozen other humans—good, yes, happy to have the refugees, but most of them did not serve the *cause*. They would be trained, of course, but for now...

And then, the salt in the wound? The other fungal tower was ripe for the taking. And they fled in some ungainly combination of hubris and fear, thinking, *We will return another day soon and destroy the second tower and the city will be free from the oppression of the psychosaur invasion.*

But the second tower changed. It sealed up. It locked down. The entire Chrysler Building was now shellacked in a thick *rind* of hard, glistening fungus: you couldn't even *see* the building beneath it.

Worse, they seemed to be working on repairing the first tower.

No fungus, yet. No "electric spire," or whatever that... thing was that Benjamin saw and helped Der Blitzmann destroy. (That caused her a small spike of pleasure and sadness: Blitzmann was always a thorn in their side but he was brilliant, in a way, a craftsman like she was, once.) Benjamin had been after her to talk about the spire and its ancient origins but she had little patience for that talk right now. Further, she couldn't see the purpose: if it was old, it was old, that's a fine howdy-do, but it still needed to be destroyed. It didn't matter what civilization's name was stamped on the bottom.

"We should be moving faster," she said. "We need to attack soon."

I UNDERSTAND THE JET-WINGS ARE NEARLY COMPLETE.

"And we haven't even done a test yet. Or training."

I'M SURE IT'LL BE FINE. DON'T YOU TRUST YOUR PEOPLE?

"Of... course."

SO PUSH THEM. COMPLETE THE ARMADA. ATTACK SOON. NOT LATER. I AM EAGER TO WIN THIS BATTLE WHILE WE STILL HAVE THE ADVANTAGE. UNLESS YOU SEE SOME VALUE IN WAITING...

"No!" Her own voice surprised her. "No, I... we need to do this."

GOOD. I AM PLEASED THAT WE ARE OF TWO MINDS.

"We are."

IT WAS A LITTLE BIT OF A JOKE.

"Oh." She couldn't muster a laugh, but she gave him a weak smile.

I SUPPOSE I WILL NOT BE JOINING THE MARX BROTHERS ANYTIME SOON, HMM? IN THE MEANTIME, LET'S DISCUSS THE—

Suddenly his voice inside her head stopped.

I HAVE TO GO CHECK ON SOMETHING.

And then, the platform silently marched out of the room, leaving her alone with her regret, her anger, and the ghosts of a fallen world.

Jet walked laps around the earthen hallways, psyching himself up. *Do it, do it, stop thinking about it, just do it.* As he rounded the corner, finally veering back toward Sally's office, he saw the Walking Mind coming right toward him.

DO NOT SQUEAK, LITTLE MOUSE.

The jarred brain kept walking.

Jet knew what the Walking Mind was talking about. But it wasn't his role to take orders from the likes of Jared Brain.

He summoned his courage and stormed into Sally's office.

She was there, standing by her desk, picking at a small bowl of deep-fried crickets. She looked up, tongue in the pocket of her cheek, and she offered the bowl to him. "They're good. Deep fried they lose their... squishy middles."

Jet blanched. "I'm good."

"What is it, Jet?"

"I want to go after Mack."

"What?" Her face darkened. "No."

"But—"

"But nothing. He left us. He *betrayed* us. He could've been an asset but chose to be a rogue agent. You said it yourself when he left: we're a team of heroes, not a team of individuals. He wants to act like that, then good riddance."

"You don't believe that."

"I do."

"You loved him."

"Once. I also loved you. I no longer have the capacity for it."

That rocked him.

He stood, feeling like he'd been both hugged and sucker-punched at the same time. He tilted back on his heels. "Ahh. Uhh."

"Are we done?"

"Hardly," he said, hearing an unexpected edge to his voice. "I also want to tell the others. At least some of them. About Methuselah."

"Absolutely not."

"We don't keep secrets like that. Not of that magnitude. It's burning a hole in me. The others should know! Maybe we can use Methuselah in some way—"

"He's already handled. I control the information here. For now his presence remains a secret."

"Sally, you're not giving me much room here—"

"Are we done now?"

"No!" he yelled. "No, we're not. You're pushing us all too far. I don't know if I trust where you're taking us. The timeline for the jet-wings is too tight, I haven't even tested one or trained anybody and it's not like you've been down in the workshop doing anything more than a... a cursory walkthrough—"

She came up on him fast. She moved nose to nose. He expected anger, for her to strike him, but all she did was begin to talk in a quiet voice:

"Every time I touch a wrench, or a hammer, or... any tool at all, my hand starts to shake. Not a little. A lot. I can't even get a wrench around a lugnut. I live with nightmares, sometimes when I sleep, sometimes when I wake, and I remember that day. For you it was a month ago. For me it was a lifetime. And it marked me. I made a choice. I used the Atlantean tool and I sent everyone away from me and I was left in a world bent on destruction. But the worst thing was that I lost you that day. I lost someone who trusted me. Who loved me."

She bent forward and gave him a small kiss. Her lips were cold but they warmed fast. Then she leaned toward his ear and whispered:

"Please, I need you to trust me now."

"I..."

"Will you trust me?"

He nodded.

Then: a throat clear.

There stood Professor Khan. Teeth bared. Jet had never seen him look like that. He looked...

Well, he looked angry.

"*You*," he said, thrusting a finger toward—well, toward who, Jet didn't know at first because he stood so close to Sally, but as she backed away and tried to compose herself, the ape's eyes followed her. "You're torturing him."

"I don't know what you mean," she said.

"The... the Conqueror!" He snarled: "You know damn well who I mean! You're starving him."

"We're feeding him."

"Scraps! You're feeding him... scraps of bread and water. He's wasting away in that cage—"

Jet watched Sally's own anger match Khan's—she crossed the room and poked her finger into his chest.

"What would you have us do?" she asked, punctuating each word with a jab of her finger. "Give him the run of the place? Throw him a jet-wing and let him go? Need I remind you that it was Khan and the Doctor who plotted this all to begin with? That it was *his* conquest of our world that began this? He won't yield critical information to us. That does little to encourage kindness from me."

"But that's not who we are," Jet said. "We don't... torture."

She wheeled on him. "I told you to trust me and that's what I need, Jet. Trust. Trust that I know what I'm doing. *Trust* that I have been leading this charge for a number of decades equal to more than *twice* your age on this Earth."

"Sally—"

Suddenly, she pulled up the eyepatch, revealing a pucker of scar tissue where the eye once was. It called to mind a pair of pursed, burned lips. "You want to know how I lost this eye? We were still fighting some of Khan's forces—pockets of primate resistance in the lava tubes not far from the chapter house on Kauai. They swarmed us. So possessed were they by his spirit, so convinced that he would come back and lead them, they fought with a willingness to die in his name. One of them had a spear and stabbed it toward my face—I narrowly moved my head, but they hit the wall with such force a chip of stone, a little piece of *obsidian*, broke from the wall and embedded in my eye. I killed that ape with my bare hands. We won the day, but I lost my eye."

"Miss Slick," the Professor said, gruff but quieter, "I'm... sorry."

"Sorry doesn't put my eye back in my head. Sorry doesn't change the fact that your... genetic template, your *father* for all intents and purposes, is a dangerous and charismatic murderer. You really want to throw in with him?"

The steam robbed from his engine, Khan took a step back. He said nothing, but shook his head. Jet suddenly felt for the big lug. He'd been avoiding him, but...

Khan bowed his head, then said, "I should go."

"Yes," Sally agreed. "I have planning to do."

"I'll get out of your hair, too," Jet said.

She grabbed his shoulder. "Trust me," she said.

He nodded, and followed Khan out.

Twenty steps later, Jet said in a low voice to Khan:

"I don't trust her."

Khan, now more sad than angry, shook his head.

Jet drew a deep breath.

"I want to know more about time travel," he said. "And there's something you really need to know."

CHAPTER TWENTY-SIX

The two guards slumped together, heads conking like two coconuts. Mary Elise gasped.

"I..." she said, seemingly struggling to find words.

"They threatened me," Benjamin said. "Over whatever is in this room." And it was true. They had threatened him. Threatened to knock him out, take him to Sally. They had no idea who they were talking to. Benjamin stepped forward, the one threw a punch—Benjamin got under it, lifted the man's arm and rabbit-punched twice in his kidneys.

Instant knock-out—the kidneys were one of the most poorly protected organs in the body. A harder punch could've killed him.

As the one guard dropped, Benjamin slipped the grasp of the other. Not to get away but to get *closer*. He darted inside the man's reach, threw a hard punch up—the man's teeth clacked together and it was lights out for him, too.

Benjamin stepped over them and opened the door.

"Hello, Mister Hu," Methuselah said over the warring phonographs.

The old mathemagician chuckled and coughed as he hung there.

It was only a matter of time before Benjamin found him. The mystical detective was like a dog trained to sniff out secrets—and he was obsessed enough he could not let things lie.

An unpleasant setback, but worth it perhaps for the look on Hu's face. Anger. Confusion. He spun around like a girl in a dress in a meadow. Taking it all in. He realized it now, didn't he?

A girl stumbled in after him. Quite pretty, this one. Eyes shining like little dimes. Now *she* would have to be dealt with, too.

"Methuselah," Benjamin said. Barely containing the fear and anger.

"Benjamin, so nice to see you again."

"These symbols—"

"You recognize them."

"Hyperborean."

"Yes. You're smarter than anyone gives you credit for, you know that?" Methuselah coughed again. "Now, what do they mean?"

Benjamin paused. Thought. The old man saw the young detective's jaw tighten. "They're an equation. The Hyperboreans were gifted mathematicians. This is like a... mathematic mantra."

"Mathe*magic* mantra."

"You're training. Training your mathemagic skills. Trying to relearn the equations. Trying to regain lost magic. You did lose it, didn't you?"

The old man scowled. "I did."

Benjamin had part of it right. He had lost his magic—for the most part. But there remained a glimmer. And that was all he needed in this timeline. These equations on the walls were not to train him but to give him a tiny opening, a small glimpse into the larger equation. It was like a window, and through this window he could see dominoes falling in endless permutations, different actions leading to different outcomes. A gift he'd always possessed internally but now, one that was woefully *external*. He looked up now, stared at the symbols until—

Until he saw one such permutation. A new one he had not considered.

Just then: The Walking Mind entered the room.

Benjamin suddenly stiffened, limbs going rigid as Jared Brain's psychic tendrils lashed about, invisible coils rooting the detective to the spot.

Methuselah sent out the loudest psychic shout he could imagine:

Stop!

Jared did not stop. Methuselah was not fond of a follower whose obeisance was imperfect. Still, again he shouted telepathically—

I said stop!

Elasticity and control returned to the detective's limbs.

WHY? WHAT WE FEARED HAS COME TRUE.

But I see a new permutation. One as yet unconsidered. His discovery of the symbols is our strength.

HE WILL REVOLT. THE OTHERS WILL REVOLT.

And isn't that what we want? They have not yet come to me to learn the truth. They do not seek directions and think they can do this on their own. But now our detective has a clue—a clue he'll take, a clue he'll use.

YOU PLAY A DANGEROUS GAME, OLD MAN.

And you should listen to your betters, Jared.

Benjamin, meanwhile, reached over and pulled Mary Elise close, drawing the scimitar that hung in a scabbard at his belt.

"You're working together," he said.

Methuselah laughed. "If only."

Benjamin began to half-circle around the Walking Mind, and Methuselah heard Jared's transmission to Hu's psyche:

I STOPPED YOU BECAUSE YOU ENTERED UNAUTHORIZED SPACE AND YOU HURT THE GUARDS, MISTER HU.

As Jared's platform tromped into the room, Benjamin kept his scimitar slicing invisible symbols in the air as a warning.

"Whatever's going on here," Benjamin said, "I promise to find out."

"Of course," Methuselah said. "If you must play detective..."

The man darted out of the room, sending the woman ahead of him.

Such chivalry.

Shame, in a way. Methuselah would've liked her as a plaything. Make her dance, make her sing, make her wet his lips with a soggy sponge.

THIS COULD BACKFIRE ON US.

I have seen the infinite futures and these dominoes fall in our favor.

YOU FAILED TO GUESS HOW THE DOMINOES WOULD FALL LAST TIME.

A spike of rage inside his belly. He hoped Jared Brain felt it—hot like forge-hammered iron. *I made a fundamental error at the very beginning of that particular equation which is an error we both hope to correct, yes?*

...YES

Then shut up and trust me.

The Walking Mind said nothing. For once.

CHAPTER TWENTY-SEVEN

The erudite ape felt nervous. Odd, that. After all the things he'd faced recently, here he was feeling nervous just drawing on a blackboard and trying to teach Jet Black the theories he'd learned. He'd never gotten particularly nervous when teaching at Oxford, but this was different. Khan knew so much was riding on this. Further, this was Jet. Relations between the two of them had been strained, and he worried that if he pushed too hard, the young Centurion would again throw up all his walls and walk away.

"It's like this," Khan said. "If we found a way back in time—a big if, I realize, since we know that the gates are all closed—and we were able to change things *from the very beginning*, the question then becomes, what happens to this reality? Will this future fail to manifest? It must, yes? If we counteract it at the start it's like salting the earth so that a tree may never grow. Ah, but—"

He circled a diagram on the chalkboard that looked like the root system of a tree. He began to erase the larger root bundle, leaving all the smaller, fringed bits drawn on the black.

"Think of it like the map of a building. Just because we block the entrance does not mean the hallways disappear. Time in this regard is written. If we are to accept endless quantum universes and an infinite host of possibilities, we can still assume that this reality will not merely disappear or even die on the vine.

It will be unmoored from the timeline we choose to create with our actions—but it will still remain. This timeline won't just... disappear. Those in it will not perish."

He saw the look of consternation on Jet's face.

"I don't know, Professor. That might almost be worse."

"How so?"

"Because... because then we really are abandoning a fight. It's like... we had a barn-fire once when I was a kid, right? We had two barns, one with the stable in it, the other connected to the grain silo, and when the one burned we didn't just abandon it for the other barn, or for some... future barn we were gonna build. We had to save the animals inside that one."

"The question," Khan said, "is whether this... barn is worth saving at all."

Jet swallowed hard. "Sally..."

"Is not the Sally you remember."

"She is. She's in there somewhere. You'd be changed too if you went through what she went through."

"Be that as it may, she's drifting, Jet. Drifting away from us. They say it can happen, you know. That some Centurions... toward the end of their times, they refuse to let go. Time darkens them. They slowly twist and become Shadows. Perhaps that's what happened to Methuselah. Perhaps once, long ago, he was a Centurion like us. And perhaps he did not want to let his century pass—and he with it."

"Those are just hypotheticals. This is real. Sally or no Sally, this world's still in danger and the people—I mean, jeez, Khan, we just saved a few dozen. I know that's just an ant on top of a mountain but it's real."

Khan held up a finger. "Now imagine that we save them all. Imagine that we go back in time and those who were lost can be reclaimed—Jet, they'd never be taken at all."

"In *that* timeline. But in *this* one..."

A sudden knock on the door to Khan's bunk chamber. An assertive, even angry, pounding.

The Professor shot Jet a quizzical look.

Jet stood, reached for the door, gently opened it.

Amelia and Benjamin stood there.

They did not look happy.

"We need to talk," Amelia growled.

As Amelia and Ben spoke, Jet felt tension gnawing away at his middle, like rats gnawing at a cable. Eventually they got to the part where Benjamin explained that the symbols on the wall were not there to trap Methuselah—

But rather, they were there to help him. How, Benjamin didn't know for sure, but he thought that the old mastermind was trying to *relearn* the mathematical magic that had been wrenched from his grip.

Jet couldn't hold it in any longer.

"I knew about all of it." He corrected himself: "*Most* of it. I didn't know what the symbols were for, I—"

Amelia stared bullets through him. "You *knew?*"

Khan echoed the question: "Jet. You... were aware of this? All along?"

"I was. Mack showed me. He wanted to figure out how we would manage to get back in time and Methuselah had a way—"

"We're not trusting him," Amelia hissed.

"Wait," Benjamin said, holding up a hand. "Hear him out."

"The... 'doctor' said he had an Arctic base where one of his gates would surely still be open—it wasn't a gate linked to the others so it wouldn't have closed when they did. And since it's in the Arctic, the reptile army wouldn't be able to follow us because... reptiles."

"Cold-blooded," Khan said, shaking his head like he'd just put a piece of the puzzle in place. "Of course. Cold would kill them. Or at least make them so slow they couldn't operate. I'm so foolish. I've been so occupied with all this I didn't even see that piece right in front of me."

"The problem," Jet continued, "was that we had no idea where the base was. Still don't. Mack thought we'd just... fly around until we found it, which proves just how drunk he was because, gosh, the entire Arctic Circle is millions of square miles. That meant we'd have to ask Methuselah, and Sally and the Walking Mind already caught us once and..." He rubbed his eyes. "I'm sorry I never said anything. I should've, but I thought that would put you all in danger. And... I trusted Sally knew what she was doing. But I don't anymore."

Amelia scowled. "You should've told us."

Benjamin held a steadying hand on her shoulder. "Give his rope some slack. Jet didn't know. We're all a little topsy-turvy."

"That still leaves us without foreknowledge of Methuselah's base," Khan said. "And no way to get there."

"I bet I know," Benjamin said. He half-laughed. "Those symbols, they were Hyperborean."

Jet gave him a questioning look. Khan took the lead:

Khan said, "*Neither by ship nor by foot would you find the marvelous road to the Hyperborean assemblage.* That, from Pindar, the poet from Thebes. The Greeks spoke of them, the Hyperboreans."

"Yes," Benjamin said. "That's right. The Hyperboreans were a race of people from the distant north. The Children of the North Wind. They arose along with the Atlanteans, the Meruvians, the Thulians, the Lemurians. The other so-called 'root races' of our world, if you believe the theory. Here's the thing: the Hyperboreans were said to have been the ones to seed mankind with an understanding of mathematics as they themselves held to an understanding paralleled perhaps only by our own, today."

"Like Methuselah's 'mathemagic'?" Jet asked.

"Maybe. A cohort of mine—an archaeologist by the name of Xian Chu—had a theory that Hyperborea's capital was on an island called Magiya Island in the East Siberian Sea—a place hidden on an ice field and concealed by such thick fog that Xian could never herself make the trip. It would make sense that Methuselah would make that his home, wouldn't it? Studying the secrets of the Hyperboreans? It's even possible that's where he began to learn his mathemagic so many years before."

"It's a long shot," Jet said.

"An informed long shot," Khan corrected.

Amelia added: "And the *only* shot."

"How do we get there?" Benjamin asked.

"If only Mack had stayed," Jet said. "He might've known a way."

"We'll have to fly," Khan said. "I believe the Pindar poem told it true. You will not get to Hyperborea via ship or on foot. The sky is the only way."

"The jet-wings," Amelia said.

Benjamin nodded. "We take the jet-wings."

"They're not even tested," Jet said.

"They're what we have."

"No!" Jet protested. "I... can't. It's already bad enough we're talking about abandoning this world for our own—I can't then take their only meaningful weapon. Before we do anything, I want the jet-wings working. I want them operational and capable. And I want Sally and the others to use them as they were intended. We have to find another way. We're *not* using the jet-wings."

The others shared a look.

"Of course," Khan said.

"We'll find another way," Amelia agreed.

"We find another way," the others said.

CHAPTER TWENTY-EIGHT

We don't have another way, Jet thought, as he strapped on his hopefully repaired jet-wing and adjusted the harness that held Steve the psychosaur to his chest. It was the next morning and he stood below the massive carved-out channel below the fake-lake of Central Park, a lake whose presence was part "smoke and mirrors" illusion from the Great Carlini, part psychic veil put in place by the Walking Mind.

Steve craned his eerie reptile head over his shoulder and hissed a greeting at Jet. "Hello, Jet."

Jet cinched the belts tighter over Steve's chest. "I've been here the whole time, Steve."

"I know! Just wanted to say hi."

"Hello, Steve."

"Hello."

Sally stood nearby. Looking up. "If it doesn't work?"

"Then I fall."

Others milled around behind her. Colin, Tara, Carlini in his cape. Behind them stood the original Centurions: Amelia, Benjamin, and of course, Khan.

Off to the side, the Walking Mind stood silent, implacable.

Jet looked to the others and gave them a tense smile.

A booming voice in his mind: IF YOU FALL I WILL CATCH YOU.

That sent a chill up Jet's spine. He looked to Sally. When he fell, she was usually the one that caught him. But perhaps times really had changed.

He advised Steve to tuck his legs.

Jet crouched.

He reached back, slapped the button behind him—

The jet-wings snapped open—

A pulse of air punched out of the back—·

And by the time he caught his breath, he was already up over Central Park.

Voosh.

From up here, the city opened up to him. It was the same as before— mist worming between crumbling skyscraper canyons, buildings cracked and shattered by the slow-moving hands of vines and roots, and in the distance, the Chrysler Building—now an orange spire, the building itself lost beneath the pulsing fungal carpet. Pterosaurs circled in the distance but Jet didn't feel threatened. Not yet. Besides, Steve gave him the protection he needed from the psychosaurs' telepathic feelers. As long as he stayed away, he was good.

For just a moment, he let himself fly. Up on heat vectors—then down, a corkscrew, a fake fall, before once more slinging back up and gliding.

It felt good. Liberating. Like all the world's problems were gone forever. No worries over timelines or villains or psychic dinosaurs or starving ape-lords.

Wind in his teeth. Goggles comfortable around his eyes. The feeling of being one with the sky.

Steve seemed to like it, too. A big, toothy smile sat plastered on his face.

Eventually, though, reality crept in—a cold damp, deep in the marrow.

Something had to be done. Sally wanted to use the jet-wings. A suicide mission? Jet didn't know. Her plan seemed sound: jet-wings to the top of the spire, attach to the fungus, cut holes through the myco-layer, destroy the electrostatic obelisk from within and diminish the psychosaur grip on the city.

But the psychosaurs numbered in the thousands.

They had less than a hundred to send into battle. And only two dozen jet-wings to claim some kind of sky superiority.

Then there was the plan—steal away to Hyperborea, find a time gate, go back in time to the very beginning, unwrite the mistakes they made...

They would need the jet-wings for that. They had no plane. Mack was gone—probably dead. His mind pored over the problem, unable to find any niches or cubby-holes in which to get a proper grip on it—

Beneath him, water. And coming up, the Brooklyn Bridge.

A sudden memory snapped back into his mind:

Sally's map. Her pointing to it.

The Brooklyn Bridge is a nesting ground for Pterosaurs.

The towers and cables of the bridge were only 100 feet below him. Already he saw the massive nests molded between towers, held to the towers and above the cables with bundles of roots and sticks and crude thatch.

The nests squirmed.

Baby Pterosaurs. And eggs.

And all the parents, too.

Suddenly, a cacophony of shrieking punctuated by the sound of leathery wings catching air—

A flock of Pterosaurs took flight beneath him.

Ten. Then twenty. Then too many to count.

They were coming for him.

"Uh-oh!" Steve said cheerfully.

"Uh-oh is right," Jet said, and gave the jet-wing a hard boost just as a tornado of Pterosaurs rose beneath him.

"They're not back yet," Sally said. Worry sat heavy in her belly as claws of tension gripped her shoulders. Not an unfamiliar feeling, but magnified this time. She told herself it was because everything counted on this jet-wing test. That little voice inside of her just said one name: *Jet.*

She looked behind her. The others were watching her. Staring, really. She felt their judgment. Once she had envisioned them returning to this world and in those visions she imagined them all reforming the team that made the

Century Club great. But time was not kind to the relationship. She'd seen things they never had. Lived through experiences they didn't even understand. They thought things were bad back then: all the villains and fighting and constant world crises. They had no idea. And that's why they stared. They *judged* her.

Let them judge.

The Walking Mind intruded upon her thoughts:

I FEEL HIS PRESENCE OUT THERE.

"So, he's all right?"

I AM NOT SO SURE ABOUT THAT, MISS SLICK.

It was like trying to fly inside a flock of crows—except these crows were a hundred times the size and carnivorous, and oh, also, *really protective of their babies.* Every time he pivoted in the air, he met scratching claws or clacking beaks—he twisted his hips, rose higher, only to almost get swiped out of the air by a rushing wing. Back down, *voosh,* through the center of the Pterosaur tornado, only to see one of the creatures—a big one, one of the Thunderbirds from before—headed straight for him like a flying freight train.

He had nowhere to go.

The sun was blotted out by wings.

The shrieks echoed in his ringing ears.

Everything was shapes and movement and shadow.

Then: a sudden opening in the flock. Three Pterosaurs suddenly danced herky-jerky in mid-air and each dropped like a stone.

What the—?

Then he heard it:

Ack-a-ack-a-ack-a!

Machine gun fire. Bullets stitched holes in dinosaur wings—their bony beaks opened to scream as they scattered or fell.

And in through the gap roared a Clipper plane—a flying boat made famous by one particular pilot, and Jet caught a glimpse of that pilot smiling through the front windshield.

Mack gave Jet a thumbs-up.

Jet couldn't help but laugh. He quick jetted off to the side to find a name painted in drippy black paint across the side:

Lucy.

The door just under the wing hung open—right underneath one of the four whirring propellers. Jet sucked in a deep breath, hoping that the jet-wing's mobility was as good as he hoped because this was like threading a needle—

Next thing he knew, he was faceplanting inside the Clipper.

The jet-wing still clung to his back. Steve still on his front.

And Mack calling from the fore: "Hey, kid. Meet the new Lucy!"

HE IS GONE FROM MY PSYCHIC REACH.

Sally stood for a few moments, trembling.

Then she whirled heel-to-toe and marched back toward the interior of the base. Sally pushed through those who had gathered to watch the takeoff.

"I'm going to get a jet-wing," she said. "I'm going to find Jet."

The new Lucy was...

Well, it was filthy. Fuzzy roots clung to a rusty bottom. Half the seats were gone, the other half were torn open, springs poking out. Spiders nested in webs in the corners. Big spiders. Spiders as big as Jet's hand.

"You're quiet," Mack called from the pilot's chair through the open cockpit door.

"I'm just... looking around."

"The spiders, right? Yeah. They ain't poisonous if that's what you're wondering. I mean, I guess they are because all spiders are poisonous but they're not gonna kick your keister into the grave." Mack cleared his throat. "I know she isn't much to look at, but it's a good start."

For a good end, Jet thought.

Jet unsnapped his jet-wing and let Steve free, then told the psychosaur to wait there. Steve, ever compliant, smiled blankly and agreed.

As the propellers rumbled overhead and the boat-plane shuddered with pockets of warm, rising air, Jet made his way into the cockpit and sat down.

Mack grinned. He looked clear-eyed.

He had even shaved.

"Like her?"

"She's loud," Jet yelled over the propeller sound. "I don't remember Lucy being this loud before!"

"Sally rigged that one up, remember? She had all kinds of... noise dampeners and stuff. Plus, this isn't a Boeing like the other one. It's a bit smaller—one of the original Sikorsky Clippers."

"Oh."

"I haven't had a drink in a month."

"Oh. That's... that's good."

"Good? Kid, I'm *clean*. I'm like a... a landing strip cleared of brush. I'm a threaded needle. What I mean is, I'm ready."

"Ready for what?"

"Don't be a clown. *To save the past.* To go back in time and... do whatever the hell it is we need to do. You find out where the Arctic base is?"

Jet hesitated. "We did."

"I knew it! I knew if I left you alone for a little while you'd get that all locked down." Mack clapped Jet on the shoulder.

"Last we left we were... *mad* at each other."

"So?"

"So then you stormed off and... I figured you were dead."

"Eh, kid, it takes a lot to rip the stuffing out of this teddy bear, lemme tell you. We almost punched the lights out of each other, whatever. Blood under the bridge. You needed time. I needed to find a plane. And I did! Flew that autogyro—which, by the way, is like trying to fly a bucket of water the thing's so damn unsteady—to an old Jersey airfield near the shore just as I was running out of fuel. Looks like I still got the old Mack Silver luck. No psychosaurs at the base—though more than a few wandering dinosaurs, thankfully none of them meat-eaters. And there in one of the hangars I found this old beaut."

"How'd you know to find me?"

"Here's where you're gonna think I'm nuts. I woke up this morning and had a dream that today you'd be out there with your jet-wing. I'd already taken to flying patrols here and there, so... I was just flying out over the water when boom, there you were. Like in my dream."

"That's kind of strange, isn't it?"

He shrugged. "Listen, kid, we're heroes. We don't need to question that. You start to question it, you lose something. It's like staring too long at a picture on the wall or trying to repeat a word over and over again. Eventually, you lose all meaning. Heroes, we go from our guts. That's how I knew you'd eventually get on board with this plan. Because you're a smart kid—but not *too* smart."

He winked.

"And what about Sally?"

Mack's smile suddenly vanished. "I don't wanna talk about Sally."

Jet said, "But—"

"No. I... hope we never see one another again."

Sally stood in the workshop, feeling foolish. Two dozen jet-wings laid out wing to wing, front to back. All around her, the tools of the shop hung on hooks drilled into the stone.

A wrench hung nearby. Shiny due to a fresh polish.

Her hands were damp. Her mouth, dry.

She told herself it was that she was a warrior now. A war-leader like Atok. She wasn't to spend her time frittering away with nuts and bolts.

But she also knew that it went far deeper. A kind of *block*. A persistent fear that had only deepened over the decades. Like a bottomless well, its water black and its darkness hungry.

Still. Now she didn't need to do anything to... fix these jet-wings. They were good enough. She crouched down, pressed her back against one and looped the straps over her shoulders.

It was time to fly.

It was time to save Jet Black.

Again.

Khan stood as Sally marched to the center of the opening. The others seemed hesitant, as did he, but he could not let this go unsaid—

As she looked up through the massive opening—a hole easily as deep as a skyscraper was tall—Khan stepped up and laid a massive but gentle hand on her shoulder. She didn't look at him, but he spoke anyway.

"Be safe, Miss Slick," he said.

"I will, Khan." She offered a small smile. "I'll be fine. I hope you trust me."

"In this, I do."

He couldn't tell how she felt about that. The small smile seemed strained, somehow. Just the same, she touched his shoulder.

With that, he backed away and she shot up through the channel and was gone.

Sally, unsteady and uncertain, shot above the city.

Her first thought was: it had been a while since she flew. Whether with Mack or with Jet—it had been so long, but the memory came back fresh as the scent off a newly-washed bedsheet. The feeling of exhilaration. Wind in her face and hair. That sense of her heart and stomach left behind on the earth as her spirit escaped the flesh and flew free, for a time.

The second thought was not so pleasant: a wave of fear came over her, making her suddenly dizzy. That little voice, no longer little and now very loud, *You can't do this, you don't fly, this isn't your place, this is Jet and Mack's place—and Mack left you and Jet no longer trusts you even if he says he does, mankind is on the edge of oblivion and you're the only one who...*

Can...

Blood rushed to her head. The world spun sideways.

All went black.

Sally Slick fell.

CHAPTER TWENTY-NINE

She awoke.

Ground beneath her hips.

Jet-wing lying nearby.

Sally looked at two feet planted on the tarpaper roof.

A gloved hand reached down, helped her up.

"Jet," she said.

"Hey, Sally."

"I..."

"You fell."

She felt two blushing roses bloom on her cheeks. "Oh."

Nearby, Steve the psychosaur stood, poking a stick into a half-collapsed pigeon coop.

"I caught you," Jet said.

"I feel so..." Her one hand formed into a frustrated fist. "I feel so stupid. You had gone off the radar and—"

"—I figured I'd try a longer flight, just to see—"

"—and then I went after you to—"

"—to save me. You wanted to save me."

She hesitated. "I thought you were in danger."

"I wasn't. I'm okay. But thank you."

"I guess you don't need me saving you anymore."

"I thought I did." He took a step back. "But I can save myself."

That one step seemed magnified, somehow. An extra foot of physical space seemed like an emotional mile. All the more confusing was that old feelings stirred up and she wanted to kiss him. But that wouldn't be the strong thing to do.

And she wasn't sure he even wanted that from her, anymore.

"I guess we should get back," she said.

He nodded. "I guess so."

They landed to applause. And handshakes. And triumphant whistles.

Jet didn't bother mentioning that Sally had fallen and that he had saved her. Even though everyone probably assumed it was the other way around.

He thought her experience up there would have taught her something about using one of the jet-wings, but she put that thought quickly out of his head as she announced:

"The jet-wing test was successful!" More applause and hoots. "That means tomorrow morning, we suit up and go to war. Eat and drink well tonight, for soon we take back our city—" Here the applause reached what Jet thought was its crescendo, but then she added: "And then, *our world.*"

Massive applause. Thunderous for the small group present. Magnified by the echo of the stone walls around them.

"Steve," Jet asked, "can you project your... mental field? Around us?"

They stood with the others—Amelia, Khan, Benjamin—in the workshop next to the remaining jet-wings. Steve gave a quizzical look.

"Steven," Khan clarified, "can you protect us from others like you?"

"Okay!" the psychosaur chirped, and his opaque eye-membranes closed for just a moment, then opened again. Again he said: "Okay!"

"Will that work?" Amelia asked. "Are we protected from... *him*?"

By "him," they all knew who she meant.

Jared Brain. *The Walking Mind.*

"I guess we'll find out," Jet said, then dove right in: "I saw Mack."

They goggled at him.

Khan laughed, a bellowing gorilla *ho ho ho.* "He's alive?"

"Alive and has a plane. I told him we're all in and that we had an idea where to go. All we need to do is meet him tomorrow for the pickup."

"That's great," Amelia said, sharing a rare smile. "Where do we meet?"

"Since the plane's a Clipper it can land in water—we agreed on the Central Park reservoir, which is only about a mile north of here."

"We can take Steven," Khan said.

"No," Jet said, fast and firm. "He stays. They'll need him for whatever is to come. I don't want to rob them of any weapons they can use."

"What about us?" Benjamin asked. "Serious question. *We* are weapons they can use."

"We're not weapons. We're heroes. And that's why we have to leave. I hope they win the city back and then the world, but I don't know that we're the ones to fight this fight. We have a bigger battle ahead of us. We have to fight for the world we lost, not for the world we made."

A hard decision, but there it was. He still wasn't sure about it, but he knew he didn't want to stay. Maybe part of it was just that he missed the world as it was. Nostalgia had its claws in him—though it wasn't that long ago for him, it felt suddenly like forever. He missed that world. That life. *That* Sally.

Some parts of this world were irreparable.

Sally was one such component.

"Tomorrow," he said.

"Tomorrow," they agreed.

Perhaps an odd sentiment for a group of heroes looking to travel back in time, but there it was.

CHAPTER THIRTY

That night, as Mary Elise slept in her bunk, Benjamin crept in and sat at the edge of the bed. She stirred. Her hand found his.

"Hey," she said.

"Hi there."

"Come lay down?"

"I can't now. I want to talk."

She kissed his hand. "So talk."

"I'm leaving tomorrow."

"But you'll come back. I believe in you. I believe that with you by their side that victory will be in your hearts—if you'll excuse the poetics, gosh, that sounds so corny, but—"

"Mary, that's not what I mean. I mean I'm... going somewhere. I'm not going to war tomorrow. At least, not for this world."

She sat up.

"I don't understand."

"I come from a different time—"

"I do too."

"But this isn't my world."

"It is your world. And it's my world. It's what we have."

"This world doesn't have a place for me. Its mysteries are meaningless. In this world, I'll never again wander the streets of Hong Kong looking for a... lost idol. I'll never trudge through a mountain cave looking for the Merovingian Gospel of the Unmade King. I'll never solve an inexplicable murder and give peace to the family and to myself. This place has no peace for me. It has no mystery."

"It has me."

"And that's why I want you to come with me."

"Where?" She seemed agitated, now. Confused. How could she not be? "I don't understand. Where are you going?"

"Not where. But when. We're going back in time. To the start of it all. To prevent the psychosaurs from ever entering the world of man. And that means I'll never be able to come back. Either I'll die and we won't be successful or... we'll succeed and this timeline will be forever cut off."

"I love you."

He bit his tongue but it was too late. "I love you too." His heart felt hot. Was it hot in here? Was he having a heart attack? Or was this just love?

"But I can't go."

The heat in his heart, crushed beneath an avalanche of grief.

"I understand if this isn't your world," she said. "But it is mine. I want to go back to that time when I had poetry and a... a cat and a job and all of that. But I have a memory of what those monsters did to me. And I want them gone from this world. Not from some... earlier time, but from the *here* and *now*."

"Oh. I... of course, I understand."

"I can't go with you. And I'm sorry you have to go."

"Me too."

She kissed him.

Then pulled away and spoke quietly in his ear:

"If you make it back to your time, look me up. I won't remember you. I won't even know you. But I'll be there. And I think that version of me will still come to love this version of you."

He kissed her again.

"I will," he said, and left.

Amelia opened Sally Slick's office door.

Sally looked up from her desk, from a bottle of whiskey. She must've just taken a sip, the way she hissed an intake of breath through her teeth.

"Stone," Sally said.

"Slick," Amelia greeted in response.

"You ready for tomorrow?"

Amelia didn't answer that question.

Instead, she said: "I don't like you."

A flicker of something at the corner of Sally's eye. Irritation? Regret? "You don't have to like me. You just have to respect me."

"I don't respect you."

Thunk. Sally set the bottle down and straightened in her chair.

"Go on," Sally said. "You seem like you have something on your mind."

She did. If she was going to leave this world in the hands of *this woman*, she had something to say, all right.

"I don't like bullies," Amelia began. "And you're a bully. I can already see the protest in your face—you're going to tell me how this is a hard world and you've had to become hard in response to it. You're going to say how this is what the world made of you and you're *tough* but *fair*. That's how a lot of bad people justify themselves. We like to think the villains we fight are evil just because they want to be evil but that's not it. They never think they're evil. They think they're the heroes in their own stories, just like you think you're the hero of this one. They have their reasons. Revenge they call justice. Selfishness they call equity. Malevolence they call righteousness. It's a tired old story, Sally, and you wrote yourself right into it."

Sally was visibly trembling, now.

"You're calling me a villain."

"I might be, at that."

Sally stood suddenly, the chair knocking back behind her. She came like a storm around the side of the desk, fists up, teeth bared—

Amelia held up a hand.

"You better cool your jets, Miss Slick, because tomorrow you go to war, and I don't think you want to fight that battle with your one good eye swollen shut."

Sally pressed her nose to Amelia's. "You seem to assume I'll lose."

"No, I *assume* I'll give as good as I get."

The two of them stood face to face like that for what felt like an eternity.

Finally, Sally offered a laugh that contained no mirth, only bitterness.

"Fine. You don't like me. You don't think I'm a hero anymore." Sally turned and walked back to the other side of the desk and picked up the fungal whiskey. "I'll prove you wrong tomorrow."

"Goodnight, Miss Slick."

"Uh-huh."

And with that, Amelia turned and left.

The clock fell past the tipping point, falling on the far side of midnight, and Jet tried to sleep but failed. Instead, he wandered the halls of the Century Club chapter house—if it could be called that—and saw the troops readying themselves for the war tomorrow. Some of them played cards. Others practiced fighting in bunk rooms and the mess hall and even in the hallways.

Didn't look like anybody was really sleeping.

Colin and Tara drank "coffee"—really a brutal black root brew that had stimulating properties—and told stories. Tomorrow she'd go up in the sky and he'd stay on the ground. Jet wondered if they had a thing for each other. Realized or unrealized or perhaps just unfulfilled. (And he thought of Sally: not this world's Sally but of the Sally he left behind. The Sally he planned to see again, one day.)

Lily-Belle the ghost zipped in and out of the earthen walls, her noncorporeal form both a gift and a curse. She saw Jet and she laughed and waved.

The Great Carlini donned his black cape and his red mask and was practicing throwing his razor-honed playing cards at a dummy against the far wall—each card either stuck in the dummy's heart or head, or shaved bits off. Stuffing drifted down after each throw.

He thought to go and say goodbye to Sally.

But he just couldn't bring himself to do it.

Atok sharpened a spear.

A hand landed on his shoulder.

"Stone," he said.

"Atok," Amelia answered.

He liked this woman. Liked that part of her name—her "last" name, whatever that meant—was Stone. It suited her. He liked stones.

"You helped me," she said.

"You helped me," he answered.

"Do you want to go home?"

He turned toward her, felt his brow darken. "Home to Hollow Earth?"

"No," she said. "Home. Back in time. First we have to fix some things in the distant past, but... we're going to change all of this."

"Atok good here," he said.

She gave him a quizzical look. "You like it here?"

He tried to explain it as best as he could that his people didn't believe in the past—and while they believed in the future, it wasn't nearly as important as the *now*. You never really left the past or entered the future because all of life balanced on the single moment in which you lived. And it was *that moment*—and the world of that moment—that truly counted.

Of course, that's not what he said. Because he couldn't communicate with her the way he could with his own people.

Seeing her look of confusion deepen, all he said was:

"Cannot retreat. Will not surrender."

Amelia nodded. That, she seemed to understand fine.

"Fight well tomorrow," she said.

He nodded, then went back to sharpening his spear.

It was nearly time.

Khan soon had to meet the others in the tunnel—they'd climb up through one of the boltholes Colin had dug throughout the park.

The Professor had one more thing to do.

He went to the captive ape-lord.

"You," the Conqueror sneered.

The Professor laid a package of food—some hardtack biscuits, a few fruits, some dried jerky—just within reach of the cage.

And on top of that, a hammer.

He'd stolen it from the workshop the day he fought with Sally in her office. That day he was angry enough he expected to bash open the cage then and there, but... he wasn't sure if it was good judgment or cowardice or some combination that prevented him. But now it was time.

"That's a hammer," the Conqueror said.

"It is."

"What good will it do me? The lock is crumpled."

"A hammer will help you open it."

"I'm weak."

"You're strong enough."

The Conqueror chuffed. "Give it here."

"You'll have to stretch to reach it. Which you will in due time. And you'll escape. And the Walking Mind will probably stop your escape but—I know you're capable and resourceful, even weakened. It's not much of a chance but it's a chance, don't you think?"

"Why now?"

"Because I'm leaving."

"Where?"

"To go back in time."

"There are no more time-gates."

"We believe there's one. Methuselah's Arctic gate."

The Conqueror chuckled. "Of course. I should've thought about that one. I've been there, you know."

"I wondered as much."

"But you never asked."

"I feared what you might ask of me in return."

The Conqueror eyed him up. "A fair caution. I'll tell you now—the Magiya Islands."

"Yes. The old Hyperborean capital?"

"Indeed. A caution: the fog is thick. And Methuselah had... protections. Automatons. Traps. And when you're flying in you'll see—there's a way to know when you're almost on top of it. There's a way the sea smoke shimmers. A ribbon of it. That's how you know. Because you'll not see the island from the sky."

"Thank you. But why? Why give me that information now?"

"Perhaps because of the hammer and the food. But we both know that's not the reason. You're smart enough to see that I'm dying."

"You will outlive yourself."

"I'm sick. I have a... cough. I feel my heart. Weak. Paltry. A sick thing sputtering in my chest. I barely hear the jungle drums anymore. I'm dying. So I might as well impart something to my son before I go."

My son.

"I—"

"You're going to see me again."

"I know."

"If you're going back far enough to stop it all, we will meet anew. And you will have to fight me to stop me."

"Yes." The erudite ape shifted uncomfortably. "Yes."

"I'll give no quarter. The drums in your heart, listen to them. But be smart, too. I was not. I was blind to Methuselah's manipulations. You'll find your way."

"Thank you." Professor Khan offered his hand. "Father."

The withered ape reached out and shook it.

"Go," the ape-lord said. "Time waits for no ape."

"Time," Methuselah said. "Time will never wait for me. Not this iteration. Not this body, this mind."

The brain-in-a-jar stood there on its platform.

YOU ARE CERTAIN? YOU DO NOT WISH TO COME?

"No," Methuselah said. "What's the point? I'm old. My magic is just out of reach. I can see it. But I cannot affect it. This world has been ruined for me. But out there is another version of me. A more vital version. That is who I serve. I serve myself of another time, another place."

THEN THE TIME HAS COME.

"It has."

WILL THIS WORLD FOLD IN ON ITSELF? AN ORIGAMI CRANE COLLAPSING IN A HEAVY RAIN?

"I do not think so. I think it will remain. Cut off from the temporal roots but present just the same. Then again: who can say? I've been wrong before."

GOODBYE, DOCTOR.

"Goodbye, Jared."

Then, the bell-jar with the brain lifted out of its mooring, floating there by the power of Jared's mind. The fluid within—which Methuselah believed was some kind of amniotic fluid—sloshed and bubbled.

The jar drifted out of the door, over the dead bodies of the two guards— Jameson and Smythe, their heads twisted at off-angles.

CHAPTER THIRTY-ONE

Three in the morning.

Finally, those of the chapter house slept.

All but those who fled.

Khan, Amelia, Benjamin.

And, of course, Jet Black.

They crept through the tunnels and found one of the bolthole shafts through the stone and soil—wooden slats forming a crude ladder up.

They ascended, and entered the park under the cover of night.

The Central Park jungle was alive. More at night than during the day. Hooting monkeys somewhere, their throat-bladders blasting loud bleats. Insects buzzed and chirruped. Some great lizard-like bellow echoed over and through the trees.

"This way," Jet hissed, flagging them on through the trees. He prayed the psychosaurs wouldn't catch them here—if they did, they were borked. He hoped that under cover of darkness they would not be seen. Or felt. Or however it was that the psychosaur powers worked.

Ahead, through the curtain of vines and twisting branches, they could see the moon shimmering on water—like jewels scattered across a black mirror.

They crept up through the underbrush and found the edge of the reservoir—fat water-skeeters, each as big as a human hand, flitted across the surface of the water, *flit, flit, flit.*

Together they crouched by the muddy shoreline, algae-topped waters lapping at the edge.

"Maybe he's not coming," Amelia said.

"He's coming," Jet said.

"He wasn't in good shape. The leg. The drinking—"

"He's clean. Clear as a window."

"If he doesn't come—" Khan started to say, but then Jet hushed him. "Listen!"

In the distance: the growling rumble of an engine.

Propellers.

A pair of red lights winked on in the sky—a plane. A Sikorsky *Clipper* plane, more to the point. Coming in for a landing over the north end of the park. The Clipper lowered toward the water, 100 feet, then 50, then only 20 feet left before—

The reservoir water suddenly rose up in a big blistery bubble. A dark shape emerged and—

A massive splash as a creature roared out of the water—an alligator the size of a city bus, jaws open as waterfalls poured between craggy teeth.

Its jaws snapped shut.

Jet and the others screamed.

Sally awoke at her desk. A small puddle of drool beneath her chin. She blinked. Tasted sour fungal mash in her mouth. Her elbow moved, nudged a bottle, and it rolled off the desk and shattered.

She wasn't drunk. But the alcohol still had her in its grip—she felt a bit wibbly-wobbly, a wee bit tipsy.

At least she wasn't hungover. The fungal whiskey had that going for it—the hangovers were mild when they appeared at all.

Out of the fog rose that little voice, this time mimicking Amelia's—

Revenge they call justice. Selfishness they call equity. Malevolence they call righteousness. It's a tired old story, Sally, and you wrote yourself right into it...

She was no villain. Her legacy was not as a Shadow to end this century.

Or are you? Weren't your actions the shadow that fell across these many decades? Your choices the shade in which we all must live?

Ugh. None of that.

She needed to find Jet. To wish him good luck tomorrow. No—good luck *today*. Only a few hours. Dawn, they flew. She'd again remind him that his trust in her was appreciated. Maybe she'd kiss him again. Maybe she should've kissed him a long time ago. *Stop that. No distractions. Get up.*

She got up.

Now go wish him luck.

The Sikorsky Clipper pulled up suddenly just as the mega-gator's jaws clamped shut on the open air where the plane's tail once was.

"Dammit!" Jet said.

"That thing is *huge*," Amelia said.

"I'm not riding *that* one," Benjamin added.

Suddenly, in the middle of the lake, the mega-gator spun and splashed and fixed its gaze upon them. The moon and stars caught in its bulbous yellow eyes.

"I think it sees us," Khan said, quietly.

Its tail lashed out of the water and splashed down—

And suddenly, the beast began swimming toward them.

Faster than any boat Jet had seen.

And then the beast disappeared under the water in a froth-capped churn.

"Run," Khan cried. "Run!"

They turned to run.

The beast rose up out of the water like a beached freighter—all massive jaws and bulbous eyes, all monster claws and armored hide.

It crashed onto the shore, pursuing them with great hunger.

Jet was nowhere to be found.

Not in his bunk.

Not in the workshop.

Not wandering the halls as he sometimes did.

Nor was he with Khan. Or Amelia. Or Benjamin.

In fact, she couldn't find Khan. Or Amelia. Or Benjamin.

The electrical spark-and-crackle of something dreadful fired in the dark of her mind, threatening to illuminate a greater fear. A fear that spoke of mutiny.

The answer to this question was easy enough to answer.

She threw open the door to the Walking Mind's chamber. But the jars of brains along the wall were alone.

Jared Brain was gone.

That didn't make any sense at all. And now the electrical sparks were snapping and hissing and throwing off showers of hot white anger, but none of the wires seemed to connect. Nothing made sense.

Something had gone very wrong.

It was all going terribly wrong.

The beast crashed through the jungle behind them. Jaws smashing trees into splinters or ripping them out of the moist and spongy earth before flinging them skyward. The dense vegetation did little to slow the creature down.

But it was doing a helluva lot to slow down their escape.

Khan managed ably—from tree to rock to tree. Benjamin and Amelia ducked vines and leapt roots. But the pack on Jet Black's back was cumbersome—snagging on vines from which he had to struggle free.

But then he had an idea.

He yelled over the crashing and cracking—

"I have an idea!"

One minute, Amelia was fleeing the beast.

The next, she heard Jet yell something over the din.

And then the ground was ripped out from under her.

Mack turned Lucy in a tight arc, trying to stay over the reservoir as much as possible. His heart was kicking like a bucking bronco after that thing launched itself up out of the water. He was pretty sure he hated dinosaurs more than he hated anything else ever.

Suddenly, something thudded behind him, toward the back of the plane.

He knew then and there Lucy had been compromised. Invaded. Time was always a factor and he knew that the psychosaurs had found him.

But then—

Jet called from within.

"Here's Amelia!" he yelled.

Mack turned over the seat, saw Amelia Stone sitting up in the middle of the aisle, looking dazed and confused. Jet gave a little salute, then dove back out.

Benjamin's promise to himself had failed.

He was riding a dinosaur again.

Well, not *riding*, not exactly.

Amelia was gone, suddenly, yanked up into the sky by what Benjamin realized later was Jet Black—

And in that moment, Benjamin found only distraction. His foot clipped a root. He went down, hands hitting the earth, elbow twisting at the joint— not a break, but a sharp stab of pain.

Then: a shadow fell over him. Leaves rained. Branches, too.

The mega-gator was upon him.

It slammed down onto him—or, rather, onto the space where he was only a half-second before—with the weight of its entire body. *Boom.* He rolled, leapt to his feet, grabbed a vine, and swung up onto the monster's shoulder.

Then he grabbed a scale and hauled himself up onto its back.

The creature must've felt him there—its head craned back on what was effectively no neck at all, the jaws snapping closed on nothing but open air.

Scimitar time.

Benjamin stood up on wobbly feet and unsheathed the blade—another jolt of pain shot through his arm but he couldn't let that matter, not now. The creature raised and lowered its head in a predictable pattern of frustration, and as soon as its head was low, Benjamin ran up to its ridged reptilian brow and plunged the blade into the thing's watery yellow eye.

It rose up.

Bellowing. Snarling. Tongue lashing the air.

It flung its head and Benjamin flung with it.

But something caught him in mid-air and—

Zoom—

He was gone.

Thuddump. Jet zipped in through the door of the Sikorsky Clipper and dumped Benjamin next to Amelia. She helped Benjamin stand and told Jet:

"You're crazy."

He winked.

From the front, Mack Silver hooted.

"One more," Jet said, then fell backward out of the plane.

Khan's back pressed against a massive rock. He held aloft broken boards from an old park bench—as he passed by, he'd snapped his foot down and caught the board as it shattered upward.

The beast—now with one ruined eye leaking clear fluid due to a scimitar sticking out of it—had him backed against the rock.

Suddenly, the mega-gator lunged. Khan cracked the board across its ridged snout—the beast shook its head like a smacked hound and recoiled.

But it did not retreat.

Then, a rustle of branches overhead—

Jet dropped down out of the sky and landed next to Khan.

"Let's go, Professor."

Khan felt Jet's arms wrap around him as the two crouched and—

They launched up into the air.

Five feet. Then ten.

Then back down again.

The beast lunged anew.

Jet moved fast, rolling over and clipping the creature's nose once more with the tip of his wing. Again the beast roared and took a step back.

"I'm too heavy," Khan said with no small amount of dread.

"Khan, we need you in that plane."

"I..."

An idea struck him.

Not a good one.

Not a safe one.

By no means a sane one.

But such was the life of a Centurion and he *was* a member of that most estimable club of heroes. He let the jungle drums rise in the hollow barrel of his chest and he growled his plan to Jet.

Jet gave him a look that said, *This will never work.*

But he took off, just the same.

Mack heard the sound of Jet landing again—and he was about to hoot once more because the gang was all here and it was time to get moving, but then Jet burst into the cockpit panting.

"We don't have Khan," he stammered.

"What?"

"But the Professor has a plan."

And then he told Mack that plan.

"That's crazy," Mack said.

"I know."

"Total apehouse."

"I know."

"But it might work."

"I know!"

Mack nodded, jammed the stick down—the plane took a sharp dive.

"Time to shave some trees!" he yelled.

The drums. The jungle drums.

Khan hit the beast again. This time jamming a splintered board up the mega-gator's nostril. It afforded him a moment. Just one. *Just one.*

He clambered up the rock.

Ba-doom ba-doom ba-doom

He leapt to a tree branch, hugging it—

Ba-doom ba-doom ba-doom

Khan hurtled himself up the thick banyan branches—

BA-DOOM BA-DOOM

The creature rose beneath him. Jaws opening.

Khan reached the open air—

The tree shuddered.

It began to give way beneath him. Swallowed into the behemoth's mouth. Little monkeys fled. Colorful birds took flight, squawking.

BOOM BOOM BOOM BOOM

He leapt.

The jaws opened all the way—

And began to snap shut.

The tip of the Sikorsky wing slammed him in the chest.

His arms scrabbled for purchase—

The massive teeth slammed shut—

Narrowly missing his heel by a scant few inches.

The plane lifted up high.

With Khan clinging to the wing.

CHAPTER THIRTY-TWO

"They left," Methuselah said.

He said it with great glee. The old doctor did nothing to hide his giddiness. And the rage it sent rippling across Sally's face like so many waves of fire pleased him *that much more*. After all, it was she who pulled the trigger so many decades ago. The literal trigger pull that ended his aspirations.

"I don't understand," she seethed.

"Nor should you. The victim of a mutiny rarely understands the mutineers. That is how a mutiny is born, my dear."

"Go to hell."

He tried to shrug from his cruciform perch.

"I'm going after them."

"You'll never catch them."

"Watch me," she said, and stormed out of the room.

As Sally raced through the halls, her mind raced through possibilities.

They were gone. Not on foot. Couldn't be. Then they'd be taken by the psychosaurs. Or dead, eaten by some T-rex.

Mack. Had to be Mack. She knew he had an autogyro. He probably used that to get a plane. He always talked about it in his drunken stupor—outlining which airfields were where, which ones were likely to have a Clipper plane like Lucy.

And the Walking Mind. Where did he fit into this? All she had to go on was the husk of his body and two dead guards. No bell-jar. No brain.

So: what?

He went after them.

That *had* to be it.

He went to bring them back. Because they all worked so hard for this, and now it was in danger. Jared Brain was hunting them down.

That didn't explain the two dead guards. Why were they dead? The possibility—*the Mind betrayed us all*—didn't add up, not after all this time. The dead guards... *they* were the betrayers. Had to be. It made sense, didn't it? That's how Mack and Jet got in there the first time. They were working toward that goal all along. Mutineers hidden in plain sight.

The next question:

Was the Walking Mind capable of bringing this train back onto the tracks? She had to admit: he *was* just a brain in a jar.

He could only do so much. Yes, the power of his mind was immense—a titanic fist, a tornado of possibilities. But he had no body.

Which meant this was up to her.

Five minutes later, she found herself in the Professor's chambers, going through his stuff, looking for some clue—*any clue*—as to where they'd gone.

Books. Papers. Notes scrawled on a chalkboard—notes that made only a lizard lick of sense to her. Then:

A map.

A world map. With no markings on it.

Oh. Wait. What was this?

No pin but—a pin*hole*.

A small island. In the Arctic Circle. Not far from Russia.

Methuselah's Arctic base. It had to be. They'd looked for it long ago but never were able to discern its exact location. There, Mack would attempt to fulfill his delusional mission of sending them back in time to "fix" what was broken.

This world. This "broken" world.

Anger flared like a struck match-tip.

She was going after them. She was going to stop them.

Colin slept on a chair. Hardhat pulled off the top of his head and positioned over his eyes so that the lights of the underground didn't keep him awake.

Someone shook him. He fell out of his chair and the hardhat bounced away.

"Muzza," he mumbled, blinking past the glare.

Sally stood above him.

"I'm leaving," she said.

"What the—what the bloody what?"

She began to spill all this information at him. He could barely keep up. Jet, the Professor, Amelia, Benjamin—all gone. Mutiny. That's the word she used. *Mutiny*. Serious accusation, he said, but she ignored him. Said she had to go after them. Then she said the worst thing of all:

"The war is off. We need them back."

He balked. "You gotta be pullin' my bells. If they're gone, they're gone. We've got the folks wanting to fight. We've got the jet-wings. So let's fight!"

"No," she said. "Not until they're back and I've returned."

"You know, all this time, you talk about them like they're the damn A-Squad and we're the... B- or C- or Z-Squad. A bunch of scabby scrubs with our thumbs up our nethers, but we can do this, Sally, we can take the fight to the—"

"Jared is gone, too. The Walking Mind already went after them."

"Wh... what? But he's what's protecting us from..." He didn't even need to finish that sentence, did he?

"You'll just have to make do. Man the fort. Stay low."

"Sally—"

But she was gone. Bolting down the tunnel like someone lit a firecracker and stuck it in the hem of her pants.

Mack had a plane. Probably a Clipper, like he wanted.

Sally marched forward, did some quick calculations in her head.

135 MPH, top speed.

A journey of 2000 miles, give or take.

Fifteen hour trip.

She needed to fly faster than they did.

And all she had were jet-wings.

She walked into the workshop. Felt her breath catch in her chest. There the devices waited, wing to wing, front to back. She chose one. Slid her hands across its contours. The thought struck her:

You can make it go faster.

This is what you do.

This is who you are.

She gritted her teeth and reached for a wrench.

CHAPTER THIRTY-THREE

"This almost feels like old times," Jet said. The plane rumbled along, bumping across invisible humps of hot air, sometimes feeling as if it were a flat stone skipping across a windswept lake. He moved his knight forward, captured a bishop. Khan moved his queen out of hiding and took the knight.

Then the plane hit another pocket and the pieces hopped like jumping beans off the board and rolled under the dingy, uncomfortable chairs.

"Yes," Benjamin said, "but Lucy was a much more comfortable ride."

They all laughed.

"That was Sally's doing," Jet said.

And then they all got quiet.

Amelia helped Khan pick up the chess pieces.

"We're doing the right thing," Amelia said.

"I know," Jet said.

"Heroic action usually feels more... heroic," Khan admitted.

It was then that Benjamin told a story. He said, "I remember this one time I was pursuing the villain known as the Scarlet Skeleton—he'd stolen this horn of plenty from an offering altar at the fore of Xibalba, and there we were wrestling over it at the crumbling lip of a massive chasm deep underground— steam rising from the chasm, streamers of dust and rock falling from above, and he sacrificed the horn. Threw it into the chasm. It landed on a shelf—one that was fast cracking and about to collapse. And the Skeleton fled.

"I had a choice, then. I could save the horn of plenty and hopefully use it to feed some hungry village or even a city until the end of time, or I could—just as he had—sacrifice it to capture him. Skeleton was a psychopath. The damage he'd done already, the people he'd killed... I worried that for those I saved, he'd undo the damage by killing twice the number just by dint of his nature. So I let the horn fall and I went after him. He did not survive the encounter." Benjamin took a deep, steadying breath. "That was a day when heroism did not feel good. It had no easy choice. Even to this day the question gnaws at me, a mouse nipping at cheese. Did I choose wisely? I do not know."

They all sat around in silence. Not sure what to say or where to go next.

From the cockpit, Mack Silver called:

"Hey, shut up back there, you goofy goons." He tilted his head out the cockpit door and they saw him beaming. "Take a look around you! We're *back*. We're a team again! Doing the whole *jump into danger without necessarily thinking about the consequences* thing. This is what we do! Flying! Continent-hopping! Invading the bases of sinister masterminds! *Get excited*, you mopes!" He hooted and clapped his hands, then the hoots devolved into a fit of coughing. "Man, I'm feeling old. And no, I'm not drunk. I'm just excited."

They all laughed. A sincere laugh, too.

"Meanwhile, take a look outside, will ya?"

They all stood up and moved to the porthole windows.

"Other side, other side."

They rolled their eyes, moved to the *other* side of the aisle.

There, out the windows, the sun was setting. Jet said, "It looks like a Creamsicle melting."

"Or the horizon swallowing a ball of fire," Khan said.

Benjamin added, "Or the face of one of the many gods shining before sleep."

"It looks like a giant ball of fiery gas standing still as the earth rotates away from it," Amelia said. They all shot her a look. "I'm not one for metaphor, sorry."

Another laugh.

Out there, beyond the sun, they saw the swooping of Pterosaurs—creatures blessedly disinterested in their presence. Below, in the water, they saw great shapes swimming—even from up here they could tell those things were big. Not whales. Dinosaurs. Sharks. *Sea monsters.* Jet thought it was all pretty, in a way, when seen at a distance. And that was the key, wasn't it? *At a distance.* Up close it was psychic intrusions and rending claws. They had ceded this world.

Was it really too far gone?

He didn't know and supposed they'd never find out.

Mankind would either survive and find a way like a fire that refused to be extinguished—or the creatures would claim this place as their own and grant the earth its greatest irony: once-extinct dinosaurs come back to the world and in turn drive humanity to extinction instead.

Heroism wasn't supposed to feel like this.

Hard choices and sad realities, indeed.

The plane flew on.

CHAPTER THIRTY-FOUR

They swept over them like a fire.

One minute they were standing around the mess hall—Tara, Colin, Carlini, Lily-Belle, a handful of others like the Praxis and Silver Shade and Digital 2000—trying to figure out just what to do next. No Sally. No Walking Mind. The other heroes, fled for reasons unknown.

The next minute: a scream somewhere. Then another. Cries of alarm.

Psychosaurs.

The creatures poured in through the channels and tunnels, crawling from above and below like a carpet of army ants. The psychic wave crashed upon their mental beaches and then—

Then they knew it was truly over.

The view from inside Colin's mind was a horror show.

Men and women of the Century Club, thrown up against walls with great psychic force, others dragged through tunnels. Psychosaurs with lips curled back over needle teeth. The sounds of their breathing. Their wet gurgles. Their hisses.

And behind all that, a wretched shame-filled frequency: *You left your home, this is not your place, they have you, it was all for naught, the only thing you dig is a hole for yourself and the others—an unmarked grave for a future dream forgotten—*

A psychosaur thrust its face into his. Tongue slathering over teeth. Black eyes, soulless and probing.

Its head split like a melon.

The psychic locks fell away from Colin's mind.

He grabbed the creature and hurled it aside.

Behind it stood Atok. Black blood flecking his scruffy cheeks.

And behind Atok:

Steve the psychosaur. Striding in with the same dead eyes as his monstrous cohorts but with a big goofy smile on his toothy maw.

"War time," Atok said.

Colin grabbed his shovel and spun it in his hands.

War time, indeed.

Methuselah hummed to himself.

The phonographs had long stopped playing. The guards never came to reset the needles—and, in fact, the two guards present were now collecting big fat hungry flies. Buzzing around like ping pong balls.

Marvelous creature, the fly. Stuck in a moment. Time had no meaning for such a creature. Methuselah yearned for that. He too wanted to be stuck—or, rather, *unstuck* from time's cruel clutches. But it was not to be. Not for this body. Not in this lifetime, or timeline, or world.

The fly was impermanent.

And, sadly, so was he.

The door to his prison—or was it his lair?—creaked open.

An unexpected sight crept inside.

Weak. Sallow. Patches of fur lost. Or was it hair?

He decided to ask:

"Do gorillas have hair, or fur? I never get that right."

The ape-lord, Khan the Conqueror, snarled in response: "Fur. Hair continues to grow. Fur does not."

"Ah. Yes. That's it."

"It's all gone to hell," Khan said.

"Yes. It has. But I've secured a different world. Not for this version of me. Rather, for another. And for another version of you, too, though I do not suspect *that* Conqueror Ape will be too pleased with his lot in life." Methuselah clucked his tongue. "You were a poor choice. Easily controllable, yes. And as your name suggests, a most excellent conqueror. But clumsy. Foolish. Ego-driven. And worst of all: *a common ape.*"

"You made me."

"I did. Perhaps I shouldn't have."

"You lied to me."

"More to the point, I *tricked you.* I used you the way one uses a gun, the way one discards a handkerchief. But I had a revelation that perhaps Miss Sally Slick would appreciate: I chose the wrong tool for the job. I answered a very early variable in the grand equation with an ape. And that is a mistake I intend to fix."

Khan snorted. He shuffled over to the two phonographs, and cast them aside in a violent sweep of his arms.

"I've come to kill you."

"Of course you have."

"It was that, or leave you to the monsters. They're here, you know."

"That explains the ruckus."

Khan stepped up to the cruciform doctor, pulled a box over from the corner and stood up on it. He thrust his primate's face into the doctor's own. Methuselah smelled rot and decay. The breath of a body that was digesting itself. Khan was sick. He was on his way out.

"You're dying," Methuselah said.

"Yes."

"Our century is over."

"It is."

"I created you."

"Irony," Khan said, then reached up and snapped Methuselah's neck.

CHAPTER THIRTY-FIVE

The sun set, and now the sun rose.

Though that mattered little once they hit the fog.

Through the cockpit window, the fog looked almost monstrous—a physical wall, a titan's flesh, a presence that threatened to consume and crush. Mack couldn't help but hold his breath as the plane plunged into the mist—

Nothing happened, of course.

Nothing but a little bump and the almost total loss of visibility.

For a while the fog seemed to glow with the light of the rising sun—but soon the sun was lost and the day was as night.

A presence suddenly next to him. Jet. The kid sat down.

"The fog," Jet said.

"Crazy, huh?"

"I don't even know how you see."

"I don't. I use these little guys—" He tapped the cockpit controls. "And this big guy right here." He tapped his head.

"I just wanted to say I'm sorry."

Mack gave him a screwed up look. "Sorry? Kid, don't insult me with apologies."

"No, I mean it. For the things I said, for not... realizing how hard it had to be for all of you who had to keep living in this world while we just skipped past it. I'm sorry for things with Sally."

"Kid, I'm good for a few things. I can drink. I can fly. I can put together a crazy-faced over-the-moon plan of action and commit to it. But I'm nobody's leader. I'm nobody's husband. I feel bad for betraying Sally like that, but... I'm not abandoning her. When our job here is done, if I'm not dead and if I can fuel up somewhere, I'm going to head back. Not to make things right. Wrong guy like me doesn't make things right. But just to see her again. And maybe to apologize to her like you're apologizing to me." Mack winked. "Just don't tell anyone I said that."

"You could come with us, instead."

"Hah. What, to the past? I'm not exactly a history buff, but where you're going, I don't think they have airplanes. And despite that stunt that Benjamin pulled, I don't think the Thunderbirds really *require* pilots."

"I guess that's a good point."

"There!" Mack said. "Look—"

The fog—the so-called "sea smoke"—shimmered, almost iridescent like sunlight through a spray of mist.

"Buckle up!" Mack yelled.

Then he pushed the flight stick down.

Lucy dove.

That was the moment Jet knew he was a bit of a control freak. He was a flier. He was used to—frankly, he even *loved*—aerial acrobatics. Barrel rolls and corkscrews and deep dives. But when Mack did it, this time and every time, he felt anxiety firmly grip his heart and he realized *he* wanted to be the one in control of the stick, the wings, the whole kit and caboodle.

Fog rushed past the windshield.

And then, suddenly: a mountainous peak.

It rose up out of nothing. As if swiftly drawn by divine hand.

They were going to crash into it.

"We're going to crash," Mack said, confirming Jet's worst fears. But then Mack jerked the stick and the first peak passed underneath Lucy's metal belly by what Jet assumed was a matter of *centimeters*, and then suddenly there appeared the black ice of a half-frozen lake, and Mack let the Clipper flop down into the shattered floes and slush-frost waters with all the aplomb of a tubby kid doing a belly-flop in the community pool.

That's when Mack whooped with laughter.

"You thought we were going to crash!" he brayed.

"You said it! You said we were going to crash!"

"Aw, geez, I only said it because I saw the look on your face. You may have to change your nappies after that one, kid." Mack laughed so hard he had to wipe tears from his eyes.

"You *knew* that lake was going to be there?"

"Well. No."

"So we still could've crashed?"

Mack shrugged, his laughing finally dying down. "It was always under control, kid."

Amelia struggled her way into the cockpit.

"I hate you," she said to Mack.

Which got Mack laughing all the harder.

The boat-plane slid along the water, ice floes bumping aside as the propellers dragged them all forward. Professor Khan stood at the door, leaning out, feeling the cold air sock him in his ape face. It was bracing. In some ways good, but in other ways, it only gave the drums in his heart greater cause to keep thudding—ever since that daring rescue back in Central Park, they'd started up again and hadn't stopped. As if they were leading up to something.

Something the drums knew, and he did not.

His chest hurt from where the wing clipped him.

Crawling back into the plane—a plane flying at over 100 MPH, lifting up into the sky—had been one of the more harrowing experiences in his adult gorilla life. Teaching at Oxford had never been so exciting.

Ahead, a dock. Icy. Dark. Thrust out into the water like an outstretched arm and eager hand. Here, the fog was heavy only far above their heads, so he could also see carved in the mountain rock a massive sculpture carved of ice and rock—a man and a woman, each with eagle's beak noses, long-limbed and forming an arch with outstretched arms and intermingled fingers. At the side of the man was something that resembled a two-bridged lute; at the woman's side, a scroll.

And all around them, carved not into but out of the rock: symbols. Like the mathematical symbols of an alien world.

"Hyperboreans," Benjamin said from behind Khan, startling him.

"Yes. So it would seem. They were... artists, were they not?"

"Artists. Architects. Mathematicians. Not warriors. They did not understand war. The legends say that is how they fell. They thought themselves so enlightened they could avoid battle for all of eternity. But battle came to them."

"I'm told there are traps inside."

"That would not surprise me. But they won't be the traps of the Hyperboreans. They'll be those of their conquerors, or worse—"

"They'll be Methuselah's."

"Indeed."

"Once more unto the breach, dear friends," Khan said.

Benjamin nodded: "Stiffen the sinews, summon up the blood."

Khan said nothing, but worried quietly that it was the blood that was summoning him with the beating of his ape-lord's heart.

CHAPTER THIRTY-SIX

Long hallways of ice and stone. Glistening and smooth. No sharp angles. Almost as if they were carved not by tool but rather by water and by breath. Gone was the Byzantine strangeness of Atlantis—the towers and mechanisms, the gilded edges and turning gears.

Amelia walked along behind the others. She watched Benjamin slide his hands along the ice—he marveled, goggling, really. It was easy to see why: behind the ice you could make out figures. Statues or carvings, she guessed, of people like those at the archway entrance—they held tablets and worked looms and performed other artisan tasks. None of which made much sense to Amelia. That was not her way. Frankly, she understood the Neanderthals better than the Hyperboreans or the Atlanteans. Fight to the death. No quarter. No surrender.

She wondered how Atok was doing.

And the others. All the others. Even Sally. A stab of guilt struck her in the belly for the things she'd said. They were true things. She believed them then and she believed them still. But what good did it do?

Another part of her felt she should stay. Save this world, not some other one. But then that name paraded itself in front of her—*Le Monstre*. The villain who robbed her life, who she'd been pursuing as her life's purpose.

This path was the way back to him. To catch him. To lock him away in a dark oubliette.

"Here!" Benjamin said, waving on somebody, anybody—he flailed out behind him, caught Amelia's wrist and pulled her close. "Look at that."

Behind the ice, a massive thing. A shape far larger than the already tall and long-limbed Hyperboreans themselves. This bulky beast with the body of a boxer and a triangular head on a set of shoulders with no neck.

"What am I looking at?" she asked as the others continued walking.

"A golem," he said. "Hyperboreans were masters of artificial life, so the poems say. That's how they moved big blocks or carved whole mountain passageways—they used golems made of ice, stone, even hematite."

"Did it just move?" she asked.

"What?" he said, giving her a look. "It's frozen."

"I swear it just moved." It wasn't a lark. But it must've been a trick of the ice, the way light refracted or... some sciencey reason that escaped her.

"It didn't m—"

A hand shot out through the ice and grabbed Benjamin by the neck. His eyes bulged. He tried to scream, but it was a wordless gurgle.

Methuselah's traps, Khan thought as the walls all around them began not to shatter, but rather melt away as if given over to sudden heat—steam hissed and great massive lumbering shapes stepped out of the dissolving walls. One had Benjamin, another lurched toward the hobbling Mack, and then—

They all collapsed.

Each and every one of the massive sentinels.

Benjamin found his footing and rubbed his neck as the thing crumpled next to him, face forward.

"Check that out," Amelia said, pointing to the back of their upside-down-pyramid heads. Sticking out of each was a sharp icicle. Like an ice pick buried in the brain or whatever passed for the creature's control mechanism.

"Someone's already dispatched these..." Jet searched for the words. "Whatever they are."

"Golems," Khan and Benjamin said in unison.

"Somebody's been here," Mack said. "That's probably bad news."

"Then we must be doubly vigilant," Khan said.

His heart stuttered and tumbled in his chest—

But then he realized there was another sound, too. Beneath the ground. A faint vibration that pulsed in time with the jungle drumbeat of his heart.

He pressed his palm to the floor.

"I feel it," he said. "The gate. The same energy pulsing that came from the gate in Atlantis—if a bit quieter."

Mack shrugged. "Then down the rabbit hole we go. Let's find some stairs or an elevator or, worst case scenario, *a big damn hole.*"

CHAPTER THIRTY-SEVEN

They found neither stairs nor elevator. A hole didn't seem to be in the offerings, either. Instead what they found was a massive spiral—a corkscrew in the ice and stone that went down, down, down. Similar in design to what they found at Atlantis, but this carved (no, *sculpted*) out of the elements.

The entire thing didn't look stable.

"I think it's a slide," Jet said.

"Then how do we get back up?" Amelia asked.

"Maybe we don't," Mack said with fatalistic glee, then dropped onto his butt and scooted down. In a half-second he was zipping down the ice, gaining momentum before he whipped around the turn of the screw and was gone.

They heard him hooting, though.

They all looked to one another.

"Once more, a mysterious plunge," Khan said to Jet.

"It's what we do," he said.

Then together, they all dropped down and slid down the spiral.

They found Mack already standing.

And gaping.

Ahead lay a massive room. Almost cathedral-like. The ceiling above looked like bones bridged together in an arch—but though they looked like bones they were made of smooth, gleaming ice. Ice as blue as Hawaiian waters, as cold as those waters were warm.

The whole room glowed that color blue.

But the room had been...

"Corrupted," Khan said before Jet could realize the word. And that was true, that's what it was. This seemed like it once may have been some kind of holy place for the Hyperboreans—a temple, a church, or just a sacred meditative space empty but for the bones above and the thoughts below, but Methuselah's markings were all over it. Blackboards and tables full of iced-over beakers. Chairs and tables knocked asunder. Cages with frozen seabirds in them. And clocks. Clocks and watches and pocketwatches. Sundials and pendulums. Signs of a man obsessed with the unstoppable ebb and ineluctable flow of time.

And in the center of the room, a massive rupture in the ice. Big as a merry-go-round. Notable for its lack of sculpted edges—these were ragged, chipped, clearly the hand of man, not Hyperborean.

Inside this space was a whirlpool.

But it wasn't water that whirled about, but rather—the very liquid of the time-space continuum. A portal. Like that of Atlantis or of all the other gates—but this one, smaller, faster, coruscating with crackles of electricity that would've given Der Blitzmann more than a little tickle.

Beyond it, another body in the ice.

Jet saw something that looked familiar.

It can't be, he thought.

He staggered past Mack and the others, and circumvented the portal by giving it a wide berth.

In the ice, he saw a female form. A body. A... *corpse*, by the look of it. Almost mummified.

On its head, a crown of ice within ice—the diadems of icicles.

Words carved into the ice, too—not by any crass human device but almost by human hands. As if by a finger, actually.

RIP ME

JACQUELINE FROST

MAY THE NEXT ICE AGE TAKE YOU

"It's her tomb," Jet said.

The others came up behind him.

"Jacqueline Frost," he said. "She's the one who dispatched those golems. She took this place as her own. At the end of the world."

"At the end of time," Benjamin said.

Frost had always been a thorn—or, at least, an icicle—in their side. Always independent. Practically never worked with the other Shadows. Had a raging hatred for some of them, too—particularly Methuselah.

"She must've come here to escape the psychosaurs," Jet said.

"For someone so cold," Mack said, "she was *so* smokin' hot."

They all gave him a look.

"What? Sorry. Jeez. Red-blooded American male standing down."

"She could've been greatly useful to the Resistance," Khan said. "We know now that the psychosaurs would've been vulnerable to the cold and she was capable of manifesting ice out of nothing."

"Frost didn't play well with others," Jet said.

Suddenly—the sound of the air cutting, *swish-swish-SWISH*—and Mack's hat lifted off his head as if jerked by a string.

It flew through the air in circles, pinned to a razor boomerang.

A boomerang that flew back to the hand of its keeper.

Sally Slick.

Sally stood there in dark goggles and a thick parka.

She scowled and hissed:

"Foul mutineers!"

CHAPTER THIRTY-EIGHT

Sally found rage in her heart.

She'd been here in the Hyperborean capital for the better part of a day. Her efforts at improving the jet-wing design had succeeded—at first her hands shook and her teeth clenched so hard she thought they might snap, but it wasn't long before her fury overtook her and her hands worked almost without engaging the mind at all. The resultant device was a thing of beauty.

That's when she bundled up, and took flight.

Through rain and wind and, eventually, fog. Avoiding Pterosaurs. Blasting just over the ocean waves as Megalodon sharks swam beneath her.

She arrived ahead of Mack and the others.

Part of her wondered if they'd ever even arrive.

She came down here. Found the tomb. Found the gate. Thought of trying to destroy it—and that's when they showed up.

Now: she faced them. She screwed Mack's hat on her head.

"That's my hat," Mack said. "Oh, and hi, honey."

She flung the boomerang again.

This time, right for him—

It scraped the ice above his head, showering him in a frosty snow before returning to her gloved hand.

"Don't," she seethed. "Betrayers. The lot of you."

"Sally," Jet began, stepping out ahead of the others with his hands in a pleading, plaintive gesture. "Please, you have to understand, this isn't our time, this isn't how we operate—"

"I asked you to trust me!" she screamed. "That's all I wanted. I wanted your trust to help me fix what was broken. But all you care about is *you, you, you*, and meanwhile I'm left as the only vanguard to save the people in *this* world?"

"You're right!" Khan said. "You're right. But we could never be the vanguard for this world. You had a fire in you we... could not match. You were far more able in this timeline—"

Mack suddenly shouted: "Aw, that's all horseapples. A bucket of fly-specked, steamy, stinky *horseapples*. Don't let them sugarcoat it, Sally. Truth was, we just didn't like this place. And we didn't much like you, either. You changed, sweetheart. I hate that you changed and I hate that maybe I'm part of the reason you did. But... things got screwed up a long time ago and I want to fix it. Not for me now. Not even for you now. But for the Sally Slick of 1935. Kind-hearted, ingenious creature that you were—this place is ruined and you got ruined with it."

His words lashed her like a whip.

She raised the boomerang.

"You never had the stones for this," she said.

"You're right," Mack answered. "I didn't."

The boomerang trembled in her hands.

"You're not going through with this," she said.

"Yeah," Mack said. "We are."

"I'll kill you where you stand."

"That's okay, baby. I don't blame you for that."

"Where's Brain? Where is he? Where is the Walking Mind? What did you do to him?"

She saw them all share uncertain glances.

Then, a voice in her mind:

I'M RIGHT HERE, MISS SLICK.

A pain shot through her wrist—

The boomerang dropped into the ice and stuck there with a *kachink*.

An invisible hand closed around her throat.

And a bell-jar with a brain in it floated into the room behind her.

He froze them all. Jared Brain lashed out with invisible tentacles that tightened around all of their throats. He felt their shock and alarm and fear feeding back to him through those noncorporeal telepathic channels.

And those feelings thrilled him mightily.

Oh, how confused they were.

He savored that confusion and for a moment he considered leaving it in place—particularly since so many villains seemed inclined to explain themselves away as if *so desperate* to justify themselves in the face of heroism. But here his explanation served a delightful secondary purpose: to make them realize just how completely he'd manipulated them all.

They'd feel like sad little shrimps in the mouth of a shark.

Then he'd crush them with his psychic teeth.

They would die. He would go through the gate.

Ha ha ha ha. Idiots.

Plus, an explanation would take no time at all—he could literally *shove* it into their minds like a mushy apple through a sieve. Jared quickly gave them the lay of the land: *I've been working with Doctor Methuselah. He directed me to this gate where I could send myself back in time and replace Khan the Conqueror as the master of the psychosaurs—since I've been practicing on conditioning them, with young Master Steven as a perfect emblem of my control. With that done, I will fix the one damaged variable in Methuselah's great equation. It will then be me conquering the world, not Khan, and Methuselah and I can rule the world properly. Me with my psychic fist, he with his powerful time-stopping mathemagics. The world will be mine. All of time will be his. La-de-da-dee, little mice. You were the delivery mechanism, a way to allow my unbodied brain—so vulnerable to the elements—to reach this gate unharmed. As a stowaway. You stupid, stupid bags of meat.*

He felt their shock. Their recoil.

The revelation of their own stupidity.

They'd been had *again*.

Such fun. Jared was a patient brain for just this reason: patience paid off. All the time. All the waiting. The stars slowly creeping toward alignment.

It felt really wonderful.

But, it was time to get on with things.

It was time to start crushing throats.

He reached for the ape first. Practice, perhaps—this was what he was going to do to the *other* Khan, the more menacing one.

Ah, but there—a curious thing.

A heavy pulsebeat traveling the length of his invisible psychic tentacle.

Ba-doom ba-doom

A sound that was suddenly familiar to Jared.

BA-DOOM BA-DOOM

It was the sound of the elder Khan's heartbeat. A heartbeat that always clouded Jared's efforts to reach into the Conqueror's mind.

BOOM BOOM BOOM

The professorial ape moved fast. He broke free of the telepathic control—

And then the ape charged.

It happened fast.

Khan felt his blood boiling, and what he once thought was a curse given to him by the man who called himself *father* was perhaps a blessing yet again— as the ape-lord suggested, it was a way to break the shackles of telepathic control, his own psychic burst like wrists snapping manacles, like shoulders shrugging off the oxen yoke that thought to steer him—

The drums filled him. *Attack. Conquer. Destroy.*

His knuckles found the ice and he galloped forward, snarling and spitting, his eyes flush with fury.

Khan leapt over the gate—fists out—

And that time was all it took.

The brain floated backward—

The walls shuddered, crackled and split and shattered—

Shards of ice and stone and snow flew toward him with unerring speed—

That's when the fist of the Walking Mind's new body slammed Khan right in the chops, knocking him backward—

And into the time portal.

NO NO NO NO NO—

He roared that word again and again through the minds of these meddling heroes—the stupid ape escaped him and *thankfully* he happened to be one of the fastest-thinking minds, if not *the* fastest, in all of history. His synapses fired and psychic tendrils shot out and exploded the walls all around them, pulling the debris fast to his flesh and forming for himself a body thrice the size of any paltry human, an ice brute with fists like boulders and no head. The brain-jar lay encased in the barrel-like chest of the body, utterly well-protected.

He smacked the ape down but then—

Then he lost control for just that moment—

He reached out but it was too late.

The ape fell through the portal.

One. One hero escaping to the far flung beginning of time.

He could manage that one hero. It was but a mote of dust in the eye—the younger Khan would be an irritant, but as long as the rest of these dullards didn't escape him, all would be well.

Time to do this the old-fashioned way.

He would hold them with his mind.

But then crush them with his fists.

Real fists. Hands of ice. Knuckles of jagged rock.

He would crush the group of them first—then savor Sally Slick as his last. He wanted to feel her body *pop* like a grape as she realized she'd been working with him all along. That he'd ruined her. Driven her to actions she would have never given herself over to if he hadn't pressed and nudged.

He grabbed the minds of the others—Amelia, Jet, Mack—and then...

Wait. There should be a fourth mind in there.

Benjamin Hu.

And yet, when he reached for the mind, it wasn't there.

It was as if his mind had retreated. All that was left was the body...

Suddenly, Hu sprung up—mind present, flaring bright, but Jared couldn't hold it, it was slippery and inaccessible and *dammit dammit DAMMIT*

Hu slid between the Walking Mind's ice-trunk legs—

Then ducked a massive fist as the body rotated 180 degrees at the waist with the sound of grinding stone.

Jared stomped after, *thoom thoom thoom*—using his mind to grab *more* debris from the walls, this time in the form of jagged ice-arrows. He flung them all at Benjamin, who tumbled forward and leapt up, graceful as anything Jared had ever seen—

And in Benjamin's hand glinted Sally's boomerang.

Hu rushed in, using it not as a thrown projectile but rather as a melee weapon, chipping bits of Jared's body off—

Jared swung and stomped and bashed.

But the body was slow. *Too slow.*

And Benjamin's mind and movements were too quick!

Wait. *There.*

A tiny mote.

Benjamin's arm—a signal of pain radiating off. He couldn't grab it with his mind, Benjamin had already shrugged off his grasp—

But he reached out with his mind and plucked a baseball-sized hunk of rock from the wall—

Just as Benjamin cut through one of Jared's icy wrists, dropping the fist to the ground like an unmoving boulder, the chunk of rock fired into the elbow of Benjamin's arm. There was the sound of bone breaking—

Benjamin screamed.

Opportunity.

He brought his one remaining fist down—

And it crashed into the ice where Benjamin once stood.

Again he pivoted his torso and Jared saw—

NO NO NO NO

Benjamin slid toward the portal—

And then was gone as he fell through it.

Sally felt his rage.

Her own matched it.

The Walking Mind had used her. Perhaps even *urged* her into becoming this dark and twisted Sally Slick. She'd lost sight of who the real enemy was. She'd cozied up with the Shadows and then wondered why she could no longer see the light? A fool's move.

And now it was all over.

Jared reattached his massive fist and stomped over to Amelia, Jet, and Mack.

He picked up Jet.

Then he picked up Mack.

And he began to squeeze.

Jared felt their pain and fed it back to her—

In her mind, Jared laughed.

THIS IS YOUR FAULT, he told her.

THEIR DEATHS WILL BE ON YOUR HANDS.

YOU CANNOT SAVE THEM THIS TIME.

THEY DIE IN YOUR SHADOW.

Shadow.

Shadow.

She had fallen into shadow. This wasn't who she was.

Jared held the mind of the woman she'd become, but not the mind of the woman she'd once been. A woman of hope and optimism.

A woman of love.

She embraced that hope. She used it to banish fear.

She cleaved to love.

And she used that love to break his grip upon her.

It wouldn't last.

But she only needed a moment, while he was distracted.

Jet cried out. Mack screamed.

She dove forward.

Hand fell on the boomerang.

It was like Atlantis all over again.

Tools and weapons.

Ancient civilizations.

The two loves of her life in danger.

The tiny voice reminded her that she made the wrong choice before. She could do it again.

She told that voice to go to Hell.

Then she threw the boomerang.

She'd gotten away from him. He felt her slip the mental leash—it was almost as if he was holding the mind of someone who didn't exist anymore. It blended, disappeared, a chameleon of sorts.

It didn't matter. These two would die, and then Amelia after.

Except—

Kachink.

Bright blooms of misery and lightning exploded.

The boomerang. *The boomerang.* He felt it—digging deep into the ice of his back. The tip of it cracked the glass of his bell-jar.

His fluid was sloshing out.

He needed that fluid. It was telepathically *conductive.* Without it—

His control started to slip.

NO NO NO NO

He dropped the two heroes, let them all go—

Reached out with everything he could—

He flung the boomerang away and pulled debris toward the injured cleft—

It closed it. Filled it. Stopped the flow.

He spun.

And found Amelia Stone standing up with the Tommy gun in her hand.

It barked fire.

Bullets perforated the ice.

Crashed through his jar.

The ice body staggered backward—

And tumbled through the gate.

He drowned in the tide of time and space.

Jet struggled to stand. Pain tore through him. His body wasn't broken but it'd damn sure be bruised and battered—he felt like a steamroller just flattened him like the petals of a crushed flower.

Sally ran past him and slammed into Mack.

The two of them hugged. She covered Mack with kisses. He spun her around on his one good leg. It stung. It shouldn't have. It should've filled him with happiness that they'd found peace and love once more. He knew it was a good thing. Abstractly, he knew it was the right thing.

But still it felt tough watching them like that.

Amelia came. Helped Jet up.

"We still have a job to do," Amelia said. "C'mon."

"Wait!" Sally yelled. She turned and hurried over to the two of them.

"Miss Slick," Amelia began, but Sally shushed her.

"You were right," Sally said. "I had turned into something I no longer recognized. And I'm sorry. You go. You save your world."

Amelia took a step back.

"Sally," Jet said. "The others have gone—I'll stay."

"You go, too. I want you to go. I want you to save the world. And then I want you to find me. *That* me. The me of 1935. And I want you to tell that girl you love her. And I want you to fight for her. And let her fight for you. Let me save you this one last time. Don't fall for me here. I need you to fall for me *there*."

"Sally—"

She kissed him. On the cheek.

A single tear crawled from her one good eye.

"Now go. Before something else happens."

"Thanks, Sally."

Amelia nodded to Jet. "Ready?"

Jet gave her a soft smile then turned to Mack.

"Go get her, kid." Then he saluted.

Jet saluted back.

He and Amelia jumped into the portal.

EPILOGUE

The Sikorsky Clipper returned to New York City almost a week later.

It was a somber homecoming.

Sally and Mack had once more found each other and they laughed and told jokes and when they refueled at an airfield in Anchorage they made up for the many lost years on a bed made of their parkas.

But they knew the time had come to go home.

And she knew what she would find:

Her people would be embattled. Jared's protection was no more.

She only hoped the Century Club had enough remnants that she could rebuild from what was left.

She stood in the back of the plane. Pacing. Practically wearing ruts in the already ratty carpeted aisle between the seats.

"Sally," Mack called.

"Not now," she said.

"Sally! Dammit, you need to see this."

She frowned, hurried to the front.

The Chrysler Building.

It had fallen. The upper third of the building was shattered and lay against the building across the street like a giant tree branch.

It was no longer covered in fungus. What fungus was left was black and charred—withered like sun-dried raisins.

"Oh my god," she said.

"I don't see any of those damn flying dinosaurs," Mack said.

"Wh... what happened?"

Suddenly, a crackle of static:

The radio came to life.

The voice of Colin came over the radio.

"The People's Republic of Manhattan to unknown aircraft," came the voice. "Repeat: Manhattan to unknown aircraft. Over."

Mack laughed. Sally just goggled.

The Silver Fox grabbed the hand-held: "Lucy here. Got Mack and Sally incoming. What in the name of all the holies happened down there? Over."

Crackle.

"We fought the battle and won the war."

Just then, a pair of jet-wings rocketed up in front of them and then swept to the side. Colin continued:

"We're sending a couple of jet-wings to help you land. Follow them into the reservoir and we'll talk more. See you on the ground. Over."

Sally shook her head.

"They did it," she said. "Without me."

"Sweetheart, I think maybe your time as leader of this crew has passed."

She nodded. "You're right."

"That okay by you?"

"Best news I've heard all day."

She stood behind him and kissed his temple as Lucy descended.

THE CENTURY CLUB
WILL RETURN

in

DINOCALYPSE
FOREVER

TRUTH AND ILLUSION

A STORY OF CHARLES CARLIN, "THE GREAT CARLINI"

BY CHUCK WENDIG

1935

THE METROPOLITAN MUSEUM OF ART, MANHATTAN

Charles Carlin—the Great Carlini—stood in the center of the Cistern Collection, a room that housed one of the world's most precious collections of unusual and inexplicable artifacts collected by one Tobias Cistern, wealthy steel magnate, antiquities dealer, and utter shut-in. His collection was home to the Anchorite Puzzle Box, the Scimitar of Hylia, a frieze depicting the courtship of the Hyperborean Goddess Silpathia, the Clockwork Pony of Krong, and so on, and so forth.

And now, it was all missing.

"It... it was all here," said Albert Edgar Putman—aka *Putt*, the museum's collection director. "I came in. I began turning on all the lights. I called out for our night watchman, Teddy Brigham. He didn't show so I turned back around—and while I was still in the room, everything just... *disappeared*. Poof! Like they never existed. As if one minute they were present before me and the next all that was left was..."

He handed Carlin a linen handkerchief. White. Pressed. Clean.

Smelled of apples and honey.

In the center of the handkerchief: a mark of lipstick. The color of a cracked-open pomegranate. Lush. Full.

Carlin's heart swooned. A smile tugged at the corners of his mouth despite his best efforts—she had her hooks in him, all right.

"You're smirking," Putt said.

"I know who did this," Carlin said. "You came to the right person. I'm all too familiar with the work of Nadya Saunders."

"The daughter of... Zardok?"

"Indeed, old Putt, indeed. She's the one who stole your precious Cistern Collection. And I aim to get it back."

2000

THE CENTURY CLUB SUBTERRANEAN CHAPTER HOUSE, CENTRAL PARK, MANHATTAN

It was then he knew they were doomed.

An odd feeling, that. Charles Carlin had long been the optimistic sort—never a scrap he couldn't escape, never an illusion that failed him, but this was no illusion. The artifice had collapsed; the effect was proven to be just a dream. The world had been taken. He had put his trust in people who took that trust and pulled the rug out from under it—the lady in the box was truly sawn in half, the card picked from the deck was always the wrong one, the top hat was home only to dead doves and deceased rabbits tumbling out onto the floor.

All his illusions were swept aside when the psychosaurs found them.

Sally Slick had gone. So had her friends from the past: Jet Black, the Professor, Amelia Stone, Benjamin Hu. Mack had abandoned them. The Walking Mind was gone.

The psychosaurs came faster than anybody ever expected.

They charged through the tunnels like army ants—crawling, shrieking, pouncing. The psychic wave crashed against the breakers of their minds, crushing them in the drowning surge, and Carlin's mind was a sudden flight not of doves but cruel, cruel blackbirds, squawking doubt and doom in his ears: *You'll never see her again, the world has moved on, you failed, all an illusion ALL AN ILLUSION—*

He'd been patient. He'd been smart. Or so he thought.

He'd been stupid, is what he'd been.

Benjamin Hu had recently proven that it only took one man to make a difference and here Carlin had forgotten that, having chosen to place his lots in with this rag-tag crew. And now, the telepathic fist squeezing his psyche, saurian claws digging into his cloak, his back on the ground as they dragged him away—

But then it all changed on a dime.

He heard gruff grunts and crass ululations—

The crack of a rifle.

The whisper of a ghost girl through the walls.

And like that, the telepathic rope around his mind went slack.

And then was gone.

A psychosaur rushed him—Carlini found his bearings fast, dipping into each sleeve with pinched fingers and whipping his hands out in a quick-draw:

Two razor-sharp stainless steel playing cards ripped through the psychosaur's neck—*thwip thwip*—and black blood jetted against the stone walls of the subterranean headquarters and the beast fell backward. Carlin mounted the beast, rescued two of his playing cards, and felt a renewed surge:

The show goes on.

1985

NEAR THE KOLOA CHAPTER HOUSE, KAUAI, HAWAII

The sea reached for him, then retreated. Again and again. Lapping higher and higher on Charles Carlin's bare feet—those feet sinking deeper and deeper into the sand.

The line where the sky meets the ocean looked like a hot lance of fire.

"I think our time here is about done," said Sally Slick, coming up behind him.

"Mm," he said, not turning around. "Shame, in a way."

"Is it?" she asked. "I never got the feeling you cared for it here."

He gave her a small smile. "I do like it. Though the beach and sun, sand and surf... it's not really my thing. I prefer the city. And adventure. This is too peaceful." It hadn't been peaceful, of course. They had to reclaim the island. From the dinosaurs. From the *psycho*saurs. They'd made it safe and sane and some of them talked about staying here forever. Making this their new permanent home. Take some of the other Hawaiian islands back, colonize, rebuild, let this be the reconstructed cradle of man.

Charles didn't like that idea.

He wanted to go home.

Even though home was... well.

"You're thinking about her," Sally said.

"I am."

"You think she's still there."

"She may be. I don't know."

"We're going back."

He spun. The surf sucked at his feet. "I'm sorry. Going back where?"

"Where do you think? New York."

The grin would not be contained. "That's good. That's very good."

"But I don't want you caught up in your own crusade," she said, lancing his bubble with a steely gaze. "This can be personal only in the deepest chambers of your heart. This is about mankind. About all the people, not just one."

"Right." He sighed. "I understand."

"We must do whatever it takes. Sacrifice is our bread and butter now."

"Of course."

She approached closer—not too close, for she was always the distant type, standing just at the margins, as if getting too close was a curse, like she might catch something (some joked that she was afraid to catch *compassion*, but then they shut up real fast just in case she heard them).

"I need your help with something."

"Oh?" he asked. "What can I possibly help with?"

"I need a new weapon," she said. "Guns aren't my thing. And ammunition is at a premium. I want something to replace the..." Her hand fell to her hip, then clenched suddenly in a fist. "I want something new."

"Why are you asking me?"

"I like your playing cards. Stainless steel. Razor sharp. Classy."

He smiled. "I used to use a boomerang in one of my acts. I always wondered if we could make it thin enough and sharp enough, yet still return to the hand. Interested?"

1935

HELL'S KITCHEN, MANHATTAN

The warehouse smelled of dust and mold and rust. Dim dark lay pinned by spears of light in which hovered slow-moving motes.

Charles had gotten the address from a fence down at the Bowery—a skeevy no-good cheat named Donny Dapper, the name an irony since he wore dirty rags and had wild hair like he'd tongue-kissed an electric eel. Donny was a poppy-head, an opium smoker always happy to kick the gong. Charles lured him out of a local hookah-house in Chinatown, made it seem like he had a couple so-called "oyster fruits" to sell: *pearls*. A string of sweet pearls that'd help Donny feed his habit. Charles laid the pearls out on a table. Donny reached for them: they popped in his hand and little puffs of swimmy green smoke rose from inside—a little bit of knockout gas.

Donny woke up an hour later suspended over a tank of water. The tank was from one of Charles' old gigs—straitjacket, chains, no keys, into the tank, daring escape. He told Donny he knew how to escape. But Donny didn't know the trick, and unless he told him where the goods were, Charles would drop him in the drink and let him drown.

"At least you're not in a straitjacket," Charles said with a wink.

Donny wasn't a dummy. He knew not to give it up easy.

Charles dunked him.

The door slammed shut above Donny's head. *Choom.*

Donny's face lit up in shock. His hair drifted like seaweed. Dirty hands pawed at the smeary glass, *thump thump squeak thump.*

He tried to get himself free. But panic was going to kill him. That was really all it took to escape the containment: a small plate at the bottom of the box revealed a key made of glass, a key you could not see in the water, a key that Charles lifted with his toes and used to unlock the chain around the padlock—then, dislocate a shoulder to slide out of the straightjacket, then hit a second pressure plate to open the top door of the box and climb out *just in the nick of time.*

Panic was the magician's enemy, of course. Most solutions were simple as long as you could keep your cool.

Donny's cool was cracked like an egg.

He would die in there, of course, unless Charles did something. He climbed up the ladder on the side of the box as Donny thrashed around like a spasming octopus—taking his sweet time, of course, no need to rush—and then he climbed to the top and cranked open the door, reached in and grabbed a hank of Donny's hair—

Then lifted him out.

Charles gave him a winning smile.

"Ready to talk now, or back in the tank?"

"*I'll talk I'll talk I'll talk*—" Donny said, spluttering, coughing, eyes pinched in fear. Donny had heard tell of the missing Cistern Collection. Who hadn't? And Donny, despite being a poppy-loving dodo-bird, knew people who knew people and had a line on where the goods were stashed. Criminal types always loved to talk about robbing other criminals—though they never did unless they had a death wish, because you never knew if the score belonged to a far bigger fish than you.

That led Charles to this warehouse.

Steel shelves stacked high.

Already he saw what he was looking for.

There: the Bronze Age Aegis of Thonodox. Over there, the clockwork bust of the Selracc Automaton. Dangling from a hook, the Scimitar of Hylia.

The Cistern Collection.

All neatly stacked on shelves.

So easy.

Which meant this was a trap.

Shadows emerged in a circle around him. Long-legged stilt-men. Legless freaks on wooden dollies brandishing straight razors. A couple clowns with teeth filed to points. Zardok's crew. Carnies and circus mutants.

Up above, footsteps on a high shelf.

A whiff of apples and honey.

"Charlie," Nadya said. Daughter of Zardok.

"Nadya," he said, giving her a faint twist of a smile.

"I thought you'd have seen this trap from a mile away."

"I thought you liked me more than this."

"I do. I really do." For a moment, she sounded sincere—not her strong suit, but it tickled him just the same. "But my father... he has other plans for you."

The circus freaks and carny thugs crept closer.

"So this is his doing, then?" Charles asked.

She shrugged. "I am my father's daughter."

Then the shadows leapt.

2000

THE CENTURY CLUB SUBTERRANEAN CHAPTER HOUSE, CENTRAL PARK, MANHATTAN

Charles rolled the top hat off his head, down his shoulders and into his left hand—all at the same time, his right hand plunged into it and withdrew a collapsible cane that served as a telescoping baton.

He lashed it across the face of an onrushing psychosaur.

Shattered teeth ricocheted off the wall.

Hat rolled back up the shoulders, returning it to his head.

As the creature fell, Carlin flicked two steel playing cards over the limp body, slicing the throats of two more saurian invaders.

The Great Carlini ran.

Everywhere he turned, the Centurions were fighting back. Neanderthals using rocks to smash psychosaur heads. A young greasemonkey kid—couldn't have been more than 16, 17 years old—cracked one psychosaur in the leg and, as it fell, a teen girl with her hair bound in a dirty handkerchief pounced with a pair of screwdrivers. Lily-Belle the ghost reached through walls and smashed saurian heads into rock. Tara Shepersky made short work of lizard faces with the jagged toothy tip of her ice axe. Then—

Around the bend: a yell. Colin. The Aussie Digger.

Charles and Colin didn't much get along—they had different ways of doing things, of seeing the world. But they were allies in this fight just the same and Colin was in danger—

He was pinned against the wall, invisible telekinetic hands holding him there as a trio of psychosaurs ganged up on him, claws out, tongues licking across needle teeth—

Two more cards thrown—*thwip thwip*.

One swipe of the baton—*whack*.

Blood gurgled from two opened throats.

The third's head was collapsed like a dented can.

Colin skidded to his feet, gasping.

"They're..." Colin coughed. "They're gonna keep coming, mate."

"I know," Carlin said. "They have a taste for us, now."

"We've got to move. Get on the run."

Nadya.

"No!" Charles said. "I have a different plan."

Then he told Colin, and the Aussie Digger smiled a mean smile.

1995

THE CENTURY CLUB SUBTERRANEAN CHAPTER HOUSE, CENTRAL PARK, MANHATTAN

The voice boomed in his mind: MY ILLUSIONS ARE FAR MORE COMPLETE.

They looked up through the massive pit that led down into the Century Club chapter house beneath Central Park—an emergency entrance, if not an exit. They had tunnels coming into the chapter house from multiple angles, but this one was key if they were ever to get people down here from the park fast. Or, better yet, if they ever needed to stage an invasion. He'd seen Sally Slick's plans. *Jet-wings*, he thought. *Could work*. She needed Jet Black to return to use his as a pattern—and that was something she took on faith more than Charles could. But then she said she had "inside information," whatever that meant.

Charles sniffed. "My illusions are far more interesting."

MIRRORS. THAT IS YOUR SOLUTION? MIRRORS.

"We can make the hole look like the lake that it once was. A little smoke and mirrors makes it look like the surface of water—with your telepathic powers, that will complete the illusion."

FINE. DO WE EVEN HAVE MIRRORS?

"Some from the scrapyard. Plus, burnished tin or polished hubcaps will do the trick in a pinch."

CRASS.

"But effective."

WELL-PLAYED, "GREAT CARLINI."

Even in telepathy, the Walking Mind's dismissiveness was keenly felt—a greasy slathering of sarcasm that coated everything.

"I am—or was, at least—one of the best."

He grinned.

1935

HELL'S KITCHEN, MANHATTAN

The first clown swung a Louisville slugger—

And it connected with open air.

Carlin's cloak dropped to the ground, for he was no longer in it. A thin micro-filament cable carried him up with astonishing speed and he dropped next to Nadya with a flourish of his black jacket.

"Helluva trick," she said, smirking. "How'd you do it?"

"A magician never tells."

Suddenly, she was gone—no trick, not this time. Instead she bounded from shelf-top to shelf-top toward the front of the warehouse.

Nadya was always fast. But she'd gotten *faster*.

It almost made him swoon.

But for now: the chase was on. He took his own leap forward—

Just as the shelves in her wake began to collapse. A series of giant skeletal steel dominoes crashing one after the next.

He lost his footing—fell forward, catching the next shelf and hauling himself up just before the other would've pinned (and crushed) his legs. Again and again he scrabbled to find purchase as the shelves fell beneath him until the end—

Charles looked up, saw Nadya crash through the front window.

And then the momentum of the final shelf falling flung him through the window, too—a baseball hurled through empty space.

2000

THE CENTURY CLUB SUBTERRANEAN CHAPTER HOUSE, CENTRAL PARK, MANHATTAN

"I don't know that I'm ready for this," Colin said.

Charles looked over the room full of jet-wings. He sucked in a deep breath, stepped under one and hoisted it up on his shoulders. It was lighter than he imagined: he assumed it would be some heavy contraption whose value was only when flying high—but then again, didn't Jet Black fight with his strapped to his back? Capably so?

The others that Colin had chosen—including Tara, a couple of the workshop greasemonkeys who helped construct these jet-wings, as well as a few of those rescued from the Empire State Building—stood around with great trepidation. As if the jet-wings may somehow spring up and bite. Didn't help that in the background they still heard the sounds of the fracas.

"I'm ready," Charles said to them all. "I used to wing-walk, you know. Out of the plane, walk on the wing. I've even leapt from one plane to another. Once you're up there, it'll feel like the easiest thing in the world."

"Let's do it," Colin barked suddenly, and began distributing guns—couple revolvers, a few M1911s, a Tommy gun. A few folks got grenades, too. He put a grenade in Charles' hand. "The great equalizer."

Charles nodded. They shook hands.

Then everyone began to step into the jet-wings.

1935

HELL'S KITCHEN, MANHATTAN

She gave a helluva chase. She always did. Like the temple run in Bolivia. Or across the girders up on the Empire State Building. Or through the Chiang Mai labyrinth. It always ended the same way, these chases: he caught her. Or she let him catch her. And then they spent the night together and before the sun rose, she fled him anew before popping back up a year or so later.

One night he hoped she'd choose to stay.

He hoped that was this time.

He'd fallen out of the window and into traffic—a Ford Model-A almost careened into him but he sprung up, ran across the hood and leapt back down to the road. There, ahead, a glimpse of her darting into an alleyway. This is how it always was: a glimpse, a dash, a daring chase. Like she got off on it. Like he did, too.

Into the alley. Up a fire escape. Across rooftops. Feet pounding on tarpaper. Leaping over the canyons between buildings until finally there were no more buildings left to leap.

There. At the edge. She spun heel-to-toe and flashed him a smile that shone like the sun caught in a beveled mirror's edge.

"Caught me," she said.

"As always," he answered.

He stepped toward her.

"One day maybe you won't catch me," she said.

"One day maybe I won't have to."

But then, somewhere: a sound. People yelling. A car horn honking followed by a crash. Off in the distance he saw shapes in the sky.

Flying shapes.

Winged things. And behind them: the black shapes of looming dirigibles. *Oh, no. No, no, no.* Something was wrong. Something was amiss. *Not now, not now.*

She turned and looked.

And that was the last time he saw her face.

The thing shrieked, launching upward—a Pterosaur with splayed claws on leathery wings, and on its back was a rider. An inhuman creature with black orb eyes and a mouth full of crooked needle teeth, a lizard-like monstrosity that shrieked and bellowed—

The wave of psychic energy swept over him—

Doubt dragged him down, crushed him under a boot—

You are weak, give in, succumb, you've lost her already, you never had her, all your life was a great illusion—

He smelled the jungle. Felt the damp hot rainforest breath on his brow— he tried to find his hands, his arms, any part of him that he could control, that he could use to reach out and stop her—

But Nadya leaned forward like a tilting tower.

And she fell off the edge of the roof.

No!

1985

NEAR THE KOLOA CHAPTER HOUSE, KAUAI, HAWAII

Swish swish swish—

The razor boomerang cut through the branch.

A coconut dropped to the beach sand with a plop.

Charles applauded. Sally Slick took a bow, the boomerang already back in her hand—it called to mind a falcon returning to the falconer's wrist.

"Looks like it's well-balanced," he said.

"It feels natural," she responded. "And it flies true. You have a gift."

"It's not the gift I expected, creating weapons like that. I have other gifts, you know. Greater plans in mind."

"Your magic? We'll find use for it."

"It seems useless now."

She laughed. "We all feel useless now. We'll find our feet again."

He watched her. "How's the eye?"

Sally fidgeted with the eyepatch as she went over and claimed the fallen coconut. She used the boomerang to pop a hole in the side so she could lift it to her mouth and drink. She offered it to Charles and then said: "It's fine. It itches. Mack says it's saucy. Like I'm some kind of pirate." She harrumphed but then laughed. "A saucy pirate. That's not the gift *I* expected."

"How are things with you and Mack?"

"Fine." But she bristled. Enough to change the subject, it seemed. "And how are you? Still dreaming about..."

"Nadya."

"Ah. Yes. Zardok's daughter." She took the coconut back and, before drinking, eyed him up. "She's still alive, you think?"

"I think so. She fell off the roof but then..." He clapped his hands together. "A second flying monster caught air just beneath her. It rose in the sky and had her in its claws."

"I remember that day."

"As do I."

"How'd you get free, by the way? So few heroes managed."

"They came for me, then. The psychosaurs. I could already feel my mind retreating from my body, like they were... trying to take my psyche and stash it somewhere very far away. I smelled the jungle. I felt the heat. But when they reached for me they triggered one of my tricks."

"Oh?"

"Indeed. Sent a cloud of acrid smoke up—it was enough to sting their bulging black bug-eyes and they lost their telepathic grip on me. I was able to flee to the river, which wasn't far."

"See?" she said. "Your magic may be of use to you yet."

2000

THE CHRYSLER BUILDING, MANHATTAN

The grenade pin hit the ground with a *ping*.

The grenade itself bumped and bounded like a tumbling rock before thudding into the cracking electro-spire at the center.

In the moment before it exploded, Charles realized just how lucky they were. Most of the psychosaurs were descending upon the chapter house—and with the jet-wings moving fast and furious, they had an opportunity that wouldn't have been given if things had been kept the same. Colin "dug" a hole in the side of the fungus outside the skyscraper—not with a shovel but with a stick of dynamite. The others—wobbly, unstable, uncertain, but aloft just the same—flew in through the gap.

The grenades let free.

And then:

Boom.

A lightshow like Carlin wished he could have on stage with him sometime—fingers of lightning like the hands of the gods reaching up and down and all around, the searing white burned into the dark of his retinas.

And then when it was all clear, he saw the fungus drying up. Hell, he *heard* it—crackling like the ice of a lake underneath a heavy boot.

His eyesight finally returned.

And then he saw her.

He called for her—

"Nadya!"

He swept her up and pulled her close—she was sallow-cheeked and filthy, her hands worked to calluses. But her eyes still shone and sparkled and her mouth still did that funny thing where it turned into a tiny wry smile, and he swore, *he swore* he could smell honey and apples.

"Helluva trick," she said, woozy. "How did you do it?"

He held her close and whispered in her ear: "A magician never tells."

MORE BOOKS FROM
SPIRIT OF THE CENTURY™
PRESENTS

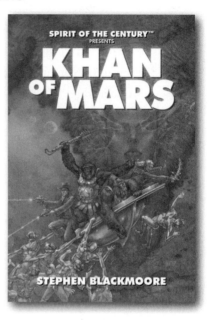

The *Spirit of the Century* adventure continues in these titles, available now or coming soon!

- The *Dinocalypse Trilogy* by Chuck Wendig: *Dinocalypse Now, Beyond Dinocalypse*, and *Dinocalypse Forever*

- *Khan of Mars* by Stephen Blackmoore

- *King Khan* by Harry Connolly

- *The Pharaoh of Hong Kong* by Brian Clevinger

- *Stone's Throe* by C.E. Murphy

- *Sally Slick and the Steel Syndicate* by Carrie Harris